HALLOWED BE THY LIGHT

TIMBER PHILIPS

ISBN: 978-1-950222-19-3

Edited by Barbara J. Bailey

Book design by Maggie Kern

Cover art by Dar Albert at Wicked Smart Designs

DEDICATION

To Kamila, thank you for helping me plot and scheme this one out.

PROLOGUE

*J*une 3rd, 1820...

It was hard to tell dusk from smoke in the char-choked air as I knelt in front of the smoldering ruins of the church. Aye, I'd barred the door, soaked the wooden structure in kerosene and had put the building to the flame. Thirty-two souls were trapped inside. I'd listened to all thirty-two of them, damn their eyes, scream and wail listened as they'd gnashed their teeth and sent up their pleading prayers to their new god, and I'd felt nothing. I was hollow, empty, my heart still echoing with her screams, her prayers to the old gods likewise unanswered as she'd burned and died, my child withering and dying with her, still trapped in her womb.

The scuff of a boot against the dirt and rock of the ground roused me. The deal had been struck, the Queen of Air and Darkness had held her end of the bargain, and now it was time to hold mine.

"Was it worth it, Jackie-boy?" she asked, her lilting voice, dulcet in tone, drifting on the swirling ash. I straightened, sitting back on my heels, and shook my head.

"I cannae say as it was," I said honestly. I had thought their demise would bring me peace, that it would bring me justice, but all it did was score more darkened memories in tortured lines across my soul.

"It is time," she intoned and the words were weighted with her magick. The vague sound of the belling of the hounds echoed through the hills, tinging the edge of her voice.

"Aye."

"You will wander in darkness for what you have done here, my messenger between the barrows and hills. Have you any requests?"

"A light, to guide my way?" I asked. She stepped 'round me, a cruel smirk twisting her lush red lips. She stalked in among the burnt timbers and cracked stones and plucked an ember from the floor. She turned and held it out to me and I shook my head. A blacksmith by trade, I'd been burnt often enough, but I was tired of burning things.

I hauled myself to my feet and staggered over to the turnip cart, abandoned by its master, one of the men who'd died inside. I plucked the iron lamp from the cart and swung open its glassed-in door, holding it out. She smiled a little less cruelly and set the ember inside, carefully avoiding touching the iron with her skin. I swung the door shut and faced my fate. I would follow my Queen wherever she would have me go.

1

October, Modern Day...

Quinn...

It was unseasonably warm this close to November. I left my rented cottage in the small Irish village that looked like it didn't belong in the modern world. It had been my business partner and best friend's idea. Olivia had thought it would inspire something new, being out here. We wrote children's books together. Well, Olivia wrote them. I did the illustrations. We'd been making up fairy tales and stories since we were kids. I would create something and she would come up with these fabulous stories surrounding my creations and then I would draw the rest to go along with the story. We fueled one another creatively, and somehow, it had eventually all grown beyond us.

The worlds we created were our own but at the same time, opened doors to a whole new one for us. The stories she created, the drawings and paintings I made to bring them to life had provided us countless opportunities, starting in high school with a scholarship to an arts college for me.

We both knew when we'd met that day in third grade, me new to a school full of strangers, that we would be best friends forever. Together, we were something magical and extraordinary.

Sadly, neither of us had counted on the 'forever' part of our friendship ending at the age of twenty-four. We were supposed to find our Prince Charmings together, have our families together. Our children and our children's children were supposed to be best friends like we were before them... but now it was just me, our friendship broken, my best friend lost to me.

I bowed my head and turned the old iron key in the lock of the cottage door. It was a quaint, adorable, one-room little thing much like a studio apartment. Unlike a studio apartment, the old little cottage was quite a bit more rustic. The interior heated by a small, iron potbellied woodstove which also served as the cooktop. While the cottage had been wired for electricity, it wasn't used much, except to produce hot water for the little shower and in the old farm sink, which still had its old-fashioned hand pump. When Livvy had told me we would be roughing it a bit, she hadn't been joking. Still, I loved it, just like I knew she would have loved it – if she were here with me.

I stepped lightly across the gravel drive and past the landlady's much larger house. Mrs. O'Leary wasn't out in her garden today, which to be honest, I didn't know what she'd been doing in it yesterday. Autumn was in full swing and it was super close to Halloween, except they called it something different in this part of the world. It sounded like 'sow-wan' when you said it, but it was spelled S-a-m-h-a-i-n. I'd noticed that about a lot of the Gaelic words and names. They didn't read anything like they sounded, and to someone like me, as American as apple pie, it made little to no sense. Still, I was glad I was here. It was like I could breathe a little more.

The culture here was vastly different than in America. Friendlier, and the fact that I was a mixed kid from Baltimore didn't seem to matter one bit to anyone here. Every time I caught someone staring I felt myself tense, subconsciously readying myself for the derogatory remark or the coming micro-aggression about the fact that I was 'other', but it never came. What issued forth was, instead, typically a genuine compliment or a forthright and innocent curiosity and it was so refreshing.

Of course, then I'd speak, and a fresh new dread over how it would go over that I was American would take root and grow like a weed. Still, nothing had come of it. No one seemed one bit bothered by the fact that I wasn't from around here. In fact, the only negative remarks I had heard about anyone was over a people they called 'travelers' and I didn't know immediately what that had meant but had quickly surmised it was a form of gypsy.

"Quinn! Where are ye off to?"

I paused at the edge of the road and looked over the little fence of piled stone in the direction of the voice that had called out. Mrs. O'Leary was straightening from one of her flower beds, although what she could be planting this time of year I had no idea. Gardening wasn't one of my things, even though I enjoyed flowers immensely. I guess it was really that I was too much of a city girl. I hadn't been raised around plants and nature, our family trips were usually museum and historical society type things. Camping hadn't exactly been my mother's bag.

"Hi, Mrs. O'Leary!" I called back, brightly. "I was just on my way to take in some of the scenery and do some drawing." I held up the tartan blanket over my arm and rattled the strap to my leather messenger bag slung across my chest for emphasis. She smiled, but it was a peculiar expression, as she did it with a frown.

"Don't ye be out after dark now, y'hear?"

I laughed lightly and, puzzled, asked, "Why? What happens after dark?"

"It's Samhain already, All Hallows Eve. The veil is thinnest, dear girl, and the fair folk will be out on the wild hunt."

I gave her a long slow blink. Surely she didn't believe such things. I had been here nearly a week already and I hadn't taken Mrs. O'Leary as the superstitious type. In fact, she was as God-fearing as they came. I didn't think someone with such strong convictions rooted in Christianity would believe in faeries.

"Oh, okay..." I said weakly.

I didn't believe in magic anymore. I didn't believe in faeries. I didn't believe in God, or that there was some kind of benevolent higher power. I didn't believe in good, or evil, or any of those things anymore. I just believed it was what it was. That life was what you made it, good, bad, or indifferent. The magic was just gone for me and it hurt. It left a gaping, aching, emotional wound that was so immense I had no words to describe it.

I did my best to avoid the topic with Mrs. O'Leary and went on my way. I just wanted solitude. I breathed deep the fall air and stepped lightly down the dirt lane. We were in the far Irish countryside, outside a little village by a mile or so, the opposite direction nothing but farmland, pastures, and trees. I liked that. I think I needed this for so many reasons and as I got out of sight of the squat little cottages on Mrs. O'Leary's property, I felt properly alone.

I felt the mantle of anxiety and even a little of the loneliness and despair lift from me. I always thought that was strange. How lonely I felt surrounded by people and how freeing being truly alone outside the presence of anyone was for me. It was a contradiction, for sure, but I think that was something of being an introvert. Sometimes you felt less lonely just being by yourself. Maybe it had something to do with being an only child and being expected to be grown up beyond my years a little bit when it came to being around my father's superiors and the like. I had to be a good reflection on him and I never wanted to be anything less. I was a daddy's girl through and through, which was why it had broken my heart so much that he had been the parent to die young.

My mom and I got along, but our relationship was always somewhat tense. I had always been under the impression she would never have had me if it hadn't been for how much my dad had wanted me and how excited he had been. If there one thing we had in common between us, it was our love for my father. He had been an easy man to love and like and I knew we both missed him something awful, but even that wasn't enough to bridge the divide between us.

My thoughts heavy with all of these things and then some, I was pretty heavily brooding by the time I picked a spot off the dirt road to lay out my blanket and unpack my sketchbook. I lay back and stared up through the orange leaves of the tree I'd set up under and watched the sun spark fire and reveal their veins and tracery with its warm golden light. I sat up and started drawing an adorable little leaf-man with an acorn in his curling little hands, wide dark eyes staring off the page as if startled and caught in the act.

I had no story for him, though. The stories had always been Olivia's doing and I'd ruined it all. I sighed and set the sketchpad aside and dug out my lunch, my stomach growling. I ate it, and satiated, lay back again to watch the leaves dance. I smiled and closed my eyes, watching the play of light and shadow on the insides of my eyelids, the sun warming me through my sweater, and tried not to think about, well, anything.

I'm afraid that my plan worked a little too well because when I opened my eyes, it was well after dark and I had no clue how to find my way back to the cottage from where I was.

"Oh, no, Quinn," I murmured to myself. "Do you seriously have to be the absolute queen of poor life decisions lately?" I looked up one side of the lane to the other, squinting in the moonlight and tried urgently to recall which direction I'd come from. For the life of me, I just couldn't. I tried not to stress, even though the direction I had picked back at the fork hadn't been one I had been down before.

Scraping my bottom lip between my teeth, I gathered up my pencils and sketchbook. Then I froze in place, the blood running cold through my veins as some animal out there let out a barking, baying howl that was entirely too close for my comfort.

Of course, right then is when clouds decided to scud over the silver of the moon, plunging me further into the deep of night that was already oppressive. I quickly slung my packed bag over my chest and snatched my blanket by feel from the leaf-littered ground. I shoved it through the leather strap between my breasts and over the satchel riding at my hip, making sure it was secure before I stepped carefully in the near perfect dark over the rough and pitted ground. The grass swished against my boots as I put my hands out, feeling for the low stone wall I had stepped over to get to my place under the tree. My toes hit it first and I cautiously stepped over it and carried on over the grass with stuttering steps until my feet scraped against the dirt of the lane I had traveled down.

"Okay, Quinn, which was it? Left or right?" I murmured and tried to think back as another baying yip from whatever animal was out there carried on the wind which rushed over me. I felt my breath catch and tried to decide which had me more chilled, the wind or the sound, even as more voices joined the chorus. I took a deep breath as the clouds moved off and squinted into the dark looking first one way then the other, trying to decide.

Stupid, stupid, stupid! I chanted at myself silently berating myself with every leaden step. The hounds or coyotes bayed again, and it sounded much closer this time. I felt my heart leap into my throat and looked back over my shoulder even as I broke into a stiff jog, then a run, trying to put distance between myself and that awful sound.

Closer still the next howl came, and as I looked back this time, I swear I saw the ice-blue shimmer of a pair of ghostly eyes skimming just above the ground. So terrifying was the sight of it, I cried out, just as I fetched up against something solid. My initial bleat of terror ramped up into a higher-pitched cry as a light loomed by my face, warmth radiating from it, a man's face beside it, nearly nose-to-nose with mine. His gloved hand closed tighter 'round my elbow and he cursed in a language I didn't know. Still, I didn't need to speak it to know it for what it was. The mad terror was closing in and I stopped resisting for the moment.

"Come on with ye!" he cried and towed me off the side of the road, holding out an old-fashioned lantern to light the way. Off the edge of the road we went, the grass swishing against our legs as I threw myself back from him. Something behind me snapped and snarled, and I found myself immediately reversing course, throwing myself back forward, plunging into the man's wake as he crashed through the tall weeds at the roadside and through the scrubby brush.

"Where are you taking me?" I cried, frightened not only by what was pursuing us but also by the fact that I didn't know this man at all and he might be just as dangerous as the creatures behind us for all I knew.

"Hallowed ground, they can't follow us there!"

"What?" I didn't think I had heard him right, I mean, seriously?

We waded through plants before spilling into a clearing where I had to gasp. I was out of breath, with a stitch in my side and my fingers wrapped in a death grip on the blanket over my satchel. It was Mrs. O'Leary's and I didn't want to lose it, plus I may have need of it. I mean, right?

Stupid, Quinn. You are so damn stupid!

"You're hurting me!" I gasped, but his grip only tightened on my arm, to the point I thought I might have a circle of bruises on the skin if he ever let up.

"Come on, lass! This way, through here," he called, and I followed him past standing stones and through the blackened opening of a stone archway.

"Where are we?" I demanded. "Who are you?"

"The old church ruin," he said, doubling over with his hands on his knees. My own breath was heaving painfully. I let him catch his breath some and just as he opened his mouth to speak, another voice, masculine and taunting, rang out from out there.

"Come now, Jackie-boy! You can't protect her forever, and I do believe I saw her first."

"Not tonight, Gwynn!" the man called back. I thought to myself that at least now I had a name for him, but I still wanted, no, needed, to know just what the hell that was, out there.

"Oh, come now, Jack!" the voice called. and I edged closer to the stone wall which was blackened on the inside and covered in moss. I rolled my lips together and peeked around the edge of the worn stone and gasped.

The speaker was white as snow, from his long, long hair that easily went past his knees and floated like spider silk on the currents of air caused by the churning mass of creatures behind him, to his pale, pale hands. He wore what appeared to be silver plate armor and held a sword before him, point thrust into the ground, those white, long-fingered hands wrapped around the hilt at chest height.

I gasped again and shrank back when I reached his face. He didn't have one that I could see, and I honestly didn't know if I wanted to see it, if it was anything like what churned behind him. His face was covered in a helmet of bone, a ram's skull, the horns curling to either side of his head, his eyes glowing from beneath the vacant eye sockets, the same white-blue light of the teaming throngs of ghastly creatures behind him that ranged out like a wall to either side of him and high above him, so high it was blotting out the sky.

"Just give me the girl!" the terrifying man in the armor called, and the cacophony of soulless fright rose higher, nearly drowning him out. The clamor was terrible, like the worst wind you'd ever heard, rattling through the trees with the clatter of bone and wailing like the wind through the house eaves and against windows. I pushed back, further into the ruins of the church, twisting and bracing my back against the wall, my chest heaving in terror, covering my face with my hands and pressing fingertips into my lidded eyes to the point of pain.

"Stop," a firm voice said, and the man who'd brought me here, who'd rescued me, pulled my hands away from my face. "Don't do that, you'll hurt yourself."

"What does he want me for?" I asked. I mean, no one knew who I was, so I couldn't fathom why anyone would want to kidnap me.

"Likely, he wants to rape you. You are quite unique."

"Please don't hand me over," I said quickly and the man in here with me - Jack, the pale man had called him - looked down at me impassively for a moment, face unreadable. I think I stopped breathing altogether. He looked back out, past the archway that had once been the church's front doors and let my wrists go gently.

"Gwynn isn't so terrible," he said. "It would be after, that you'd have to worry about. You would be forced to join the rest of the souls for all eternity..." he trailed off and pursed his lips. "And that? That is a fate worse than death. Come away from there, further in here. I don't want you going mad, which you will if you look at them much longer. I'd hate to put in all this effort for nothing, and we're going to be here a while."

"What do you mean?" I hated how hollow, how defeated, my voice sounded.

"We won't be able to leave until dawn at the earliest. It's All Hallows Eve, the veil is thinnest. You picked the worst night to be out, lass. We stay put until dawn and you'll be free to go, though I don't recommend you tell anyone about this."

"I doubt anyone would believe me," I said and he nodded.

"Aye, I doubt they would."

I stepped away from the wall and looked up. The wailing specters swirled above the absent ceiling of the old stone building but a goodly way up. I remembered what he said about not looking and dropped my gaze immediately. The sound diminished the closer we moved to what used to be the chancel and apse. Um, that's the place where the altar was, and the hollow at the head of the church where the crucifix lived, if it were still a church and had one, that is.

Though I wasn't technically a Catholic, I had gone to some of the best Catholic schools that money could buy. My father believed in going to where I was going to find the very best education and I had belonged to some of the best private schools as a result growing up. We'd even gone to church every Sunday, but I don't think either he or my mother was what you would call firm believers. School functions and Sunday services were the only religion that was really practiced in our house. We didn't pray at meals, or before bed, or anything like that.

"There is best." He pointed up against the wall and I nodded, laying out Mrs. O'Leary's blanket on the dirty, leaf-littered floor.

"What happened here?" I asked, looking at the sky, stopping short of actually looking at the creatures that wanted to make me one of their own. I let my gaze wander along the blackened stone walls before returning it to my unlikely savior.

"A fire," he said softly and shifted uncomfortably. He was handsome. A white man, like most of the guys around here, with long dark hair in a ponytail.

"Who are you?" I asked.

He smiled, and said, "You ask a lot of questions, you know that?"

I shrugged. "What else is there to do?"

He chuckled. "A fair point, lass. A fair point."

"So?"

"My name is Jack. Jack O'Laughlin."

I frowned, "Your name is Jack O'Laughlin... doesn't Laughlin mean 'lantern' in old Irish?" I'd had a discussion about names with the girl in the village café my second day here, and Laughlin had stood out because it almost sounded like 'lantern.'

"Indeed, it does!" he cried, and he sounded delighted. He had a nice smile, but I quickly dismissed that notion when I blinked, long and slow signaling silently that I thought this was some bullshit.

"Jack O'Lantern... and you expect me to buy that?" I said. "That I just so happen to meet a guy named Jack O'Lantern on Halloween night? Seriously, what is this? Is this some kind of a trick or a show? Where're the cameras?"

"No tricks, no cameras," he said sincerely. "I swear to ye, this is as real as it gets. Outside, the Wild Hunt is after ye. You've seen it with your own eyes, and surprisingly, remain sane, and yet having seen that, you don't wish to believe that my name could be what I say it is?"

"Okay, not a trick. No cameras," I said, eyeing him carefully. He was way too serious, way too calm. I tried rationalizing in a different direction. "I'm dreaming, right? Like, any second now I'm going to wake up back at Mrs. O'Leary's and this is all going to be a bad dream."

"Alas, for your sake, I wish it were so," he said apologetically, "But this is as real as it gets."

"Bullshit," I muttered, simply not wanting to believe it.

"Oh, aye, then you'll be going out to chat ol' Gwynn up, then will ya?" His grin was a slightly reckless one when he said it, but it did nothing to take the sting out of his words.

"I didn't say that," I said, my mouth suddenly dry just from the thought.

"You know he's not so bad to look at, when he's got that old ram's skull off his head," he muttered, gazing in the direction of the collapsed doorway, out into the madness out there.

"I'll, uh, take your word for it."

He chuckled again, and turned around, swinging his lantern and bringing it up higher so I could not only see his face better, but I imagine, so he could see me better.

I swallowed hard. He really wasn't bad to look at, at all. He was probably in his late twenties, maybe early thirties. His eyes were dark, like his hair, over a neatly-trimmed Van Dyke beard. His long coat was something straight out of the history books. Maybe a 1700's kind of revival fashion – unless he was one of them, like the man outside that clearly wasn't human. Maybe Jack O'Laughlin was a ghost, too?

"What is he?" I asked, swallowing hard, working up the nerve to ask.

"Gwynn?" he asked. I nodded. "People now have it wrong when they declare him a King of the Tuatha Dé Danann. He's more like a crown prince. He's the Queen's brother."

"The Tuatha Dé what now?" I asked, stumbling over the unfamiliar words, my initial train of thought derailed.

"Faeries," he said and I blinked. I quickly got back on track, deciding to roll with what he just told me.

"And you? Are you a Faerie?"

He smiled and it held an echo of sadness. "I am just a man," he said. "A man in the Queen's employ."

"Explain."

He shook his head.

"Enough about me," he said. "Who are you?"

I wasn't sure what to tell him, so I kept it simple, raising my chin defiantly I said, "I'm Quinn. Just an American tourist."

"Ah, ha," he gave a knowing nod, and I hated that he was mocking me. Still, I figured I had it coming, whatever was going to come out of his mouth next. "And what were you doing out on a night like this, Quinn? Did no one tell you of the dangers you could face?" He laughed, a short bitter sound, and added, "Especially tonight, of all nights."

I felt heat rise to my cheeks, even though the rest of me had started to tremble finely with the first stirring of shivers. It was quite a bit cooler than it had been when I'd left earlier in the day. I stared at my clenched hands in my lap behind my upraised knees and startled when his boot scraped against the ground.

I whipped my attention back to him. I'd been staring at my hands, which had really been just an attempt to pointedly look anywhere that was not at him. I swallowed as he swept off his coat and sat down close beside me, covering both of us with it. He mirrored the way I sat and kept his hands to himself. Still, I was on guard. I mean, there was obviously some things he was hiding from me, not telling me. Of course, I was being evasive, too.

"Thanks," I said softly and he said nothing, just arched an eyebrow and set his lantern in front of us, twisting the dial at its bottom, the shutters on the inside of the glass raising, the light brightening and the heat coming off of it increasing.

"Wow, neat trick," I murmured, trying to deflect his interest.

He leaned back and sighed, and it held an edge of impatience and I sighed back, a sullen sound, even to me.

"Mrs. O'Leary said something, yes, but I don't believe in those things."

"What things?" he asked curious.

I looked up at the absent ceiling and the swirling miasma of ghosts and creatures beyond it, high above us, but I didn't look too hard or for too long. If I let my gaze linger, shapes would resolve and they were honestly shapes of things I didn't want to see. That, and his warning kept rattling around in my brain. '*Look too long you could go mad*'. *Great, that's just great.*

"You don't believe in things your own eyes can see?" he asked, amused.

"No, I don't believe in fairies or ghosts," I said, and he laughed. "I don't know what that is." I was being stubborn for the sake of being stubborn and I knew that, but I really, honestly, and truly didn't want to believe what I was seeing, even if seeing was believing.

Jack may have been part mind-reader to add to the bizarreness of the evening because he said,

"Seems tonight, of all nights, both of those things chose to believe in you, Quinn."

I sniffed and looked away, staring fixedly back at a random point on the floor away from us.

"It'll be alright come the dawn," he said a short time later, voice conciliatory. I nodded, sniffing. I didn't want to look at him. I didn't want him to see me cry.

He shook out a handkerchief and handed it to me wordlessly. I took it, and dabbed at my eyes saying, "Thanks."

He nodded, not something I could see, as I was looking away, but I felt it, where his shoulder was pressed to mine so that we could both take advantage of the cover of his coat.

"So," I started and had to clear my throat. "Are you the Jack O'Lantern?"

He harrumphed and I turned to look at him, startled to realize his eyes were fixed on me. He didn't answer and I figured he wasn't going to at first. I mean, I hadn't exactly been forthcoming. I may have regretted that for half a second because now I really was curious. When he didn't say anything, I tried a slightly different tack.

"We're going to be trapped here all night," I murmured, and he nodded.

"Aye."

I sighed and straightened out my legs in front of me from where I'd had drawn my knees up tightly to my chest.

"Sorry, let me start over... Hi, I'm Quinn. I'm from America."

"Jack O'Laughlin, from Ireland," he said carefully.

"Isn't 'O'Laughlin' old Irish for 'O 'Lantern', like the myth?" I asked again.

He smiled and it once again held that echo of sadness.

"Aye. Aye, it is, Quinn."

"With what's going on out there, I guess it's not that hard to believe that you're the Jack O'Lantern, but I just thought that was an old myth. Pumpkins and gourds carved to keep evil spirits at bay. I didn't know there was a real Jack."

"Aye, there is," he said and he stretched out his long legs.

"Please, I would really like to hear that story."

"The story, or the truth?" he asked.

"Both, I guess. I mean, I didn't know there was more to the story than that. I thought that was it. Just something people did to keep," I rolled my eyes upwards without actually looking, "That, away."

He chuckled darkly.

"This," he gave his lantern a little kick, the iron ring on its top rattling against its housing, "Will do more to keep that away than any carved fruit or vegetable."

"What is it?"

"My cross to bear. That ought to make sense to a Christian like you."

"Tell you a secret," I said and he tipped his head in my direction, listening. I leaned against his shoulder slightly and whispered conspiratorially, "I'm not a real Christian."

Real Christians didn't do what I had done. Guilt swirled through me and I looked up to the sky, briefly wondering if I should just turn myself over and be done with it, the guilt coating me so thick I almost couldn't breathe for a moment.

I said it out loud, almost breathing it out with a sigh and it honestly felt good to let a little of it off. "Christians don't do what I did."

"They don't do what I did, either," he said and looked at me like I'd done something interesting, finally.

"What did you do?" I asked, and he cocked his head and his lips into a charming, devil-may-care little smile. I felt my breath catch and tried to decide if I had maybe over-shared.

"You first," he said.

2

J ack...

She searched my face, lips still parted in surprise but slowly coming together in a grim line of resolve.

"I don't want to talk about it," she said and closed herself off again.

"Aye," I said. "Then a long night's ahead of us both if it's to be a night of silence."

"I just don't want to talk about that," she said. "I didn't say I didn't want to talk at all."

"Oh, aye, but maybe I do want to talk about that. It's the first interesting thing you've said so far. I can't be letting it go that easy."

She scoffed, those lush lips of hers parting in surprise, high spots of color drowning out the adorable freckles across her nose and cheeks, like faded ink spattered across old parchment, only slightly darker than the page itself.

"Wow," she said sarcasm thick on her tongue, "You really know how to keep a conversation rolling."

"What did I say?" I asked bemusedly.

"The first thing interesting I've said? Way to be a jerk."

I hung my head and chuckled without humor. She had a point. It wasn't one of the finer things to come out of my mouth. Honest, yes, but not terribly polite. I had, perhaps, been too long among the Fae, who prized being rather direct and literal, but perhaps, didn't practice the finer points of human civility as a result. They found humans tiresome and boring. I didn't always disagree, except in the case of the fine creature at my side this night.

"Great," she muttered. "Now you're laughing at me."

"Oh, now you're just jumping to conclusions. I was laughing at me, lass."

She looked back up at me, her hair a static cloud of soft curls around her adorable round face. I found myself wondering if those very curls were as soft to the touch as they looked but resisted the urge to ask. She searched my face with almond-shaped brown eyes that were several shades lighter than my own. A rich Irish coffee with a touch of caramel cream, versus the deep darkness I held in mine.

"Why?" she asked.

"I was thinking to myself, perhaps I have lived too long among the Fae. I don't seem to be able to hold a proper conversation with another human anymore."

She leaned back a bit, fearful. Her posture tightened with the emotion, though her face gave nothing away quite yet. She was fair good at hiding behind those walls of hers.

"You are one of them?"

"Ah, no. I'm one of you, I'm just, well..." I didn't know how to explain it so I changed the subject. "Tell me something about yourself other than that you're from the Americas."

"Odd way of putting it, 'the Americas'," she said. "I'm from America, as in 'the United States of America'. How old are you?"

She was quick, I'll give her that.

"Twenty-nine," I answered amicably.

"By all appearances, but you said you've been living with them too long. How long?"

Her eyes were narrowed in scrutiny and I smiled cheerfully and gave a nod. "One hundred and ninety-eight years or so."

Her eyes widened and she swallowed hard. "You're two hundred and twenty-seven years old?" I smiled, pleased. She was indeed quicker than I'd initially given her credit for.

"Why, I suppose I am, and you?"

"I just turned twenty-five."

I inclined my head, "Happiest of belated birthdays to you, Ms. – "

I realized she hadn't given me her surname. In my day, it would have been rather improper, but the times had certainly changed and, unlike the Fae, I had no trouble stepping into the future and adapting. I'd found it necessary to some extent, while so many of the courts were simply too enamored with the past and the glory of days gone by.

"Just call me Quinn," she said softly. "No real need for formality."

It was refreshing, to be sure. The Fae lived and died by their formalities. Often times, however, their version of formal was vastly different from that of a human's and it was easy to misstep without the proper guidance.

"To be sure, it doesn't feel like one hundred and ninety-eight years have passed," I said with a sigh.

"How many years does it feel like?"

"Ten, maybe a few more, maybe a few less."

"I don't understand how that could even be."

"You don't know your fairy lore, do you now?"

"It's not something widely talked about in America," she said, defensively.

I chuckled lightly. "Time doesn't work the same in the Rath."

She frowned, "I'm not familiar with the word, unless you mean 'wrath', like 'anger', but that's not right. Not in the context you're using it in."

"Ah, no, a Rath is an earthen mound, the land of Faery is inside it."

"I have no idea how that would even work," she said and made a face.

"Magick, of course."

"Magic... right." She sounded dubious and I looked skyward, her eyes began to follow but when she realized I looked towards the Wild

Hunt, she dropped her gaze quickly. A wise decision to not look. She was strong to have not gone completely mad with how much she'd seen already.

"You've made your point," she said with an exasperated sigh, when I simply looked at her without saying a word.

She shifted and pressed her back into the stone behind us, trying to find a more comfortable spot. Alas, there was none to be had. She let her gaze wander the ruin and said, "I wonder what happened here."

I knew all too well what had happened here, though it wasn't something I was willing to share in great detail.

"A fire," I said simply. "Long ago."

"I'd guessed that from the scorch marks, but honestly, who burns a church? Well, assuming somebody did burn it. Better yet, why didn't they rebuild?"

"Why would you assume someone burnt it?" I asked.

"I guess, the fact that they didn't rebuild."

I nodded but didn't elaborate. Of course, someone had burned it. I had, and the deed done, most of the town dead inside, it was decided that the place was cursed. Thirty-two souls perishing in the same spot? The tale making the rounds that the devil himself was involved... I'm rather amazed they simply left it and didn't salt the earth and raze the standing shell to its foundation.

"A very astute young woman," I praised her thinking.

"You don't look much older than me," she said.

"Ah, but we both know that I am far older than I appear."

"How do I know you aren't pulling my leg? That that out there isn't some kind of elaborate prank by the locals?" she asked, and she sounded as if she almost wished that were true. That I would laugh and tell her she was correct. I almost wished I could. Gwynn had a fondness for the hunt and she made for a rather beautiful quarry. He also had quite the fondness for pain-- other people's pain- and had a rather impressive sadistic streak.

"You're more than welcome to step out beyond the old church

grounds and find out," I said dryly and put just the right amount of foreboding in my tone.

"No, thank you!" she said quickly.

The silence stretched between us and she shuddered and pressed her lips tightly together, face pensive for a time.

"What are you thinking about, then?" I asked, my curiosity burning as brightly as my kept ember in its lamp.

"How do I know you're telling me the truth? That you're not just lulling me into a false sense of security over here to do something later yourself?"

"Are American women so naturally suspicious?" I asked.

"I think women are, period," she replied. "We sort of have to be. I mean, look at what we live with."

I thought about it and I couldn't say I disagreed terribly with her assessment. One of the things about the Fae is they did have a penchant for living in the past. While I preferred it for my own reasons, there were things that I could live without. Their murky morals when it came to consent was one of them. I knew the world had changed drastically. I read voraciously in my spare time and regularly bartered and bargained for books to keep myself abreast of the advancements in the world I'd left behind. The concept of the suffrage movement and feminism was one advancement I was glad to see had been made. However, I was well aware it had far to go.

Fear was a man's favorite weapon against the fairer sex, and she had a right to be afraid. The interesting conundrum here was how to convince her that my intentions were both pure and true where she was concerned, when I was being less than forthcoming with her. I settled on simply telling her the truth and hoping it was enough.

"You're safe with me, lass. You need have no doubt about that. On my honor, I swear it to you."

She searched my face for a long time, expression somber and let out a breath she'd been holding.

"I guess if it's a choice between in here with you and out there with them, in here is definitely the lesser of the two evils. You could be lying to me for all I know, but for right now, I'll choose to believe you. You haven't screwed me over yet."

Her frank honesty was refreshing. The Fae, while not overt liars, were so fond of doublespeak and their games of smoke and mirrors that honesty wasn't something I encountered very often. Quinn was beginning to make me miss the land of humans and appreciate being human the more I spoke to her. Too long had being human been a detriment to me for me to consider it anything less than a burden.

"What are you thinking?" she asked and I met her gaze with a smile I knew was nothing less than sad.

"You remind me to appreciate being human."

Her eyes widened and her expression went slack with surprise. I had to smile with amusement. The expression made her absolutely adorable and I had to look away, off in the opposite direction.

"What is it?" she asked, assuming I had seen or potentially heard something that way.

"It's nothing," I said, playing along, utilizing the double-speak skills of the Fae that I'd learned. It was the truth, but at the same time, the furthest thing from it. True that nothing had drawn my attention, but still the exact opposite of the meaning of the word. Quinn, her surname protected, for now, was certainly something. What, I just didn't know yet and I didn't think it was best I find out.

I just wanted to get her through the night, return her to her world and its people, the way I could never go back. Not cursed as I was, and truthfully? I wasn't sure I wanted to. As much as life among the darkling throng had its dark moments, it was true that the world of the Unseelie held beauty to it as well.

It was too late for me, but it wasn't too late for Quinn and I would see her safely to what passed for home while she was here.

I caught her eyes straying upwards and said, "Don't look too often or too much. It's apt to drive a mortal quite mad if you're not careful."

"Good to know. What else should I avoid doing?"

I smiled; there was a lot of don'ts when it came to the world of Faery. I drew a breath and tried to decide just where to begin.

3

Quinn...

He lifted his shoulder, nudging me awake, and I jumped. I blinked and looked up, blushing once again and mumbled, "Sorry."

"Don't be, I told you that you were safe, didn't I?"

I swallowed hard. I didn't even remember falling asleep. My stomach growled and I stretched out from my curled position. I'd brought my legs back up under his coat as the temperatures had dropped.

Now, I glanced up at the sky and gasped when I realized that the swirling blue-white miasma of angry creatures and spirits had disappeared.

"Aye, they're gone," he said and I pushed to my feet. He followed suit, and when I stepped out from the alcove and glanced out the vacant holes in the stones that used to hold windows, I could see a glimmer of light, out on the horizon. The first touch of dawn was painting the hills and lightening the deep of night into something a little gentler.

"You go back the way we came, through the graveyard there, and up that way you'll find the road."

"You won't walk with me?"

"Nae, I can't go with you. You'll be fine now, I swear it."

I swallowed hard and stooped, bringing up the blanket we'd sat upon and shaking it out.

"Thank you," I said.

"Remember what I told ye about going out at night, lass."

"Never alone and don't stray from town," I recited.

"Aye."

"You're sure you won't walk with me?" I really wanted him to and I was hoping he would change his mind, but he was steadfast.

"I'm sure. My business lies that way." He pointed in the opposite direction, at the line of trees beyond the old church, along what I would have to guess was its back side.

"Well, thank you again," I murmured, at a loss for what else to say. He shrugged into his coat and adjusted the collar, standing it up.

"Be safe, and enjoy the rest of your stay in Ireland."

"I will, thanks."

"Goodbye, Quinn."

"Um, goodbye, Jack."

I struck out in the direction he'd pointed me in, pausing at the edge of the graveyard, just beyond where the frightening man in armor with the ram's-skull helmet had stood. I stared down into the grass where he'd been, expecting for it to be different somehow, but there was nothing there to show he'd ever been.

"Go right!" Jack called from the shadow of the ruined building.

"What?" I called back.

"When you get to the road, go right!"

I nodded and he raised a hand. I raised mine in return, and turned back to the gently-rising slope then took one last look behind me. Of course, he was gone, and I couldn't be sure I hadn't imagined him completely.

I started a careful march in the direction of the road, my breath pluming the air, and thought to myself that if it hadn't felt like fall the day before, it certainly did today. Today it seemed like the season was trying valiantly to make up for lost time, too.

I made it to the road, slightly out of breath from the climb, that had turned out to be a lot steeper than it'd looked. I looked back at the ruin of the old church and stared, looking for any sign of him. Of course, there was none. Just the gently waving green grass and the eerily still burned-out remnants of the weathered stone.

"Right," I murmured to myself, and turned in that direction. I walked for a long time. Far longer than I recalled walking the day before.

Reaching a crossroads, I followed the white signs with their black letters in the direction of the town I was staying near and, with a modicum of effort, arrived at Mrs. O'Leary's tired, but unscathed.

"Quinn!" she called out from her kitchen window, as I stuck the key into the lock of my cottage door.

"Hi, Mrs. O'Leary," I called back, tiredly.

"Were ye out all night, then?" she asked, concern evident in her brown eyes.

I stepped back from my door with an inward sigh and said.

"Yes, I'm afraid so!" I called. "I fell asleep by the side of the road and got horribly turned around. I found an old church and waited there until it was light again and I could find my way back."

"Jesus, Mary, and Joseph!" she cried, crossing herself. "You poor soul! You must be freezing."

I nodded. "That I am, and hungry, but I'm fine, really! Learned my lesson, that's for sure, and glad to be back unscathed."

"Please, come inside!" she called. "Let me fix you something to eat and a hot cup of tea."

I actually wanted to ask her about the church and about some of the stories of the area, see if anything came up that matched what I'd seen last night, but I didn't want to tell her any of what I'd seen. People would think I was crazy, and I couldn't be sure I wasn't. I accepted her invitation, even though I wanted my rented bed and some real sleep more than I wanted life itself.

"I'd like that," I said. "Thank you!"

"Come 'round the front," she called and ducked back inside her kitchen window, sliding it shut. I went back the way I came to the little front garden gate and let myself through. She met me at the front door and fretted over me, taking my hand to lead me inside and exclaiming over how cold my hands were. She led me into her small kitchen and I took a seat at her little kitchen table while she put around filling the kettle and putting it on to boil.

"The old church!" she cried. "No place for a young lady all night like that."

"I noticed the scorch marks on the stone, what happened there? Why didn't anyone rebuild?"

"An awful story, that one. One my grandmother used to tell me when I was a wee lass."

"I'd love to hear it, I found it so strange, it being out there all by itself like that, and in such a state."

"Oh, aye, used to be the center of town it was, way back in the beginning. Such a tragedy, but it was different times, then."

"Wait, whatever happened there was bad enough they moved the whole town?" I asked.

"Aye! A terrible Sunday, it was."

"Did somebody die?"

"Oh, no. Thirty-two lost their lives that day. I'll start from the beginning.

There once was a blacksmith and his wife. Two miserable souls. She was a witch and he was a miserly sort, but his work was next to none and the town had no other with his sort of skill."

I tried to reconcile Jack with the blacksmith of the story but quickly dismissed it. I mean, it wasn't very plausible.

"One day, the wife, she tricked the devil into changing into the shape of a coin and tricked him into her purse on which she'd worked her magic. She then gave the purse to her husband, who refused to free the devil unless the devil did his bidding."

I smiled and said, "This all sounds far out," I said and Mrs. O'Leary eyed me as she took down two saucers and cups.

"I swear, this is just how my grandmother told me the tale."

"Okay," I said.

"Old Jack, the blacksmith, took the devil, trapped in the shape of a coin, to the market and bought his wife all manner of fine silks. Everything her greedy heart could desire, and no sooner had the purchase been made, he would call the devil back to the purse his wife had given him, robbing the poor townsfolk blind."

I listened, rapt, as she told how the poor town suffered and how it was the pastor of the church who discovered that it was the blacksmith's wife who had been consorting with Satan, causing all of the town's ills. She said the town had captured the wicked blacksmith's wife, and as with all witches, they'd put her to the flame – and not a moment too soon, as her belly was swollen with the devil's child.

The blacksmith had been enraged and had called upon the devil to aid him, but free of the blacksmith's wife's spell, the devil wouldn't help him – not without making a bargain. The blacksmith pledged his soul in service to Satan to exact his revenge.

While the townsfolk had gathered for their Sunday service, Jack, the blacksmith, had set the church aflame with the townsfolk inside. The power of the devil kept them trapped as the church burned and they had all died, horribly, burned alive as Jack's wife had died at their hands.

The devil had come to collect the debt owed to him as soon as the deed had been done and had cursed Jack to wander in darkness, gathering souls for him. Jack had asked the devil for a light to guide him through the dark and the devil had given jack a burning coal. With nothing to hold it, Jack had carved out a turnip, his favorite food, and had placed the coal inside to carry.

"Mrs. O'Leary, did you just tell me the origin story of how the Jack O'Lantern came to be?" I asked, as she sipped from her cup of tea.

"I swear to ye! It's how my grandmother told me the tale."

"I don't know," I said, skeptical. "I mean, I believe the church burned down; I was there in the ruin and saw the marks the fire left plain as day, but did thirty-two people really die there?"

"Aye, they did." She looked solemn and I stared across the table, wide-eyed.

"And the whole town moved because of this?"

"Oh, no! Not because of that. The village out this way just grew faster than the town and so folks just happened to move out this way."

It was true, I'd walked into the little coastal town many times since I'd been here. It was tiny as compared to most towns and villages in the Irish countryside, but after a tragedy of that magnitude– I mean, thirty-two people!– I wasn't awfully surprised that the survivors had moved away. I can't imagine there were many people left, it sounded like it was small to begin with and that most of the town had been in the church.

The village here, now, only boasted a population of around maybe a hundred or so people. Its population swelled considerably in the summertime with tourists. It was a popular destination during fair weather, but that was why I was wintering here. One, the town could appreciate the extra money more, and two, it wasn't crazy-pants. That made it much more peaceful and conducive to creative endeavors, which I think was exactly what Livvy was going for by booking this trip at this time of year.

"You look tired, dear girl," my landlady said, and I nodded.

"Very. It was a sleepless night, listening for wild animals and all."

"Surprised the ghosts and spirits didn't get ye," she said, crossing herself.

"Ah, if I'd known then what I know now, I probably would have found a different place to shelter," I said, laughing nervously and taking a final bite of the rolled oats she'd prepared for me.

"Probably the best place for you, on second thought. Those good people I am sure would recognize the good in you, girl."

Yeah, I wasn't so sure about that but I didn't say so. Instead, I just smiled and did my best to stifle the yawn that barreled through all my prior efforts to keep it contained.

"Oh, look at me keeping you with my stories!" she cried. "Off with ye, now!" She made a shooing motion with her hands.

"Oh, um, let me clean up..."

"Oh, no! Leave it, dear girl. I'll take care of that now. I'm just glad you're all right."

"Thank you," I said and got up. "For breakfast and for the worry. I'm fine, really."

"Oh, of course, you are! Clever girl that you are, now off with ye! Get yourself settled."

"Thank you, really. I'll just see myself out."

I let myself out the way I came and went to my small cottage. Once inside, I built a fire in the little wood stove and changed into a warm sleep-set. I dropped onto the edge of the rustic brass-framed bed and stared at the licking orange flames through the three vertical slits in the old iron stove.

It reminded me of a Jack O'Lantern, a bit, and my thoughts wandered back to the mysterious Jack O'Laughlin.

After what I'd seen last night, I had no reason to disbelieve his claims, and I fleetingly wondered if he could be the same Jack from Mrs. O'Leary's church legend.

I decided I would have to have a look through the little village's newspaper archives or records if they had any. See if I could match anything. I sighed, and in the meantime, pulled my sketchbook from my leather satchel. I opened its pages and turned to a fresh one, unrolling my pencil set and selecting my favorite brand graphite drawing pencil from its slot. Pursing my lips, I set the tip to the page and skimmed its surface, leaving the first line of a fresh drawing in its wake.

4

———

J ack...

"Jaaaack, where is your head at?"

Eibhleann's voice was in that playful pouting lilt that I had once found adorable. Of course, that was before I realized what a cruel streak she held. Still, we had been lovers off and on for the last fifty years or so and she was quite good when it came to sex. It was too bad I was, indeed, distracted.

"Ah, nothing to worry your beautiful head about," I said and smiled and her playful demeanor turned very serious in the blink of an eye. She sat up and placed a hand on my back.

"Jack, what is it?"

I smiled a bit wistful and said, "All Hallow's Eve is on my mind."

"You're seriously not still on about that little spat with Gwynn, are you?"

"Mm, not Gwynn, but the girl. I haven't been able to stop thinking about her," I told her truthfully.

Her hand disappeared. "She must be quite something if it's her you think on while in my bed."

Ah, shit. Another quality of Eibhleann's that I didn't like. Her jealousy could be unparalleled, which was rich, considering that like most of the Sidhe, Eibhleann couldn't seem to help herself or remain faithful. Not that I could, or even would, ask it of her. I was far below her station as one of the court's nobility, a lowly human to her place among the glittering throng. Still, even though there was no exclusivity between us, nor no bargain for it from me, it was as if she expected that I would not stray nor want anything more for myself. Rather than argue or fight over the matter, I took the easier route.

"My apologies, my beauty. You are quite right." I turned around and lay beside her, resting my hand against her pale, petal-soft skin with its undertones of lilac. She was willowy and lithe, taller than most Sidhe women. She was also just as beautiful as her name implied, for that is what Eibhleann meant: pleasant, beautiful, and radiant.

Her skin was porcelain smooth, and very white, except when she moved you could see the lilac undertones to it. Her hair matched those undertones. Long and like silk, it fell straight past her knees, and was a stronger lilac hue than her skin. The only thing to rival her exotic hair and skin coloring was her wide and lovely eyes. The irises were a deep purple with flecks of silver in them, framed in long, dark lashes.

She was every human girl's dream of just what a fairy princess should look like and every man's fantasy about how one should behave in the bedroom. It filled me with a wistful sorrow that she simply could not be what I needed beyond the physical satisfaction we found in one another.

It was my deepest and most secret heart's desire to love and be loved in return, to recapture the emotion that I'd had with my beautiful wife all those long, cold, decades past. To feel that again, even if it were with someone new. That is what I wanted but I knew I could never have. Not without damning a woman to this cursed life with me. That was a fate I had become comfortable living with by the necessity to do so, but one I had no desire to inflict on someone else.

To date, the cruelest joke fate had ever played upon me was making me believe I would never heal from my Rhiannon's death.

Though I don't suppose, I ever really had. That is a pain that never goes away.

However, it had become much more tolerable in the intervening years. I missed her, to this very day, but I no longer actively mourned her.

Still, it would be a cruel fate, indeed, to find love again, even in this day and age. Especially with one who wasn't Sidhe or of Faery, for they would not be as long-lived and as I said: I refused to curse anyone to a life down here.

"You are thinking of the past now," she said with a derisive sniff, and I smiled a little sadly. "You always get that look when you do."

"I am," I agreed, for it was a grave insult to lie among the Fae and she knew me well enough that there was no point in denying it.

"Stop," she ordered. "You're nowhere near as fun when you go back to that time and place."

She turned over, reaching for her bedside table and plucking the silver goblet of wine off of its surface. She turned back to me but I was already up, pulling on my breeches.

"Oh, come now, Jack! Don't be like that." Her lips were set in a pouty bow, but her eyes held rage and cruelty. I smiled and once again knew it was sad. I'd genuinely liked Eibhleann in the beginning, there were parts of her I even loved, but I had learned, as most men did, that to love one of the Fae often times went unrequited.

"Ah, my beauty, I am afraid that tonight I am rather unfit to be in your company. You deserve so much more than I can offer."

"Well, now," she said, eyeing me up and down and that cruel streak of her paying me a visit. "That I simply cannot argue with." I was rather immune to her barbs by now, shielded as I was by my indifference. She sighed and I could tell that she was already thinking about other things, and that I had, in effect, been dismissed.

I leaned across the bed and put my lips to hers in a quick chaste kiss of apology, for I didn't wish to make her, or anyone, feel disrespected. The kiss was one she did not return. Her eyebrows going up, she cast a look in my direction that would have emasculated a lesser man.

"You can be quite cruel when you want to be, lover of mine," I murmured.

"You're in quite the mood this evening, aren't you, Jack?"

"Aye, I suppose I am," I agreed, backing off and swiftly gathering the rest of my things. I didn't bother to finish dressing. My chambers weren't far if I asked the magick of the Rath to take me there. I slung the rest of my clothing over one arm, pinching my boots between thumb and the rest of my hand, and gathered the ring atop the iron housing of my lantern with the other. I went to the door, and depressed its handle with my elbow, nudging it open with my foot, all while Eibhleann looked on in amusement. I didn't expect her to get the door, despite the fact that she didn't even have to get out of the bed if she should so choose. Her talent lay in moving objects with a mere thought.

The door opened for me, despite my full hands and Eibhleann cried, "Well done, Jack!" laughing at my retreating back as I slipped out into the hall. The door slammed shut behind me and I sighed, looking down the hall that appeared before Eibhleann's door where there should be none.

"Thank ye," I murmured to the Rath, and went down the hall it gave me by four or so doors to that of my chamber's. The hallway to my quarters, by all rights, should have been across the Unseelie Rath from the hall that held my lover's chambers, but the Rath had sensed my need and had taken pity on me, acceding to my humble and silent request for aid.

When I got to my door, I turned to look back at Eibhleann's but it was gone. Instead, I looked down the hall my chamber shared with many of the other human inhabitants of Faery, instead.

I sighed and leaned my back against the inside of my chamber door. The smell of iron was strong in here, as I tended to ply my old trade of blacksmithing when I could. I looked around the shop portion of my dwelling and felt comfortable. Cold iron was the antithesis of the Fae and made the bearer immune to their magick. The Rath, however, was wild earthen magick and iron was of the earth, so it minded not that I had it in here. The presence of the iron and my work ensured my privacy was respected and kept all but the lesser, more earthly, of the peoples of the Fae out of my chambers.

I sighed and dropped my clothes in a heap by the door and went to the forge. I tipped the ember loose into its cold depths and topped it with wood from the pile by the door. A few pulls of the bellows and the wood caught, burning brightly.

I crafted all manner of things from the fires of my greatest shame, for it held great power, coming from the Queen's magick as it had.

I labored intensely, working to the exclusion of everything else, especially that beautiful face with its light brown skin with golden undertones and that star-scatter of the most adorable freckles I'd ever seen.

I couldn't stop thinking about Quinn, and I hoped, with the time disparity between the land of the Fae and the land of mortal men, I wouldn't see her again. It was truly for her own good.

5

Quinn...

"Oh, now that's a cutting figure now, isn't it?" Saoirse asked me, setting down a coffee nearby my sketchbook. "And who is he meant to be?"

"Um, he's someone I met, actually."

She laughed and slid onto the hard, wooden-backed bench across from me. She had a name like Samhain, spelled completely different from how it sounded. The pronunciation more like 'sear-sha', which made me wonder where the hell the 'o' came into play at all when she'd spelled it for me the one time.

I'd been in a playful mood that day and had sketched her name with flowers and leaves around the letters, playing with a font idea. That was a hobby I did on the side which also brought in a little bit of money. One wouldn't think that designing typefaces would be a thing, but indeed it was. I mean, somebody had to do it.

Saoirse laughed and said, "Well, he's not from around here. I think I would remember a look like his. Was he dressed like that?"

He was, but I lied and shook my head, "Oh, no. That's just my imagination."

"I see, well, if you happen to see him again and you have no claim of your own, please do send him my way." She winked at me and pushed up from the table, wandering around the little taproom and tending the other few customers that were in this late.

I sighed and leaned back, picking up my coffee and sipping, smiling sadly when I found it doctored with a bit of whiskey. I set it back down and didn't touch it after that. I didn't drink anymore, but Saoirse had no way of knowing that.

She was a local, but my age. Her long red hair was pulled back at the temples and fixed with a beautiful old hammered-brass oak-leaf barrette. She tended to wear jeans and sweaters in earthy tones that complimented her fair skin and light eyes.

I enjoyed talking with her and came around regularly, mostly because this was the only place in the small village to get a decent cup of coffee. The food wasn't bad, either.

I turned my attention back to the drawing of Jack and turned the page back to the one before it, and the drawing of the man in armor with the ram's-skull helmet. A shiver went down my spine and I drew the fashionable knit shawl of undyed wool closer around my shoulders. I'd bought a few things since I'd first arrived, but this piece was by far my favorite.

Sighing, I turned the page back to Jack and pursed my lips. It had only been a couple of days since our encounter, but I couldn't stop thinking about him. I kept turning the tale Mrs. O'Leary had told me over and over in my head and I just couldn't reconcile it with his kindness, because I couldn't see his protecting me from that thing as anything but kind.

"Quinn?"

I jumped and looked up into Saoirse's gentle smile.

"I'm sorry," I murmured. "I must have gotten into the zone."

"That's all right," Saoirse drawled. "It's just closing time, and you're my last customer."

I looked around and sure enough, Saoirse's boss, the owner of the establishment, was the only other person in the bar, polishing glasses and putting them up, eyeing me like I was something unusual, which in this place I suppose I was. There weren't many here who would stay so late.

"I'm so sorry," I stammered and she smiled.

"Not at all, love. If you'd like, I'll walk with you out that way. My place is on that edge of town."

"I'd like that, thank you. Let me just pack up my things."

I slid the pencil I'd been using back into the fabric roll I used to house them, and rolled it up, securing it with the sewn-on ribbon by wrapping it around and tying it into a bow. I looked down at the drawing I'd been working on. It was of the lantern Jack carried, sitting on the church floor, dried and brittle leaves scattered around it.

One thing was for certain, I was inspired to draw. It just hadn't been the sort of inspiration I had been searching for. Nothing that filled the pages of my sketchbook was very children's-book-like.

I closed my sketchbook in its leather case, and fastened the flap, winding the leather thong around the raised button to secure it. By the time I finished thrusting everything into my satchel to carry it, Saoirse had bid her boss goodnight and held the door for me.

I slipped out and she slid out right behind me, shutting the door tightly and sticking her key in the lock. Her boss lived upstairs.

"Right, then," she said and held out her arm. I wrapped my shawl closer around my shoulders to ward off the growing chill, having not expected to stay out so late. With a slight laugh, I linked my arm with hers and it was bittersweet. The last person I had done so with was Livvy, and it hurt my heart that I never would again.

Saoirse and I chatted amicably and I was glad she didn't ask about the sketches. Rather she had a million and one questions about the American music scene and they were all questions I was happy to answer to the best of my ability, which admittedly was extremely limited in scope. If she had asked about books and publishing I could have answered questions for days, but in some ways the two were similar and so I tried my best.

"Ah, well, this is me," she said and gave me a hug. "You're sure you're all right making it all the way out to Mrs. O'Leary's all by yourself?"

I smiled and nodded, "I've done the walk after dark before. It's only about an hour more and along the same road. It's a lot safer here than it ever was for me to walk alone back home," I said in an attempt to put her more at ease. She looked a bit dubious and nodded.

"Is it really as bad as they say? The crime, I mean."

"Probably worse," I murmured. "Even though, statistically, the crime rate is better than it's ever been, at least historically-speaking."

"Really, now?" she asked.

"A conversation for another day," I said with a smile.

"Aye, you should go before it gets much later." She gave me another quick hug and waved to me, letting herself into her little apartment.

It was a different sort of building than I was ever used to. Just four little units in a row, in a white-washed one-story building. I imagined, once upon a time, it had a straw-thatched roof. I mean, it looked like that sort of a place. Now it held clay tiles with moss growing on them and it was still just as picturesque and adorable as anything I had ever seen back home.

I huddled around myself and struck out at a good pace along the side of the road in the direction that led out of town and into the countryside. It was about five kilometers or a little over two American miles from the edge of town to Mrs. O'Leary's. For me, at a sedate pace, that was about an hour. Probably more like forty-five minutes at the brisk walk I was taking it at now.

I was at the corner of her white picket fence when a soft male voice called out, "Quinn?"

I looked up, startled, and nearly stumbled. Jack held up his lantern, standing in the middle of the road headed the opposite direction I had been going in.

I blinked, surprised, and blurted, "What are you doing here?"

He frowned slightly and, ignoring my question, asked one of his own, "How long has it been since you last saw me?"

"You first," I declared, standing up straighter, breath lightly fogging the air.

He smiled a secret little half-smile that was entirely too charming and said, "Official Queen's business. Now you."

I frowned. "That's not really an answer, and it's only been a couple of days."

Jack frowned and gave a nod, like I had potentially confirmed something, and sighed.

"How far are ye from your lodgings, then?" he asked, glancing around into the dark. I shifted nervously and pointed and he gave a nod, waving me forward. I moved, wondering if he were worried about the man in the armor, Gwynn, making another appearance.

I went into the drive with Jack at my elbow, and on to my cottage. He nodded and held up his lantern for me so that I could fit my key into the lock. I gave it a twist and went in, turning to him.

"Do you want to come inside?" I asked.

"Ah, lass, that might be a bad idea."

"Please," I said gently. "I have questions, and the least I can do is make a cup of tea to say 'thank you' for what you did."

He debated silently for a moment, then two, before finally acquiescing and stepping forward. I stepped aside and let him in.

He set his lantern on the scarred, two-person table and looked about. I shut the door and took the satchel I carried off over my head. I took the pencils and sketchbook out and set them beside his lantern and hung the satchel and my shawl on the hook set in the back of the door.

When I turned around, Jack was already kneeling in front of the woodstove, building a fire.

"Thanks," I murmured, and making myself useful, moved to the tiny kitchen to fill the kettle with water.

He tended the little stove with what looked like the ease of long practice and I returned, setting the kettle on one of the cast iron raised burners on the woodstove's flat top. He sat back in one of the chairs at the table and watched me move as I brought down two mugs, a tea box with a variety of teas, and a jar of honey.

I stacked the items on the kitchen counter, intending to carry them all over to the table at once. However, by the time I turned around from the task to ferry things between the kitchen and the table, he had my sketchbook open and was already turning pages. I felt my face flame.

"That's private!" I snapped, but it was too late. He'd flipped the page to one of the images of himself and I pressed my lips together tightly, about to die of embarrassment.

"They're quite good," he said shortly, and raised his eyes from the page to mine.

I swallowed hard and voice trembling slightly said, "You think so?" I was trying to play it cool. Like I hadn't just spent the last two days obsessing about the man who was sitting at my table looking over the proof. *Quinn, girl, you are so dumb!* I chastised myself silently.

"I do. I especially like this one." He turned the page and tapped the image of the armored man, Gwynn.

I shuddered and said, "I don't, but I can't seem to stop dreaming about it. Well, nightmares, really."

I set my small pile of things down on the table and slid it against the short expanse of wall below the window. The diamond-shaped panes making up the window were so old, they were warped, and the image of the driveway beyond rippled as though you were looking at everything through water. Each one had a bubble in the center as if the panes were made from glass bottles and the bottoms of those bottles hadn't quite smoothed out all of the way.

Mrs. O'Leary had called it crown glass and had said they were very, very, old. So old, that if you looked closely, you could see the panes were thicker at the bottom than the top as gravity had worked its magic on them over the years.

I know, it was stupid, putting so much thought into the damn window when I still had so many questions about that night, but I wasn't entirely sure that I wanted the answers to those questions. I was honestly afraid of what they might be, had spent the last two days building things up in my mind with my flights of fancy. I wasn't sure I wanted the truth now. It was bound to be far uglier than anything I imagined.

"Tell me," Jack said softly and his tone was gently imploring. I sank into the seat across from him and pressed my lips together, debating.

"First, tell me what really would have happened to me if we hadn't hidden in the church."

He shook his head slightly, expression somber and said, "You don't want to know that."

"If I didn't want to know, I wouldn't have asked," I replied calmly.

"A fair point, well made," he said. "Perhaps I just don't want to be the one to tell you."

I leaned back and sighed. "I supposed that's fair enough, but who else could I ask?"

"Touché," he murmured and chuckled lightly. He thought about it for a moment and heaved a great sigh.

"I wish it were not as I said, but indeed, Gwynn would have likely raped you. Depending on his mood, you may or may not have liked it. Then, you would become one of them for the rest of eternity."

"You weren't just saying that, then?" I hated how disappointed I sounded, realizing just how childish it must have come across.

He chuckled but it held no humor. "No. I say what I mean and I mean what I say."

"Noted. You said I would become one of them, what does that mean exactly? I mean, would they have killed me? Would I have died?" I asked, but I think I knew the answer. I just wanted to hear him say it.

"One of the Wild Hunt. One of the ghosts or wraiths that you saw that night and I don't know precisely how that part works. I believe it would be something akin to a living death."

I shuddered and wished the kettle would whistle, except I was pretty sure that no amount of hot tea would alleviate the chill his revelations brought.

My thoughts drifted away from thoughts of dying back to rape, which wasn't exactly 'better' per se, but that's just where they went. Out loud I mused, "I don't understand what you mean about whether I would or wouldn't like it. I mean, I'm the one who decides that and I am like a thousand percent sure that, no. Just... no. You know?"

He chuckled and it held that dark quality to it again. He leaned back in his seat, hands on top of his thighs, and sighed.

"Gwynn, like most of the Fae, has a little more than his fair share of power. While not as adept at glamour as some of the others, he possesses enough to make human women see just about anything. He could come to you in the guise of an old lover. Seduce you appearing as an ordinary man and you would be more than happy to lie with him at the time. All told, you would be none the wiser that it was even he that you took to your bed."

I stared at him agape. "That's still rape," I pointed out. I mean, holy shit. It was like a date-rape drug without the drugging but no less skeevy or rapey. That was just gross!

"Oh, I agree," he said. "The Fae are absolutely adept at lying without lying. However, they are also much less concerned about the willingness of any human participants when it comes to sex." Something flashed across his face and I was almost certain he was speaking from experience there. I didn't want to get trapped in a rabbit-hole of conversations about what constituted consent, though. I could already tell Jack and I were on the same page about it and I was honestly much more interested in not thinking about the 'what if's' of that night now.

"Well, I suppose I should be glad there wasn't some sort of medieval torture on the menu," I said, trying to keep my tone light, an effort to begin transitioning to another subject.

"Gwynn was well put-out over the fact that I helped to stop his plans where you're concerned," Jack said and I paused.

"Oh, yeah?" That didn't sound good at all.

I wanted him to go on, but all he said was, "Aye, the court is all a-titter about it."

"Could he come back?" I asked carefully, and Jack heaved a sigh.

"The magick of the Fae is much diminished in this time of mortal men. The Hunt only rides during certain times of the year, or when magick, for whatever reason, is heightened. That being said, Gwynn Ap Nudd is not specifically tied to the hunt. He could, in theory, come back on his own."

"Oh." I thought about it, mulling it over, and hugged myself.

"How do I know you aren't him just appearing as Jack?" I asked.

Jack chuckled and nodded, "That's good, very good of you to be cautious." He sighed and said, "I swear I am the true Jack O'Laughlin. What's more, I am afraid that by helping you, I may have made you the object of his latest obsession. He does enjoy a good hunt, after all."

"How do I protect myself?" I cut right to the chase. I didn't know the first thing about Faeries or magic in the really real world. My only exposure to anything fairy up until this point was Disney's Tinker-bell. There was absolutely no denying what I saw that night, though. I was afraid that it was either accept it and move on, roll with it, or go absolutely crazy picking it apart. I mean, the most obvious answer tended to be the simplest, and the simplest answer for what I saw was that fairies and magic were absolutely real, something I would never have believed as a girl or even now if Livvy hadn't come into my life and shown me a world of imagination beyond anything I'd ever known before her.

"Salt around your dwelling is a good start. Though I suspect Mrs. O'Leary has done that for you already, it wouldn't hurt for you to do it on your own."

"Okay."

He opened his coat and plucked something from the inside lapel. I watched him as he reached up and let down his hair, unwinding a long, seemingly-waxed piece of thin leather thong from around itself.

"Stay indoors after dark if ye can," he said, and took the leather, working it around whatever he'd plucked from the inside of his coat. Curiously, I watched. My attention was quickly drawn away, however, by the whistling of the kettle. I went to fetch it off the stove and poured two mugs of hot water. I set the honey aside and opened the tea box, plucking a bag out for myself.

"What kind do you like?" I asked.

"A strong black tea if ye have it."

I made him Earl Gray and myself a nice herbal, adding a generous dollop of honey to my mug.

"Honey?" I asked, as he concentrated on whipping the cord he worked with to and fro, tying it securely.

"Aye, if you please."

I fixed his cup and when I was through, he held up the finished product of his small labors. Dangling from the leather cord, which he'd fashioned into a necklace, was a small, square, black nail.

"Wear this," he said and I dipped my head so he could hang it around my neck.

"What is it?"

"Cold iron. The only substance to harm one of the Fae. Though this won't do much rather than annoy one of the greatest of Fae nobility, it should allow you to see through any glamour if you keep it against your skin. It's not above Gwynn to use guile and seduction until a mortal is firmly trapped in his web. That should help you see it for what it is."

"Thank you, I think."

"Now will you tell me of these nightmares of yours?"

I blew on my tea and took a sip.

"Hmm, well, you did show me yours so I suppose it's only fair I show you mine."

He laughed and it was a good sound, like water tumbling over stones. Sure and swift, it was sadly gone before it'd really had the chance to lighten the mood much. I couldn't join in even though I'd been the one to make the joke and the easy smile that'd come to his generous lips slid away.

"It really frightens you," he observed, and I nodded carefully.

"How could you tell?" I asked, with a wry little smile that held absolutely no humor.

"Your reluctance to talk about it is a start," he answered simply.

I let out an explosive breath and searched his face. I supposed he'd earned a bit of trust from me and so I told him about the dream. About how it always started out pleasant enough, with sex, and hot sex at that, but how mid-way through, when I looked, it wasn't with the man I'd started with. Instead, I was staring into the dark and vacant eye holes of a ram's skull and how the harder I screamed, the harder he thrust and there wasn't a damn thing I could do to stop him.

I guess that's why I so readily believed him when he said a bit ago that this Gwynn guy's modus operandi was to shapeshift or whatever. I mean, I knew a dream was a dream, but that had been way too close to be a coincidence.

I waited for him to ask for more details about the dream, like who the sex had started out with, or to make fun of me, but he did neither. Instead, he nodded a bit tiredly and stabbed a finger at the nail resting on my blouse.

"Keep it against your skin and the dreams should stop. The magick of glamour is weaker the further the caster is from the subject the casting is upon. Even a small bit of iron like that should make all the difference."

I swallowed hard and nodded, a hand drifting unbidden to my throat.

"Is it true?" I blurted, hoping that since I'd shown a bit of vulnerability with him that he might return the favor and open up a bit more to me about himself.

"You're going to have to be a bit more specific than that, lass." He gave me a reckless grin and took a drink of his tea.

"I know, it's just... I don't know if I should ask now."

"Ask," he said, and the weight of his gaze told me that it was okay, that I should.

"Is it true you burned down that church? That you killed all those people?"

"Ah, been listening to stories have you?"

"No, I mean, maybe. I just can't fathom it, you know?"

"Afraid I don't. Why can't ye?"

"You went out of your way to help me."

He nodded and gripping the handle of his mug a little tighter than necessary, took another drink. He lowered the mug and stared down at it as if it would provide the answers for him if he just looked long enough.

"Aye, it's true. I made certain the doors were locked and set the church ablaze with them all inside."

I frowned and the question rushed out before I could stop it.

"Why?"

He smiled and it held the weight of such sadness that my heart throbbed an echo. I knew that look. I knew that feeling.

"Ever heard the saying that history is told by those who win?"

"Of course, I have."

"Aye, well, in this case, it was told by the only man who survived it."

"I see." I mean, I got what he was saying, but I seriously hoped he would elaborate because while it made sense it didn't tell me much.

He shook his head and heaved a great sigh. "Thomas Fitch lived through it. He was little more than the town drunk and beggar. He wasn't in the church that Sunday, but he was there when they killed my Rhiannon."

"Your wife, the... the..." I stuttered over saying it. It seemed so rude.

"Witch? Oh, aye, that's what they said." He chuckled but it held no humor or warmth. "Healer is more like it. A firm believer in the old ways. She drove me half-mad with her superstitions about every-thing, but I loved her so."

I rolled my lips together and just sat, my hands curled around my own mug, waiting for him to go on.

"She was heavy with my child when they put her to the flame. I tried to save her, was chained and forced to watch. The town had been convinced by that charlatan masked as a preacher that I was firmly under her spell."

"I don't understand why they would do such a thing," I whispered, my heart breaking at the thought of it.

"The preacher was a jealous, spiteful man. A boy took ill and he swore it was by God's will alone that the boy would live or die. Rhiannon mixed her herbs and medicines, sat with the boy day and night and sure enough, she cured him. Brought him back from death's door. She and that preacher butted heads and he used that boy's recovery to condemn her."

He braced his elbows on his knees and put his head in his hands, scrubbing at his face. He looked up at me and huffed out a breath.

"It was no devil I bargained with to take my revenge on them all. Those who my wife tended. She healed their hurts, nursed their sick, and they turned on her without a second thought. No, I begged Rhiannon's old gods and the Fae for aid and the Queen of Air and Darkness herself answered."

"So you did do it, but you had a good reason," I murmured. I understood, but still, I couldn't fathom killing all those people. I was the type of person I would probably have just killed myself. Internalized all my rage and pain versus externalizing it.

Yeah, I'd had some therapy in the wake of Livvy's death. I'd needed it to keep myself from doing just that. So I understood what Jack was saying, understood why he did it, though I didn't think I could or would ever be able to condone it. Still, it was almost two hundred years ago and if a man can't grow and change in that amount of time I didn't think anyone could.

"Aye, I believed so then, and I do now." His expression was grim and so terribly unhappy. He still hadn't forgiven himself. It was as clear as day on his face, still, I got it. I hadn't and couldn't forgive myself either, no matter what other people said about it.

"Still not as bad as what I've done, especially in that context," I said softly and let some of my own pain leak out around my edges.

He smiled a one-sided little smile that was watered down and said, "Are ye sayin' you believe me, then?"

I nodded. "The story didn't feel right when it was told to me. It feels right coming from you. I mean, my gut tells me you're telling the truth and I've learned to trust my gut."

I just wish I'd trusted Livvy's.

The fire crackled and popped in the woodstove, filling the silence between us. He considered me, expression somber, then said, "You said you've done worse. What did y' mean by that?"

I swallowed hard and whispered, "I killed my best friend."

6

———————

Jack…

I don't know what I'd expected but it hadn't been that. I shut my gob and raked her with my gaze. She was pointedly looking into the bottom of her mug of tea and not at me. I stared at her and willed her to look at me.

"If you don't mind me saying, lass; you don't strike me as the murdering type. If you want to tell your story, I'll listen. No judgment." After all, I'd shown her mine. I hoped that she would show me hers. I didn't make the joke in return, however. By the look on her pretty face, it would likely be ill-received.

She was silent for a long time before finally speaking. Her voice, when it came, was so quiet and unsteady my heart went out to her.

"I shouldn't have said that. I mean, I don't want to talk about it."

I let the quiet linger a moment before softly saying, "I don't believe that."

She looked up at me sharply, eyes narrowing and I cocked my head, searching her face. I sighed and said, "If you didn't want to talk about it, deep down, you wouldn't have said anything at all. I think you do want to talk about it. You need to, and I meant what I said. I can and will listen. No judgment. After all, I murdered thirty-two people in cold blood. Burned them alive while they attended church on Sunday. Who am I to judge?"

She swallowed hard and dropped her gaze back to the mug of tea she held between her hands in her lap.

"I wanted to go out and I wanted Livvy to come with me but she didn't want to go. I was being selfish, wouldn't let her out of it even though she said she just had a gut feeling. That it was a bad idea and that she just wanted to stay home and read."

She rolled her lips, eyes welling but not spilling, not yet. She was being carefully vulnerable with me and I did not want to cock it up. I knew from personal experience how much agony and anger could be avoided just by someone listening and being neutral. I had lived it. I had been angry for decades, and it simply could have been avoided had I been shown just a little sensitivity when I'd needed it.

If I could prevent another person going through what I had, then I would do my best. It cost me so very little effort to simply listen to her story and not do anything else. Besides, it was a much better view, looking upon her lovely face rather than upon the cold and lonely road.

"I badgered her into going. I thought it would be fun... We went to the club and I had a few drinks but she was just being such a drag. She wanted to go home early but I wouldn't leave and I knew she wouldn't leave without me. We left just before close and..." She trailed off just as the moisture in her eyes spilled over and trailed down her skin in twin tracks.

"Go on," I urged quietly and waited her out.

"I probably shouldn't have been driving, but I went to head through the intersection and the next thing I know there was a flash of light and then I woke up in the hospital. We were hit by a drunk driver. He hit Livvy's side of the car, and she died."

She rocked a bit in her seat, the pain evident and rampant and I knew that feeling. Like you were filled to bursting and it was all you could do to hold it in and keep it from tainting the rest of the world around you.

"It was all my fault," she said, breaking down, her voice tripping over a sob. She pressed her hand over her mouth and her eyes leaked, her shoulders trembling as she tried to contain her sorrow and it'd like to break my heart.

I remained silent and still. I wasn't unfamiliar with the modern age. I just simply didn't prefer it. I knew what a car was and I knew how modern young people were, but none of this sounded like it was truly any of Quinn's fault. Still, I had promised not to judge, so I kept my mouth firmly shut. In this case, however, I was certain I was looking at the guilt of a survivor rather than the guilt of a woman who had committed some form of any real atrocity.

"I am truly sorry for your loss, lass," I said quietly, and, under better control, she lowered her hand from her mouth and put it with the other around her mug. Still, though she'd regained the majority of her composure, her hands shook from where she gripped the thick stoneware. She raised it, liquid sloshing inside from her trembling and took a fortifying drink.

"It's my fault. If I had just listened to her, hadn't been such a selfish shit – "

"Hey," I gave her a look of reproach. It was automatic. I didn't like her self-deprecation. Not over what, to me, was clearly something outside of her control.

"So much for not judging," she said and her gaze became shuttered. I pressed my lips into a grim line and sighed.

"I know what you're thinking," she said, and there was a hint of accusation in her tone.

"Oh, aye? You do now, do ya?" I asked, eyebrows raised in amusement.

"It's not my fault; that it's just survivor's guilt, and I need to get over myself, right?"

I felt my expression slacken and shook my head, "Aye, to the first one, perhaps a little of the second, but none of the third, lass. There are some things you just don't get over. My wife, for example. That is a pain that never goes away. It just becomes more tolerable the more that time drags on."

Silence fell between us, drifting like gossamer from the little cottage's low ceiling and settling over us comfortably. She lost her tense posture and diverted her eyes from me to the flickering firelight in the little wood stove's grate. She stared for a long time and finally said, "Nothing will likely ever convince me that it isn't somehow my fault. If I'd only not been such a selfish dick. If I hadn't pressured her. If I hadn't waited until last fucking call before we left..." She trailed off and made a helpless noise and closed her eyes before saying, "She had a bad feeling and I just didn't listen."

The words *That still doesn't make any of it your fault,* clung to the inside of my mouth with the bitter tang of uselessness. Instead, I raised my mug and said, "To us, two broken souls taking a bit of refuge from the world in one another's company."

She gave me a sad, one-sided smile and raised her mug, clicking it gently against mine saying, "I suppose I can drink to that," before taking a hearty sip. I took a final swallow of my own brew and set my mug on the table.

"Will I see you again?" she asked as I stood and I looked down at her.

As much as I would honestly have loved to say yes, I told her, "Likely not, lass, and it's probably for the best that way."

"Why would you say that?" she asked, and insecurity moved behind her golden-brown eyes.

"The last part of the tale, in my case, is true. I am indeed cursed to wander in darkness."

"I was always a bit of a night-owl," she said and locked her eyes with mine. "Besides, you're the only person I've met since Livvy died that I really feel like I can relate to."

Bollocks. I didn't say it out loud. I didn't want to be a jerk, not to her. Not now. Truth was, I felt the same. I liked talking with her and I wished I could again.

"If the fates wish it," I said, "Then our paths will cross again."

She looked disappointed but nodded.

"They have no reason to, but I guess here's to hoping they smile on us a little."

I nodded once and, gathering my lantern from her table, saw

myself out. I turned up my coat collar once outside against the chill and it felt like I had to tear myself away from her door. Unfortunately, I had a message to deliver and only a few hours yet to make it to the Rath of the Sluagh.

Reluctantly, I struck out toward the road to continue fulfilling my end of the bargain with my Queen.

7

———————

Quinn...

It was strange. I felt like I'd suffered a loss all over again, much smaller than the scale than the loss of Livvy, but at the same time, the hurt just seemed to compound itself. It was frustrating to me and I realized, finally, after a couple of days that I was lonely. So incredibly, painfully, lonely, and I hadn't realized it until Jack had made me feel just a little bit less lonesome.

I filled my days with walks that ranged out further and further from Mrs. O'Leary's and the village. My evenings, I ate dinner at the pub and talked with Saoirse. She helped take the edge off a bit, always a bright and shining wit with a wicked edge of sarcasm, but she was typically very busy, which made it so our conversations were fleeting at best.

Additionally, I tried conscienciously to make it back to my cottage before full dark, heeding Jack's warning that the leader of the Wild Hunt, Gwynn, could return if he cared to. I really hoped that he wouldn't but I couldn't be so sure. Of course, as the days got shorter, getting back to Mrs. O'Leary's before full dark fell began to get harder and harder. I tended to get lost in my drawings and stayed later than I intended. In the same vein, the more days passed with nothing happening, the sillier I was beginning to feel about my paranoia. Still, it wouldn't completely leave me.

I still dreamed, but every time I woke from one of the nightmares, it was to discover that Jack's necklace had drifted away from my skin. I fell asleep every night clutching it in my hand and if it managed to stay there, the dreams remained my own. It was a frightening thing, not knowing which was which, and it gave me an insight into just what a bastard that this Gwynn guy was. I mean, I was sure I wasn't the first that he'd done this to, especially if he were as old as the internet had said he was. I admit, I had Googled the name, though I also admit some confusion when I'd discovered it was a Welsh and not Irish name, something I had no one to ask about unless the fates allowed me to see Jack again.

I doubted it very sincerely, but I have to admit, I nurtured a small ember of hope, lingering at my window late into the night, only going to bed when I could barely keep my eyes open. I even kept an eye out on my walks during the day for a glimpse of him in the trees, but so far, nothing, and I swear I felt the disappointment more keenly every day that went by. It was frustrating missing someone I barely knew and I just didn't know why. I didn't know how he'd gotten past my walls so quickly but, much like I didn't question the existence of fairies too hard, I also didn't question this. I figured if I did, all it would do was drive me some sort of crazy.

Today, on my wandering journey, I found myself back at the church with the sun low enough in the sky that if I were to make it back to Mrs. O'Leary's before dark, I didn't have much time to explore. Maybe ten minutes or so. If I stayed any longer, I would be spending another night on hallowed ground and the nights were getting quite a bit colder now. That, and without Jack and the heat of his lantern, I didn't think I would make it a whole night unscathed this time.

I wandered through the graveyard attached to the ruins of the church. The standing stones were weathered, the majority of them so much so they were unreadable. I didn't linger, cold dread ticking down my spine like spider legs when I wondered to myself if Jack's victims had been buried here. I stopped looking at the stones too closely. A real-world reminder beyond the scorched out remnants of the building was a little too much to bear, I think.

I understood why he had done it. I didn't entirely disagree with it, but I had to wonder what kind of person that made me.

I reached the other side of the ruins and looked into the woods beyond. It was beautiful. The light came through the trees just so, painting the fall leaves in a riot of color. Golden light fell in angled shafts through the canopy to the leaf-littered and yet still-green forest floor. It was breathtaking, and I couldn't resist becoming a part of the scenery and so I stepped into the tree line.

I was so engaged with wonder, stepping from tree to tree; orange capped toadstools among their roots, ivy climbing their trunks. It wasn't hard to see the magic here. I followed a trail, too wide to be just from the game, too finished to be anything but man-made, yet overgrown enough that it had to be old and disused.

I clutched the small nail in my hand out of habit, which is why I think I saw them. At first, I thought they were dragonflies. The wing configuration was similar, shiny and iridescent, catching the light in blues and lavenders, sparking fiery pinks and winking reflections of green. They weren't dragonflies at all, though. One, it was too cold, and two, dragonflies didn't wear clothes.

One flew in front of me and I smiled, watching as she hovered, cocking her head to the side. I mimicked the movement and she startled and let out a musical sound before zipping away. I didn't follow. Having listened to Mrs. O'Leary's stories, I didn't know if it was okay or safe. Instead, I walked on and watched them gather in pockets and along the ivy leaves.

I dipped off the raised path and went down a gentle incline when I spotted what looked like another ruin, only to find a clearing and an ivy-covered embankment. There was a ring of stone, but they seemed to be more natural than carved, covered in moss, drifts of dried leaves gathering at their bases. Still, natural as they may be, they most definitely looked deliberately placed, though how I wasn't sure. They had to be hundreds, if not thousands of pounds.

"Quinn?"

I jerked my head up and looked where the soft voice had come from and felt a smile, a real one, split my face.

He was tucked back, away from the light, in the recess of a rock wall rising on the other side of the small clearing from where I'd come from. The ivy draped the rock, and a couple of the little sprites I'd seen dotted the leaves, looking on in curiosity.

"Jack!" I exclaimed and took several steps forward, stopping short at the war of expression on his face.

He seemed to make up his mind and waved me forward and I went. So very glad to see him I didn't even think about it. I just folded myself around him and hugged him tightly, his arms falling lightly around me in return. I looked up and he touched my face as if in wonder, like he couldn't believe I was really here and I murmured softly, "I guess the fates smiled on us after all."

Jack...

I'd been restless and wandering, though now was typically the time I would sleep. Suddenly, the Rath spawned an opening to the human world before me and I carefully edged closer, sweeping some of the ivies to the side to reveal her standing among the ring of stones that marked this entrance.

"Quinn?" I'd asked and she'd whirled. Some of the pixies clinging to the leaves looked from me to her curiously.

I hung my lantern on the hook among the ivy leaves as she cried softly, "Jack!" her voice an excited whisper-shout. She'd come right to me, molding herself against my body and she fit so nicely. I'd missed her; had spent days resisting the urge to go to her, to see her, and I was so torn over how to feel in this moment.

My heart surged with gladness at her presence, but my mind did so much the complete opposite I was nearly dizzied by the stark contrast. She looked up at me and I swept some of the lush curls out of her face, much softer than they looked. I couldn't resist trailing a thumb lightly along her cheek as if to assure myself that she was indeed really here and that this wasn't a cruel joke.

"I guess the fates smiled on us after all," she said lightly and dispelled any doubt. My resistance to the siren's call that was her company shattered, and I brought my mouth to hers, kissing her firmly.

She made a small, surprised sound and tensed and for a moment I thought I'd misread the situation, but then, then she melted into me so beautifully. Her lips parted and she kissed me back and I swear, it was like I felt the sun on my face, for real. For the first time in what felt like forever. Only I didn't burn from it like I did from the real sun. I warmed, and the crackling frozen chambers of my heart that I thought would remain that way forever began to thaw and throb with life again.

I let my hands slide around to her back and clutched her to me, carefully, gently, as if she were this fragile thing that I could crush too easily and were it not for the amount of iron on my person, I would believe this to be a cruel vision by Gwynn, or perhaps even Eibhleann. I knew Gwynn remained cross over my besting him and Eibhleann was cross with me as well. Jealous was she, over the fact that Quinn hadn't been far from my mind since our first meet.

She broke the kiss, breathlessly and her eyes fluttered open to take me in. She smiled slightly, with that familiar edge of sadness, and said with an edge of nervous, almost shyness, "I'm really glad you missed me, too."

I smiled and laughed slightly and said, "Aye, lass. Aye, I missed ye."

She rested her head against my chest, and sighed out, arms clutching me loose around my waist. I sighed and held her back as the light out there began to fail and the gloaming turned to full effect.

It was too late for her to walk back to her cottage alone, and I was torn. So tempted to take her into the Rath. To show her the whole of my world, for it was a terrible beauty, wild and something to behold. It was also so very dangerous.

"It's growing late," I admonished gently. "There would be no way you would make it before dark. Quinn, you have to be more careful."

"I know," she said, voice muffled in the front of my coat as she held tight to me. "I just let myself get carried away, it's so beautiful out here and then I saw them and I really let myself get distracted."

I glanced out over the sunken stones and caught flashes and flitters of light where the dying sun sparkled along the glassy chitin wings of the pixies in the area. I nodded and said, "The glamour is strongest with those ones. I'm amazed you saw through it."

"You gave me the nail, remember?"

"Aye, but it only does so much. A pixie's glamour is far stronger than that of one of the court."

"Oh, what's that mean, then?"

"I don't know," I told her honestly. "There are several possibilities."

She stepped back from me and looked me in the eyes smiling faintly.

"Name one," she said and I thought about it.

"Could be that you hold some magick of your own," I said and her smile grew. I checked the light outside and satisfied the sun had dipped a sufficient amount, took down my lantern from where I'd hung it.

"Where to?"

"I have a rare night free. I thought I would see you safely home."

"I'd like that," she confessed, falling into step beside me, fingers loosely threaded through mine and hugging my arm slightly. It made me feel quite the gentleman.

"Have you eaten?" she asked and I shook my head.

"No, not recently."

"Are you hungry? I'm not exactly a renowned chef, but I'm not terrible."

I laughed gently. "I've been known to enjoy cooking myself."

"What are you proposing? A team effort?"

"Aye, I think we could do some damage, you and I."

She smiled and I believe she blushed, coyly averting her eyes to the ground as if she watched her step.

"Context is everything," she sang out lightly and I laughed

bringing the back of her hand to my lips, pressing a kiss along her knuckles.

"Aye. Aye, it is."

We talked, strolling leisurely along the old lane. Our chatter idle, mostly plans for supper. She named things I'd never heard of before and with some discussion, we came to the conclusion that, with the ingredients she had, a simple fare of stew was in order.

We made good time once I decided it was safe to exit the tree line and step into the open. Twilight deepened gently into the night and the stars sparked icy fire against the black. None of it, and I do mean none of it, compared to the radiant beauty of Quinn's freckled face. The longer I spent in her company, the more besotted I became, and it was so very hard not to fall under her spell which wasn't a spell at all. It was just her.

She held so many twists and curves, so many secret places that I had yet to discover. What made her happy was still elusive, her smiles rare and something to be cherished. The sadness casting shadows in her eyes was something I wanted to chase away. One thing I knew about her, that I was certain beyond any shadow of a doubt, was that she was so very hard on herself.

Our time was finite, she would eventually have to return to America, and as much as I had tried to stay away something had brought us together again, and rather than resist it, I was choosing to embrace it and the hurt that her leaving would likely bring. Still, opportunities like this were fleeting and something rare. Opportunities like this must be respected and lived to their fullest, and so I would do that and let come what may.

Decision made, I felt a weight off my shoulders and was all too happy to speak softly with her, learn what I could of her, and see where this chance encounter would lead for the time being.

It was almost too easy to forget how short her time with me would be but the Rath had taught me a thing or two about the currents of time, namely to enjoy every bit of what time you had before it rushed downstream and out of sight and finer memory.

Quinn sighed out and I turned my attention to her. She smiled up at me faintly and said, "You're a deep thinker, aren't you Jack?"

"I have been known to get lost in thought from time to time."

"I like that about you," she said.

"Oh?"

"Yeah. I feel like I don't have to fill the silence all the time, every time with you. I can just be and that's okay, too."

I nodded, understanding perfectly what she meant. We'd lapsed into silence a little while back, while my mind got away from me, but it was a comfortable thing and had been a long time since I had the luxury of being myself in another's presence without any pretenses.

"It's nice," I said and she nodded in silent agreement, which made me smile.

"Of all the things you regret, what is the one thing you regret the most?" she asked softly sometime later, as we turned onto the lane that held her cottage.

"I have a lot of regrets, lass. Probably far more than you."

"In fairness, you're a bit older than me, and as such, you have lived a little more."

I chuckled darkly. "Aye."

"So, honestly, what is your biggest regret?"

I paused and drew her around to face me, cupping her cheek in my hand and committing every line, curve, and freckle of her face to memory by the light of the moon and my lantern.

"Regrets and living in them means you're living in the past, Darlin'. I choose to live in the now. Here, in this moment, with you."

Her breath caught and her eyes bore the shine of a rare emotion. I felt the world still around us and determined to live the moment fully, I kissed her again. She kissed me back and I could tell she was there, with me, completely. It was a special and treasured gift. A moment I would treasure for a long time to come. An eternity past when she would be in the grave.

I refused to let the thought linger. Shoving it into the back of my mind as I drew her closer to me still.

She broke the kiss first, and stammered something about going inside. The moment disintegrated around us and I agreed. I would like nothing better to be in a close and cozy space. Just me and her.

9

Quinn...

Everything about the city-wise and street-smart girl I was wanted to say that Jack was being slicker than owl-shit. That things were going way too fast and that he was hiding something from me, or trying to get into my pants. The trouble was, they were all false constructs, nothing more than lingering ghosts from every other guy who'd hurt me or tried to pick me up for a one-and-done...

This wasn't that. Jack could have been a real damn good liar, but I didn't think anyone was that good. I was a natural skeptic one hundred percent of the time; I had to be, but this? This felt entirely different than anything I had ever experienced before. This was something genuine and rare. Incredibly special as if the universe and the powers that be watched us closely, holding its collective breath in anticipation; waiting to see what we would do. Everything about this felt right and fated and my gut told me not to screw this up, whatever it was.

You know, no pressure or anything. I thought to myself.

I lowered myself flat on my feet and swallowed hard, looking up at Jack and the sky beyond him with its hundreds of thousands, its millions of pinpricks of light.

I'd never seen anything like it before, but then again, I was a city girl and this was as far from the bright lights of the city that you could get and still pretend to be a part of the civilized world.

"Let's go inside?" I asked, and sounded as breathless as I felt. His kiss had that effect on me.

"Aye, a good idea to be sure," he said softly and he sounded breathless, too.

We continued down the road, drawing even with Mrs. O'Leary's garden fence, walking its length to the drive. Jack made the turn first, and we strolled to my cottage door. He held up his lantern for me so that I could find my key in my satchel.

"Thanks," I murmured.

"Not at all."

That thick Irish brogue of his sent shivers down my spine that had nothing to do with the chill in the autumn air. I turned the key in the lock and pushed open the door and he indicated I should go before him.

I slipped inside at the same time I slipped my satchel over my head and turned. He'd come in behind me and shut the door tight, setting his lantern in the center of the two-person table beneath the front window.

I liked the diffuse glow it gave off and rather than switching on any electric lights, I thought about lighting a few of the jar candles I had placed around the cottage. Before I could do anything, though, Jack's fingers were curling into the back of my coat collar.

"Oh," I said, surprised, and hung my satchel on one of the iron hooks in the back of the door. I unfastened the buttons on my coat and let him take it. He hung it on the same hook as my bag and began working at the fastenings on his own coat.

"I was thinking about just lighting a few candles for a little more light," I said.

"I'd like that," he said and I moved to do it as he crouched in front of the little woodstove with its cooktop, opening the front to stoke the fire.

I hesitated a moment and deciding to live in the now, stoked my courage into asking him, "Jack, how exactly does your curse work?"

He leaned up and turned, looking over his shoulder at me, his eyes roving my face from chin to eyes and back again, deliberately, the weight of his gaze such a physical thing I felt it against my skin like a caress.

"I burn," he said finally.

"Like, with any light?"

"Just sunlight. I haven't been brave enough to try with artificial light, like electricity."

"Yeah, I don't know that I would be either," I said, and leaned back against the edge of the kitchen sink.

"Aye, I miss it," he said and I raised an eyebrow.

"I didn't ask that," I said.

"No, but you were wondering it, plain as day." His grin was disarming and I felt a smile of my own answering it. I bit my lip to keep from laughing. He was right, I had been thinking it.

"Is that your biggest regret?"

He bowed his head and sighed, nodding, but not in answer, more like he'd come to a decision about what to tell me.

"I don't regret for one moment burning those people, Quinn. They had it coming for what they did to my wife. Do I regret not feelin' the sun on my face? Aye, I miss it, but not enough to wholly regret what I did."

It was monstrous and disappointing but not at all surprising that he felt that way. I grappled with what I was feeling. Trying to decide if his revelation was a strong enough deterrent to want me to make him leave. I suppose, the most surprising thing about it, was that the answer was 'no'.

I wanted him to stay. I wanted him to stay and have dinner with me, and have just one evening of domestic bliss even if it was just pretend. I mean, I didn't really see this working between us beyond just a fling while I was here, in Ireland. He couldn't leave, and I couldn't stay... could I?

"A lot of thoughts just went across your face, Love."

His voice was guarded, carefully neutral, and I smiled and I knew it held that edge of sadness. It was familiar to me now. Like a favorite old blanket. Threadbare and not quite warm enough to be comfortable but at the same time, so familiar, too familiar to let it go.

"I guess my heart hurts for you," I said and it wasn't a lie. Far from it.

"Don't," he said. "I came to terms with what I've done a long time ago. It's not the life I wanted for myself, but I've made the most of it and suddenly, if ever there was a silver lining, I find myself grateful for it."

I looked up sharply and asked, "Why?"

"It led me to finding you, didn't it?"

I pressed my lips together and dropped my eyes, nodding a bit too rapidly. I felt bad, suddenly. I mean, I was a real shitty consolation prize. I heard the rustle of cloth and the scrape of his boot on the unfinished wood floor. I didn't look up, even when the rough fabric of his shirt came into view.

He tipped my chin lightly with two fingers and I met his eyes with mine. He smiled and it was a mysterious one, one I couldn't readily read.

"I didn't like the look of that, lass," he murmured and his voice was husky with... something, I don't know.

I licked my lips quickly and his eyes fixated on the motion. Whatever I'd been about to say died on my tongue before I could say it, and then the aforementioned body part was suddenly otherwise occupied, tangling with his.

He was a skilled and phenomenal kisser. I'd never felt anything quite like it before. It wasn't just lips, tongue, and his hands smoothing down my back to hold my hips. It was a whole-body experience. Everything went awash in tingles as if a light electrical charge had suddenly lit the air, making everything stand on end. Goosebumps marched down my arms and it was the most pleasant feeling, but I couldn't help myself, I wanted more.

I wanted to forget all the sadness, drown my sorrows, and with alcohol out of the question, sex with Jack seemed like a really good idea right now. When he kissed me, everything fell away. While I had the little voice in my head practically screaming that it was a bad idea, that it was bound to end painfully, I couldn't help myself. I pulled myself closer and let his arms go around me and kissed him back deeply. I didn't hold anything back, and when his hand tugged my blouse from my jeans and slipped beneath its hem, my heart surged with a mixture of relief and triumph.

He backed me up against the sink and small kitchen counter and I let him. My arms found their way around his shoulders, much broader than I'd initially realized and I clung to him. He lifted me and set my ass firmly on the edge of the counter and made a small sound of surprise which he quickly swallowed. I had never had a man pick me up like that before and I had to say, I liked the sensation. I wasn't a particularly large girl, nor was I small. I was pretty much smack-dab in the middle of everything. Perfectly average in every way. At least I thought so.

Jack made me feel beautiful in a way I couldn't explain or even fully understand. Only two other people in my life had ever made me feel like I was worth anything and that'd been my daddy and my best friend. Both of whom were gone now. So, I cherished this feeling while I had it.

"Is this okay?" he asked against my mouth, and I felt my lips curve into a smile.

"More than okay," I whispered back. "Don't stop."

He groaned and surged forward, capturing my mouth with his once more. His hands smoothed against my skin and I shivered delightedly while I worked his long, old-fashioned shirt out of his pants. He let me lift it over his head, raising his arms above his head to allow me to strip it away and holy God, he had an amazing body. Chest and shoulders broad and muscular, but not from lifting weights. No, he was chiseled from hard labor and hours of lifting a heavy hammer. His stomach was flat but not super-defined. A man who was a product of his craft, which I could appreciate more than the guys back home that obsessed over their abs with their eating and their gym time.

"I like that you like what you see," he murmured and I startled. He chuckled darkly and kissed me again until I was breathless.

"What's not to like?" I asked, smoothing my hands over him.

He didn't answer me, just gave me a half-charmed, hooded little smile that could have meant anything and swept my hair aside to put his lips to the side of my neck. I made this impassioned sound, not quite a gasp, not quite a moan, but something in between the two. My body bowed toward him unbidden and I held onto his shoulders. The pleasant feeling of his kiss had just intensified by like a thousandfold, but strangely, just half of my body reacted and it was the half that his lips didn't play against.

I shivered and couldn't help the joyous little giggle that poured from my mouth which just seemed to encourage him. I closed my eyes and breathed him in, masculine and clean overlaid with the warm scent of burning wood with just the barest underlying bite of burning metal. It was uniquely Jack, and I scooted closer to the edge of the counter, wrapping my legs around his waist, encouraging everything he was doing while simultaneously begging him for even more.

He lifted my boho-chic peasant blouse over my head and I raised my arms from off his shoulders so that he could sweep it over my head. I think he dropped it in the sink, but I didn't care. He lifted my cotton camisole over my head next and dropped it, as well. When he encountered my bra, he raised an eyebrow.

"Just how many layers have ye on, lass?"

"Last one," I said and unclasped it for him. It was a front clasp and I couldn't be sure he'd encountered a bra before though I guess I shouldn't assume anything. The look of relief that crossed his face, however, told me that I may have been correct in my assumption. He skimmed the thin straps off my shoulders and down my arms leaving the garment to rest somewhere behind me.

I held my breath, a little nervous at being topless in front of him but if the way his eyes lit with the dark light of desire was any indication, I'd had nothing to worry about.

He went straight to my mouth first, then to the side of my neck he hadn't paid attention to yet. Marching his lips along my skin, down the side of my neck, lingering in that spot that drove me crazy, before continuing along my collarbone, down my chest, until he took one nipple gently between his teeth, teasing it with his tongue until I gasped and forgot just how to properly breathe.

I pressed my lower body into his and felt the hot, hard length of him press back into me between our clothes and suddenly, there was just way too many layers between us. Thankfully, he worked at his own pants, because I was way too frantic to try and figure out the old-fashioned catches and ties, buttons, or whatnot that were involved in keeping them up.

While he worked at his, I worked at the laces on my boots, raising first one knee, then the other, bracing my heel on the edge of the counter. I toed them off my feet as he did the same to his. Then he dropped his pants and I automatically reached for him, wrapping gentle yet firm fingers around his length.

He shuddered, eyes closing and dropped his hands limp, to his sides, letting me do what I wanted. I slipped off the countertop and to my knees in front of him and, smoothing back his uncut foreskin, took him into my mouth.

"Oh, lass..."

He raised his hands and gently touched my head. I continued what I was doing, sliding him along my tongue and carefully into my throat, timing my breathing, holding my jaw just so to negate my gag reflex. I wanted him to feel good and judging by the even, gasping moans coming from above me, I was doing just fine.

"Lass, lass, lass!" He stopped me, breathless, voice strained, and reached down, helping me up swiftly to my feet, pulling my body against his, his mouth fiercely claiming mine and his hands delving into the back of my undone jeans, beneath my panties, to grip my ass and use it for leverage to haul me closer still.

His cock trapped between us, resting against our stomachs, pressing hotly into my skin, just made me ache to have him inside me and I didn't think for one minute that it wasn't going to happen. We were both far too gone on each other to not go there. He pushed my jeans and underwear down and I stepped on the cuff one at a time and pulled my legs free, my panties just naturally following suit. I stepped out of the material and wrapped my arms around his shoulders, flattening my breasts against his chest. He let his hands move from my ass down my legs, cupping the outsides of my thighs and urging me to give a little leap. I trusted him and did so, wrapping my legs around his waist as he picked me up.

His cock pressed into me at the apex of my thighs and I ground my wet pussy against him. We were at the wrong angle for him to get inside me, and it was absolutely maddening because by this point, I was on fire and it was all I wanted. He turned and walked us to the bed, laying me down on it, following me up onto the firm mattress and getting back between my legs, grinding against me, heightening the want between us, kissing me fiercely.

Eventually, even he couldn't take his own teasing anymore. Reaching between us and guiding himself to my entrance, he slipped inside so easily, and I pressed down over the top of him, with a satisfied hiss. He eased into me as slowly as I would let him and once all the way in, leaned over the top of me, meeting my eyes with his and smoothing some stray curls from the side of my face.

It was sweet, and strangely more intimate than I was used to but I liked that. I liked it a lot. Satisfied with whatever he saw in my expression, he moved his hips back, withdrawing almost to the point of leaving my body completely before thrusting forward again. His every movement was slow and deliberate, building the pleasure between our bodies carefully.

I touched every bit of him I could reach. Smoothing my hands along his ribs, over his back, gripping his ass and pulling him into me, which judging, by the way he closed his eyes and bowed his head, he liked.

I liked how warm he was, how safe I felt caged and pressed

beneath his larger and much stronger body. The care he took in making love to me was exquisite and so very beautiful. It was emotionally moving and striking in a way I had never experienced before.

I closed my eyes and completely gave myself over to just feeling and it was so worth it. The sensual gratification built at a slow pace, rolling up and out from the center of my being like storm clouds through the sky, slowly taking over. He felt so good. Warm, inviting, stroking over places inside me I didn't even think had nerve endings. The attraction between us was something absolute, the chemistry between us out of this world, which is where we took each other. To otherworldly heights, bodies aglow with a light that wouldn't burn him and that wasn't visible to the naked eye.

"Oh, yes, Quinn..." he murmured, and I knew exactly what he meant. I was close, so very close, one ray of that imaginary sunshine away from bursting into flame like some sort of phoenix and he held me there, in the palm of his hand, nurturing and coaxing me into the absolute best orgasm of my life.

10

Jack...

    I lost myself in her body, mind, and soul. I can't say it was the worst thing I had ever done, but I couldn't say it was the best thing, either. I knew it would have to end. She knew it would have to end, but I didn't think either of us had much control when it came to the matter and so, for now, I was determined to enjoy what time we had.

I loved how she twined around me. I loved how her body fit inside the curve of mine just so, and how it gripped me, pulling me deeper. Her gasps and moans, her scent, her warmth, all of it so alluring. She was so honest, so raw, and so free once she gave herself over to me; it was a beautiful thing for sure. I couldn't deny her any more than I could deny the fates who so obviously wished us to be together. Had they not, they wouldn't have drawn us together. If it was one thing I learned, it was to never try to cross the fates, nor to question what they had in mind or in store for us. I would simply have to wait that part out and see.

She gasped and I kissed her as I moved inside her, swallowing her next moan. It was sweeter than any faerie food I'd tasted and that was saying a lot. She held onto me and was such a responsive lover. She knew what she was doing, but at the same time, she held such an innocence to her. She was the perfect amalgamation of dirty and clean and I couldn't want for anything else.

The sensation of her wrapped around me. The silken wetness of her sweet cunt like to drove me mad... and the way she looked at me. Gods, old and new, she ensnared me with her gaze, and the way she held me with it felt like coming home.

There were no games, no manipulations with her, and I adored her company for that. She hid behind her walls, certainly, but that was for fear of being hurt and it was plain to see. It was also plain to see that she was desperate to connect and I was becoming happier by the moment to be the one to ground her.

"Oh, God, Jack!" she cried and her back bowed, thrusting her perfect breasts into my chest as her body clenched around mine. She shuddered and I bowed my head, struggling not to find my own release. Not yet, not just yet, but it was impossible. I followed her into the light that had nothing to do with the physical realm yet everything to do with it at the same time.

I came back to my senses laying atop her, barely holding my weight from crushing her. Her body was soft and yielding, vulnerable beneath mine in that way that made me want to protect her from everything.

She captured my face between her hands and we stared at one another. Worlds passed between us on a thread of silence and I lowered my mouth to hers and kissed her. It took several moments – and for my arms to start to tremble – before I moved off of her and lay by her side.

"That was... that was... wow," she whispered, and I smiled.

"My sentiments exactly, Love."

She tucked herself against me and I held her, rubbing her back lightly, loving the feel of her soft skin. She had beautiful skin, even and as smooth as one of the Fae themselves.

Our breathing slowed and I glanced down at her. She had closed her eyes and was simply basking in the warmth of the fire from the stove. I let her, and I let her sleep when her breathing deepened and evened with slumber. I waited for a time until I was certain I wouldn't wake her and got up.

I had no intentions of slipping out and absconding. I had every intention of dressing and crafting the stew we'd planned on the way here. She was thin, but not terribly so. Still, I felt she should eat, and I knew I was famished.

I pulled on my breeches and fastened them and assured she was resting fast, set to work in the small cottage kitchen. I put the stew on and stoked the fire. I sat on one of her kitchen chairs and watched the flames, glancing at her table which turned into a fixated stare on my lantern and the ember that burned within.

The bitter tang of regret filled my mouth and clenched my jaw.

It was true that I didn't regret what I'd done, but for the first time in a long time, I regretted the consequences of the bargain I'd struck. I would so love to see Quinn in the light. The full light of the sun, golden on her curls. I mean, there was one way, but I couldn't risk bringing her into the Rath. While I was near-certain Gwynn was no longer fixated, there were still far too many of the Dione Sidhe that could and would harm her for their own amusement.

No, it was best for her to remain out here, with her own kind, of which I was no longer a part. I'd come to that realization, confronted that truth, a long time ago and it'd long since stopped hurting, but the scar of it throbbed and ached.

Gods above and below, I'd forgotten how much I missed this; how much I'd loved watching my wife sleep. Watching Quinn sleep, I realized that Rhiannon and Quinn couldn't be more different but the feeling was the very same, an echo from the past, yet so fresh as to be new.

Of course, Quinn was new. There was no comparison between her and my Rhiannon. Singularly unique in both their beauty and their personality, yet something bothered me, nagged at me, and I couldn't quite put my finger on the reason for the unease and discord deep below the more pleasant emotions looking at her sleeping face brought to me.

"She's pretty."

I blinked and looked over; the voice came from Mags, a familiar lesser Fae of the Brownie persuasion.

"Ah, I doubt she knows the customs, Mags. I'll go ahead and apologize for her and rectify the situation when she wakes."

"Pish, posh, Jack! The lady of the main house handles all of that. Sets out a saucer for every cottage on her sill."

Mags was an aged and wise Brownie. She limped along with the use of a cane carved from a honeysuckle vine, light and twisted. She wore a floral housecoat, her brown and weathered skin leathery, her hands gnarled but strong. Her ears pointed, her nose non-existent, lips drawn and teeth gnarled, she was the picture of beauty for her race but to the rest of the worlds, both human and Tuatha Dé Danann alike, she could hardly be called so.

"Besides," she said, tottering over and stopping by my chair to stare into the fire, "the girl leaves me better than milk.

"Oh, aye? What does she leave you, then?"

"Drawings. Some of the most beautiful little things on scraps and bits of paper in the bin. My little treasures."

She stood by my leg and barely reached my knee. She looked up at me and I down at her and we traded smiles.

"I don't think that quite counts, Mags."

"Oh, aye, it does!"

"Does it now?"

"Aye!"

"How?"

She scoffed. "Because I say so, ye git!"

I fought not to laugh. I didn't wish to wake Quinn.

"She's a sweet girl, Jack," Mags said in her raspy, low voice.

"I know, Mags. Believe me, I know."

"Aye, I know you know."

"So why tell me, Mags?"

"I'll let ye figure that out on your own," she said. "Now clean up after yerself, so I don't have to do it."

"Ah, so the truth comes out. The girl's a clean sort and leaves you little to do."

"Oh, aye, but you know there's always something to be done, Jack. Always something you humans miss."

"Truer words have never been spoken, Mags, and aye, I'll have a care."

She limped her hobbled walk to the door, waving over her shoulder at me and disappeared, in the blink of an eye.

Oh, aye, I would have a care to clean up after myself. Either that or face havoc back at my forge, in my chambers in the Rath. You didn't cross a Brownie, and I should have expected they were rife in the village, even still.

I turned Mag's words over in my head and tended things while Quinn napped, not really sure where I should go from here.

11

Quinn...

I didn't remember dozing off, but I must have because the next thing I knew, I was waking up to the vision of Jack's broad back as he lifted a lid off a steaming pot on top of the woodstove. Fragrant steam billowed from the top as he peeked inside, and I smiled.

He'd cooked. He'd pretty much boned me into a blissed-out mini-coma and then he made me dinner. That was incredibly sweet.

"Traditionally, you buy the woman dinner before you take her to bed, but there's something about this that I like so much more," I said with a bit of dry humor. He looked over his shoulder at me and grinned.

"Of course, you say this before you've tasted my cooking."

I pushed myself into a sitting position and raised my knees, hugging them over the sheet that draped them.

"If it tastes as good as it smells, I don't think it's going to be a problem."

He chuckled and ladled some out into one of the cottage's stoneware bowls. He portioned some out into another and brought both bowls, complete with spoons, over to where I sat on the bed. He handed me one and I took it between both hands, sticking it under my nose and breathing in the steam.

"Seriously, Jack. This smells fantastic."

"Why, thank you. It's missing a good crusty bread, but there isn't anything I can do about that. Not at this hour."

"I'm sorry I fell asleep," I said, and I was. I missed out on the opportunity to see this fine-ass man at his domestic finest.

"Don't be," he murmured and touched the side of my face, following the curve of my cheek in a ghostly little caress that made me shiver in all the right ways. He smiled and I laughed a little bit. It was a nervous laugh because I don't think he, or any guy for that matter, could know just how far the little things like that tapped into a woman's soul. It was a dangerous thing, taking Jack O'Laughlin to my bed like I had. I was never very good at flings. It was too easy to fool myself into believing it was more than it actually was. I couldn't keep my emotions out of it like some women.

I was more than flirting with the man, I was flirting with disaster and I knew it. Still, I couldn't help myself.

"Ah, what's that look for then, lass?" His voice was soft, warm, and inviting me to spill all my secrets and what's more, it made me want to.

"Just thinking," I said reluctantly. I didn't want to tell him, but I didn't exactly know what to tell him instead.

He smiled and leaned in, kissing me softly and saying against my lips, "Its fine, keep your secrets."

"It's not like that," I said gently, suddenly feeling guilty. He raised his eyebrows and his silence was an invitation. It was one I wasn't brave enough to take, not yet.

"It's all right, love. Any man can see it plain, you've been hurt before and often."

"What's that supposed to mean?" I asked defensively, and he smiled this charming little smile and leaned forward, cupping the side of my neck, planting a kiss on my forehead.

"Nothing bad, darlin'. I just see the hurt in your eyes, the caution."

I took a bite of my stew so I wouldn't have to comment and he graciously let it go, dispelling some of the sudden, awkward tension. At least it was awkward for me. He sat there looking perfect and perfectly fine. It was a calm and tranquility that I didn't see on many people, let alone on a guy, and I had to say, it did something for me.

It made me feel at ease and like I really didn't have to worry about myself around him. It was the first time I felt like it was legitimately okay to be me. That had, honestly, only ever happened with one person before, and that person had been Livvy.

"I have," I said plaintively, staring into the bowl of my stew, almost too afraid of looking at him and what might be on his face.

"Have what?" he asked softly.

"Been hurt. A lot and often," I said.

"Aye, I'm listening," he said softly, and I heard his spoon click against the side of his bowl.

I didn't want to look at him. Call me a coward, but I had never been good at confronting the things that hurt me. I knew I didn't have a whole lot to bitch about, I mean, first world problems am I right? But a lot of what hurt worst for me was that my mommy, literally didn't love me enough as a child or even now as an adult, and when my dad had died that had been a serious rug pulled out from under my feet. The only person who had kept me sane and who had kept me together had been my best friend and I felt like it was all my fault, that I'd killed her.

It hurt opening up to people only to have them turn around and leave. Be it by dying, which I understood was completely out of their hands, or like my mother... She didn't care one bit about who I was. Didn't care about any of my accomplishments. None of it mattered because it wasn't who she wanted me to be, or the path that she'd chosen. She never let me live it down what an utter disappointment I was, either.

"Quinn..."

I looked up sharply at my name and chickened out. I felt my eyes well and grow hot, but I couldn't bring myself to speak, to say how lonely and alone I felt. To tell him about how much I just wished that once, just once, someone could love me as much as I loved them back, but at the same time, how so very afraid I was to love anyone ever again...

So many thoughts and emotions were caught in this sudden and fierce maelstrom crashing against the insides of my walls and I couldn't make myself say any of it.

The list was just never-ending and uninteresting, anyway.

His eyes pleaded with me to just say it, to say anything, and I did what I do best; I shut down. Drew myself back behind my walls where it was safe, regained my composure and said simply, "It's nothing, honest, I really don't know what my problem is right now."

He nodded slowly, the familiar lines of disappointment etching his expression and murmured, "I'm going to have to go soon."

I swallowed hard, my heart leaping off a cliff and plummeting with a disappointment of my own, even though I knew it was going to happen eventually. He would need to leave and be safely spirited away to whatever world he belonged to, because as much as I wanted him to belong to this one, I knew it couldn't be. No matter how many times I had to remind myself of that fact because I ached to have him stay.

What does it say I finally find a man I'm willing to maybe open up to and he basically turns into a pumpkin and has to go rushing off on me?

"I know," I whispered back and, again, there was the gentle touch against my cheek.

"I wished I didn't have to, love."

"Me, too," I said honestly, and he nodded.

"I'd like to see you again if the Rath and potential time difference stays true and will allow for it."

"I'll be here," I said and tried to keep the hard edge of sarcasm out of my tone. He smiled and I knew I'd failed, but I also knew he hadn't taken any offense.

He lifted one of my hands from the side of my bowl and placed a kiss against its palm, a sweet gesture that just made my heart give a hard throb which set it to aching all over again.

I wanted him to stay. I wanted to be alone. I didn't want to be alone. I needed to figure my shit out. Trust him, don't trust him, but I knew I was sending out mixed messages and that that wasn't okay.

We finished the meal in a silence that was surprisingly companionable. I was grateful that my post-nap awkwardness hadn't completely ruined things. He'd waited patiently for me to dress and see him to my door and I stopped him before he could step out into the dark with only his flickering lantern to guide him.

"Hey, I'm really sorry," I murmured.

"For what?"

I gave him a slightly withering look and he smiled and started to shake his head, which only made my look intensify.

"I don't want you to think I have a case of buyer's remorse, or that I regret sleeping with you because I don't. Far from it. I just... I guess I have a lot more to deal with than I thought."

His look softened and he cupped my cheek, leaning in to kiss my forehead. I closed my eyes and savored the touch of his lips to my skin, savored the peace and the stillness it brought to the raging tempest of my emotions.

"I understand," he whispered and leaned back to look me in the eye. "I'm a patient man, Quinn..." he trailed off and raised an eyebrow and I blushed deeply.

"Carter," I said, embarrassed for having kept it from him for so long. "I illustrate under the name Quinn Cassidy, though." Livvy had thought I should have a pen name too, and had given me her favorite cat's name as a last name for me to adopt. We'd found the kitten together when we were fifteen and her parents had let her keep it.

"Carter, though I quite like Cassidy, as well."

"Tomorrow night?" I asked and he gave a nod.

"If the Queen has nay for me to do, then aye. Tomorrow evening."

I nodded and he'd kissed me then, a fragile thing that felt like thinnest glass to me. I committed the feel of his lips against mine to memory, just as I'd committed the feel of them against my forehead a moment before.

I had a feeling that if Jack were anything like the men of today, I'd never see him again. I immediately felt guilty for the thought, because Jack had pretty much proven time and again he was nothing like anyone I'd ever met before. 'Close to' wasn't the same as 'the same as' at all.

"Good night, Quinn Carter."

"Good night, Jack O'Laughlin."

And that was how we parted.

12

Jack...

I re-entered the Rath the same way I'd left it, by the entrance near the standing stones. I was near instantaneously greeted by an angry Eibhleann.

"And just where have you been?" she asked imperiously.

One of those moods, then. I didn't answer her immediately. I wasn't beholden to her, but to not answer at all would simply cause a more dramatic response than I was willing to deal with.

"I escorted Ms. Quinn Carter back to her current residence," I said coolly and braced for her reaction.

Her eyes narrowed and I felt my heart sink like a stone, I knew that look and it wasn't good. She leaned forward and her eyes slipped shut as she breathed deeply. They flew open, the deep lavender of her irises locking on mine.

"I knew it," she declared. "You're fucking her, aren't you?"

I hedged my bets and took just a touch too long to do it. Eibhleann's mouth went agape and she demanded to know, voice haughty, "You don't fancy yourself in love with her now, do you Jack?"

I hesitated, to ask myself that very question, and it was the wrong thing to do. Eibhleann's voice poured from her like so much bitter and broken glass as she laughed and laughed. She stabbed a finger into my chest and said, "Be careful, Jack. She's human and she can't ever understand you as well as I do."

"Eibhleann, it's not like that," I said and frowned, confused by Eibhleann's intensity. I'd only ever been just a passing flight of fancy for her. Never anything more.

She gave me a significant look that left me mystified as to its meaning, fixing it on me as she turned slowly away. Finally, she dismissed me by giving me her back completely, gliding up the hall away from me. I scowled.

"Eibhleann!" I called after her but she simply raised a hand and waved me off without turning.

She was angry, angrier than she honestly had a right to be and I felt more than a little disturbed by that.

"Be careful with that one, Jack."

I startled and looked down. Mags was standing at my knee, staring down the hall at Eibhleann's smooth retreating back, her light purple gossamer gown plunging at the back to reveal it.

"Mags?" I queried and the Brownie shuddered and looked up at me.

"The centuries tend to drive some of them mad. That, and their inbreeding, I suspect, has something to do with it." She snorted.

"Look at you, bold as brass," I muttered. The Sidhe would be angry at such an assertion, even if it were also a truth.

She scoffed, "I'm old, Jack. Older than a lot of them. I remember, have suffered just about every torture their pretty little heads can come up with. When you've lived as long as I under their thrall, there's not much left to frighten you."

She sounded old at that moment. Old and tired. I couldn't say I blamed her. I felt much the same despite my youthful appearance. I could only imagine how someone who had lived every moment of every passing year felt. Mag's years numbered in the thousands. Mine had barely scraped a couple of hundred.

She was right, however. As beautiful as the Sidhe of the dark court, the rulers of the darkling throng, were, they were also the stuff of nightmares. Beautiful nightmares, but nightmares none the less. Some of them, their moods were as unpredictable as the wind and just as temperamental.

"I hear your warning, Mags. I simply don't know what to do about it."

She made a rude snort and laughed bitterly.

"That's the problem, Jack. There's nothing you can do about it. There's no being forewarned or forearmed when it comes to the likes of her. The best you can hope for is to brace, hold, and to make your best move after something has already happened."

"That's not terribly comforting," I said with a bit of dry humor I didn't feel.

"It wasn't meant to be comforting, Jack. It was a warning. Look for harm to come to the American girl. I told you, I like her, but that one," she pointed up the hall where Eibhleann had disappeared, "won't let it go. She's the jealous sort, Jack; you know that though, don't you?"

"I've seen it, I just never thought she had a care one way or the other where I was concerned."

"You'd be surprised, Jack. You would. You know this is a world where they will hold your greatest weakness against you. Would you wear it on your sleeve?"

I didn't answer because I was too busy thinking. I was afraid I may have done just that or given the appearance that I had. Quinn wasn't precisely a weakness, but she could become one. I would need to make peace with Eibhleann, and soon, but though we'd been lovers for many years, I didn't precisely know how to go about that. I didn't think there would ever be a need for it. I hadn't for one moment ever gathered I'd meant a thing to her beyond a good time, and always on her whim.

To say I was shaken by the potential of our latest exchange was an understatement. I was afraid I had gravely misjudged Eibhleann's feelings for me and what was worse, I couldn't say I felt for her the same way she may or may not feel for me. Perhaps once, but certainly no more.

"Ah, you poor, confused lad," Mags said with humor and sympathy, and patted my booted calf.

"Thank ye, Mags... I think."

She cackled, and I carried my unease like a growing burden into a restless day that was meant for sleeping.

13

Q uinn...

I rose early despite being tired. I packed my bag with my pencils, pens, sketchbook, and wallet, before carefully choosing what I would wear for the day. It looked overcast and cooler, and I wanted to be out but comfortable so I layered up. I picked a pair of my more rugged jeans and a pair of sturdiy boots, then chose a camisole, blouse, and a thick sweater to put over them. I held my wild curls back with a wide headband and swiped a bit of ChapStick across my full lips, rubbing them together and making sure that the tube went into my bag with the rest of my things.

I made sure the cottage was locked tight and made my way into the little village to eat at the pub before going on my grand nature walk. I wanted to go back to those stones where I'd seen the little fairies and had ultimately found Jack the day before. Not because I was hoping to find him again, although it would be nice, but because I wanted to explore the area more.

Well, I wanted to explore the area more and have the time to make it back to the cottage well before dark. Hence, the super-early start.

Saoirse looked up with a smile as I came through the door and asked, "And what are ye doing up so early on this damn fine day?"

I laughed a little and told her, "I found this truly inspiring little grove out past the old church ruin yesterday but it was too late to get any drawing done and get back before it got too dark, so I wanted to get an early start today, so I'd have time to get back there and sketch."

"You know the old timers around here say those woods are cursed or haunted," Saoirse said with a wink and I smiled big.

"The way Mrs. O'Leary tells it, I have more chances of being kidnapped by fairies than I do running into a ghost."

Saoirse's eyes shone with laughter and we both burst out in great peals of it, all while I more than happily held my secrets inside.

"I bet the stories that old bat tells are plenty of inspiration for you."

"Yes, yes, they are," I agreed, slipping into a seat at my usual table.

"What'll you have, then?" Saoirse asked, tossing some of her long red hair over her shoulder.

I opted for the thick and delicious steel-cut oatmeal the pub put on every morning. Saoirse smiled and gave a nod and headed straight into the back to the kitchen behind the bar to dish me up a bowl. She returned with it on a tray along with a steaming mug of coffee and a plate full of trimmings for the oatmeal.

She opened her mouth to say something but was cut off by the bell above the door chiming as some of the village's older regulars came through. She shot me an apologetic look and went to get their coffee and food ready. I smiled and went to work on my own meal, doctoring my coffee and oatmeal to my liking.

Saoirse was kept busy for a while, which was slightly disappointing. I would have liked the company this morning before spending the entire day by myself. She eventually made her way over and dropped into the seat across from mine with an exasperated noise. I laughed a little at her and she rolled her eyes.

"Aye, I know it's my job, but it doesn't make it any less annoying."

"Oh, I know. I used to waitress in high school. It was a royal pain in the ass!"

We laughed together a little while and she gave me a rather pointed look.

"You be careful out there," she said. "I don't much like hearing you're venturing so far, and off the marked paths and trails to boot."

"That's why I stopped in here to tell someone roughly where I'd be going." I raised my eyebrows and she gave me some side-eye.

"Fair enough," she declared. "Shall I expect you for dinner, then?"

"No idea. Depends on what time I get back this way."

She nodded and opened her mouth to say something but was interrupted by one of the old men eating at the bar, "Oi! More coffee then, girl!"

"All right, all right! I'm coming," she barked back.

"No rest for the wicked," I sang out and she smiled and wrinkled her nose. It was totally impish and entirely too cute.

I finished my meal and had had it often enough I knew exactly how much to leave with a tip. I fished in my bag and brought out my wallet, laying the money on the table and suddenly eager to get walking.

"Bye, then!" Saoirse said as the bell above the door chimed. I waved at her and ducked out under the overcast sky.

I walked briskly out of town and back past Mrs. O'Leary's making good headway towards the church ruins. I stopped there for some water and to snack on some granola I had spirited away in a corner of my bag. I sat on one of the big, crumbling blocks of stone and looked out into the tree line beyond the old building. Hit with a bit of inspiration, I turned to a blank page in my sketchbook and slipped a pencil from my roll.

I lined, shaded, and smudged a rough outline of what I wanted onto the page and satisfied I would be able to pick up where I left off later, tucked the book and drawing utensils back in my bag. I huffed out a big sigh and jumped down, my leather satchel bumping into my hip. I gripped the strap riding across my chest with both hands and scanned the tree line one more time before setting off for it and the old track leading into it.

About forty-five minutes later, I was back in the little grove of moss-covered standing stones. I stepped up to the circle of them and leaned against one, scanning the ivy-covered rock face for the entry into the land Jack called home.

There were no fairies out today and all there was before me was rock and ivy. I couldn't help but feel more than slightly disappointed.

I took a seat on one of the rocks and pulled out my sketchbook again. The moss made for a softer seat as I brought out another drawing pencil and opened it up to the page I had been working on before. I liked to finish a drawing before beginning a new one and so I went to it, smoothing and restating lines. Working the image of the trees past the church, and of the man I'd slept with last night holding up his lantern as a beacon from those same trees. A mix of what was there and what wasn't. An amalgamation of imagination and reality.

Engrossed in my work, I didn't hear the clatter of chitin wings until the being they belonged to alighted on the page near my hand. I froze. She was beautiful. Long pale hair was held by the teeniest, tiny crown of what looked like stained glass, though that couldn't be right. She was barefoot and looked up at me with wide blue eyes, her features long and angular, humanesque, yet too beautiful to really be believed. I blinked, long and slow, but when I opened my eyes, she was still there. Her thin, pale-blue gossamer gown stirred around her legs in the slight breeze like strands of spider's silk on the wind.

She carefully looked down and cocked her head, and I licked my lips and asked softly, "You know Jack?"

She looked up at me and cocked her head the other way, and I couldn't be sure if she spoke or understood English. She padded across the open face of my sketchbook to the corner and took it up in both hands, tugging on it adorably indicating she wished it to be turned. Then, she took to the air with a rattle of her glassy wings. I smiled and obliged her, turning the page to a blank one, and she set back down onto the crisp new paper.

She looked up at me expectantly and sprawled out on her stomach, propping her chin in her hands. I smiled like a loony person and took it for what it was.

"All right, then... let's see here."

I studied her for a moment and swept my pencil lead across the page. She watched me draw her, much larger than she was in real life. I carefully restated lines and shadowed just so under her sharp cheekbones. Working and reworking the sweep of her hair and the crease in her dress, I sketched quietly; all the while, she watched with utter fascination.

Her wings, while celled and glassy like a dragonfly's, weren't shaped anything like the wings from one. Instead, they resembled a butterfly's, only crystal clear with an essence of color to them when she shifted in the dappled light through the trees. They were glassy and iridescent like a soap bubbles. Not at all dark or shaded. It was both the most natural and unnatural thing I'd ever seen and I carefully emulated it as best I could by breaking out my tin of expensive brand colored pencils once I was through with the initial grayscale sketch.

I took my time and when the drawing was finally done, put all my pencils away and slid them back into my satchel.

"There," I said. "All done."

She leaped to her little feet, tiny hands planted on her equally slender and small waist and considered the drawing carefully from the corner of the page.

"What do you think?" I asked.

She let out a sound like the peal of high silvery bells and twirled on one foot. Her hands went to her chest and she threw them up and out in an expression of pure joy, her wings fluttered and with a burst of light, she took off, performing quite the display of acrobatics in the air, her tiny figure hidden by her glow.

I laughed and clapped my hands, shoving my sketchbook back where it belonged. She dove and hovered right in front of me, emitting a series of sounds that could have either been begging me not to leave or a scolding, I couldn't tell.

"It's getting late," I said timking a sad face. I didn't want to go, but I needed to if I were going to make it back in time. She seemed rather insistent and I sighed.

"I would love to stay, but I really do have to go. I could come back tomorrow, though."

She swept up and plunged down, doing a figure eight before rising up right in front of my nose. I laughed and she blew me what looked like a kiss but some sort of sparkling powder flew from her hand and enveloped me in a cloud. I flinched as it got into my eyes and I couldn't help but sneeze. She backed up and then cautiously came back forward, but I couldn't quite focus.

"What did you do?" I asked, suddenly alarmed as the world just refused to come back into focus all the way.

"Precisely what I asked," a masculine voice called and I jerked, turning in the direction it came from. I blinked my eyes blearily as my vision swam. The last thing I saw as the ground rushed up to greet me was a ram's skull, long white hair flowing out from underneath. The last thing I remember was my heart seizing painfully in my chest as my fear swallowed me whole.

14

J ack...

"Oh, Jack! Jack! Come quick, lad!"

I thrust the iron rod I'd been working back into the coals and turned to the open doorway to my chambers, squinting through the heat distortion.

"Mags, is that you?"

"Aye, aye, it's me! Come quickly, boy, afore it's too late!"

"What are you talking about?" I demanded, but the agitation she was displaying had me moving to comply. There wasn't a thing you could do if a Brownie went into a rage and I didn't quite feel like being on the receiving end of one of Mag's terrors.

"Oh, he's gone and done it this time," she seethed. "Once worshiped or not, I'll have his guts for garters, I will, if he harms a hair on her head."

"Catch me up, Mags. I don't follow," I said, even as I kept pace with her up the hall. She was in a right state., Eyes aglow, hands wrapped 'round her cane, she was floating at about my shoulder's height, now. It was a use of power she didn't often bother with, but I gathered she was just that upset over whatever it was.

I had a sinking feeling, but I couldn't and wouldn't commit to it until I had all the facts.

"Bloody Sprites," she spat. "Always looking to curry favor, willing to do just about anything to get one of the pure Sidhe to notice them. Well, that Fearbán féir's gone and done it this time, messing with one o' ma charges like that!"

"Quinn?" I asked, touching Mag's shoulder. The old Brownie woman whirled and raised her cane as if to strike me.

"Why else would I be here collecting your dumb arse, ye git?" she demanded.

"Aye now, where she be?"

"I told you, Gwynn brought her down here, into the Rath!"

I froze mid-step.

"Where did he take her?" I demanded.

"Oh your guess is as good as mine," she declared. "All I know is that he used that Sprite Fearbán féir to lure her!"

"Right, where is she, then?"

"This way, my boy! If anyone can make that little – oh!" So angry was Mags, she couldn't come up with a derogatory name befitting the Sprite in question.

I tried not to laugh, lest I draw the Brownie's ire, and followed Mags through the twists and turns of the Rath. I could barely keep up. The more of a state she worked herself into, the less I would likely have to do aside from extricating Quinn safely. Gwynn had certainly run afoul of old Mags, and I somehow doubted even he of considerable power could reason with an angry Brownie woman.

We stepped out into the underground cavern that held the Sprite's realm and Mags bellowed, "Fearbán féir, come out here this instant!"

The silvery chatter, much like the babble of brook water flowing over stones, suddenly evaporated. The light cast from the tiny beings' flight dimmed and those very same points of light stopped zipping about and merely hovered in place, while some disappeared completely into the ivy and flowering vines covering the walls.

The longer Mags was forced to wait, the more the leaves rustled in an ever-growing wind. They all moved in the same direction, as if caught in a cyclone, the eye of which was the angry lesser Fae, though I wouldn't suggest to Mags right now that she was less than anyone or anything else.

It was a misnomer, really, declaring any Fae 'less' than any other. Much like humans, it was a matter of race more than species... and much like humans, the Fae weren't free from the grip of racism. While it was different in some ways, it was also much the same. Rather than skin color or looks separating the different types of Fae, it was varying degrees of power. However, with time, those degrees of power had shifted in many ways, and those that were once very powerful beings had lost that power with the loss of their believers, and now it would be a near thing going up against the likes of an angry Mags.

While it was true that Brownies weren't typically near as powerful as one of the full-blooded Sidhe, there wasn't much out there to rival the power of an angry Brownie. There was even some thought that the Queen of Air and Darkness herself might not be a match. Of course, the mere thought of actually testing that theory was like to cool even the fiercest of tempers. That, and there was something to be said about consequences after the anger had passed.

More than one rogue Brownie had been put down in the thousand-year's war, long before the time of humans.

Mag's voice deepened and echoed with a long-forgotten power when she cried, *"Fearbán féir, come to me or I shall tear your houses asunder and nail yer wings to the stone!"*

All of the Sprites in attendance disappeared, their lights zipping into the ivy and branches, disappearing into the shuddering over-sized-acorn houses and hanging hollow gourds they called home. A lone flash at the edge of our vision revealed one lone Sprite, hair like corn silk, slender body draped in blue gossamer. She floated this way though her wings stopped flickering. Caught in an eddy of Mag's power current, she drew near.

"Where is she?" Mags demanded and at first, Fearbán féir, which meant Buttercup of the Meadow, quailed, but Mags shouted, a long and wordless, fierce roar, and suddenly Fearbán became quite animated.

I had learned some Sprite and Pixie over the years, but Fearbán's fear made her so animated and her speech so quick I couldn't begin to follow her, but Mags seemed to have no trouble keeping up. The wind surrounding us calmed and the glow to Mags' eyes diminished until it was gone altogether.

"She's in the Winterlands, Jack. My old bones and the cold are quite disagreeable. Go and get her, lad." She gave me a pointed look and I didn't argue, simply held up my hands as if to ward off her ire and loped off back the way we came, asking the Rath silently to speed my way.

I turned down the next hall and relief flooded my veins when a blue door was at the end of the next hall instead of the Hall of Willows that was supposed to be there.

"Thank ye," I muttered and strode up the stone corridor. The painted blue door opened for me at its end and the cold billowed out to meet me, as did a swirl of white flakes.

I plunged through it without stopping, determined to find Quinn. Knowing Gwynn, I would find them at the edge of the lake, which is where I headed first. I cursed my bad luck that Mags had caught me at the forge; plunging through deep drifts of snow at knee-height, shirtless, wasn't my idea of a gay time.

I caught sight of the white pagoda with its peaked blue roof and iron railings around the edge of the Winterland's lake and rushed in that direction. I could see her, lying on one of the benches there and my mind immediately went to what Gwynn was playing at. He was nowhere to be seen, but that didn't mean he wasn't watching.

The board was set, the game was on, and knowing Gwynn, the pieces were already moving across the board. It was the way of the Fae. They loved their games, the longer the better. Some had even been matched against one another for centuries, far longer than even I had been alive.

I had been able to avoid engaging in a game with any of them myself, but apparently, I was engaged in one now. Quinn, unwittingly, had been declared the prize.

I didn't like that. I didn't like that at all.

I reached the actual path leading to the pagoda and rushed into its shelter, collapsing to my knees against the stone at her side.

"Quinn? Quinn? C'mon, love." I cupped her face between my hands but she was cold, her lips tinged slightly blue. She was unconscious, likely bespelled, and completely unresponsive.

I rested my ear over her heart and listened, reassured by the steady thump of her heartbeat, slow, but there, within her breast.

I shivered myself and worried. For as layered as she was, she was too cold, which meant she had been here a while. I lifted her carefully and once again asked the Rath to aid me, this time in getting her back to my quarters, near my forge, where it was warm. I could worry about waking her once we were there. However, if I succumbed to the cold, I would do neither of us any good, so I had to move.

I picked her up, and I was a strong chap, having spent a couple of centuries at my forge. Still, though Quinn wasn't a large woman by any means, I was just a man, and there wasn't much remarkable about me or my strength. It was fallible, and I wouldn't be able to carry her forever.

Muscles screaming, I made it back to the door leading to and from the Winterlands and opened it, blessedly, to the hallway leading to my chambers.

"Thank ye, I feel I have been asking too much of you lately," I said apologetically, knowing full well the Rath would hear me. I also knew that the kindness it afforded me lately could just as easily be taken away. That the next time I asked it for aid, I could find myself farther from my intended destination.

I reached my door, which opened of its own volition, a further kindness of the Rath so I supposed, until I heard Mags say behind me, "That's it, lay her down and let the heat do its job."

"Can ye be in here?" I demanded, worried for her safety with so much iron along the walls.

She scoffed. "My great-grandfather was a Redcap, iron jackboots and all."

"Good to know," I said, with a secret smile, but my eyes were for Quinn and Quinn alone.

"She'll sleep a long while yet, damn Fearbán's eyes!"

"Pixie dust?" I asked.

"Aye, a deep and dreamless sleep."

I let out a harsh breath. At least there was that.

"Rest then, love. I'll be here when you wake," I murmured, and pressed a kiss to her forehead, but Quinn Carter might as well have been dead to the world.

15

Quinn...

My head throbbed with every single rhythmic clang.

Clang! Clang! Clang! Clang! Clang!

The oppressive heat wasn't helping, either, but that damn noise!

Clang! Clang! Clang! Clang! Clang!

I groaned and wrapped my arms around my head, but it didn't do a bit of good.

Clang! Clang! Clang! Clang! Clang!

"Stop!" I cried. "Just stop it already!"

Clang! Clang! – Whatever it was clattered to the surface it was banging against. I was

frantically trying to sort through my memories, trying to figure out where I was, but every time I tried to open my eyes what little light there was in the room, which wasn't much, bored painfully into my brain. Whatever I was lying on sank a bit as someone sat near me and it came rushing back.

The little fairy, the empty eyeholes of that damn ram's skull!

I gasped and tried to push back when a familiar and soothing voice reached out from the dark.

"Quinn! Quinn, it's me, Jack. Shh, it's okay."

I gasped with relief and his thick, calloused fingers wrapped around my wrists, pulling my arms around him and I shrank for a moment before the rest of my senses kicked in and the familiar smell of man and burning metal, of iron and campfire, wrapped around me. I gasped and sank against him and he held me tight, safe, against his chest.

"I can't see," I whimpered, and he made soothing sounds.

"It's all right, lass. Give it a moment, give it a little time."

"What happened?" I demanded. "How did you find me? Where am I?"

"Shh, I don't know precisely; I was here working my forge when Mags found me. She'd heard that Gwynn had gotten you with the help of a Sprite. We went and found the Sprite; she told us we could find you in the Winterlands. I went and found you but you were alone. You were cold, I brought you here."

"My clothes – were they..?"

"Intact. Do you feel all right?"

I thought about it, focused on my body and squeezed my eyes shut tight, then tentatively opened them and squinted against the bleary image of Jack's lap and a stone floor beyond. His boots looked fuzzy against the deep, dark gray of the rock.

"I'm okay. At least, I think I'm okay. I don't feel any different. Where am I now?"

"My chambers, in Faery." He sounded grim, and I couldn't say I disagreed.

"Am I trapped here?" I asked, after seven solid heartbeats.

"Tell me, did you eat or drink anything that you know of?"

"No, I don't think so."

"You would have had to do so willingly."

I shook my head cautiously, relieved when it didn't swim on me and my vision didn't go on a vertigo-riddled bender.

"Then, No," he said. "I would caution you against eating or drinking anything that I don't give you, though. I have a store of food but if anything Faery in origin passes your lips you would be trapped for seven years."

I swallowed hard and asked, "Is that how they keep you here?"

He chuckled and I looked up into his handsome, smiling face, relief flooding my system that it really was Jack that held onto me and not that... that thing, one of those things from that night. I couldn't help but shudder despite the oppressive dry heat, and Jack held onto me a little tighter, his hand smoothing up and down my arm.

"I'm so glad you found me," I whispered and he tipped my chin so that he could kiss me. I closed my watering eyes and kissed him back, the fear of what could have been chilling me to the furthest reaches of my soul.

He held me close and just kissed me. He didn't try to take it further, which I could appreciate, but I wanted more. I wanted him to touch me and caress me the way he had back at my little rented cottage the night before and so I made the move, rising up on my knees, going in for another kiss.

He kissed me back, holding very still as I moved to throw a leg over both his own and straddle his lap. He sat up very straight, putting his arms around me as I wrapped mine around his broad shoulders.

My coat was gone, and so was my bag, and I stopped when I realized that meant my wallet, along with my passport, was missing.

"Did you find my coat or my bag?" I asked.

"You were wearing your coat. I put it just there over the chair." He nudged his chin in that direction and I turned to look. My sight was back but held a haze around it as if I'd been swimming for too long with my eyes open under the water. "You had no bag with you when I found you," he said gently.

"Shit!" I swore softly and bowed my head.

"It's alright. We'll find it," he assured me, his hands smoothing down my back and resting on my waist.

"It has my passport, all my identification in it," I whimpered.

"We'll find it," he said solemnly and it fell like a vow from his lips.

I couldn't not believe him, and it struck me just how much in such a short time he took care of me.

I traced the tips of my middle fingers along the edge of his forehead and swept a piece of his long dark hair out of his eyes, tucking it gently behind his ear. His dark eyes were soft as he swept my face and I closed my eyes and bowed my head, touching my forehead to his. His hands tightened on my hips and I got the distinct impression he was struggling not to let them dip lower, to grip my ass over my jeans and I almost ached to have him touch me like that.

"I want you," I murmured and I heard him chuckle a bit darkly.

"Are you reading my mind, love?"

"No. I wish I could," I confessed.

"Oh?" he asked.

"Mm, I sometimes wonder what you really think of me. I worry I'm a hot mess. I always seem to be in some sort of trouble around you, and I promise I'm not trying to be a damsel in distress. I'm actually pretty street-smart where I'm from."

He laughed softly and one of his hands disappeared off my back, reappearing at the side of my face, cupping the side of my neck, his thumb grazing my jawline as his other hand drifted agonizingly slowly, down, down, down, to grip my ass.

"Oh, no, don't go doing that now, love. I don't know that I could help myself if you do that."

I froze. I'd unconsciously been grinding against him and his words had stopped me, but only for a moment. I gently pulled back just enough so I could look down into his face and the careful, controlled look he gave me back, the naked desire in his eyes, sent an electric little thrill down my spine.

I rolled my hips deliberately and he sucked in a breath, closing his eyes and tilting his head down and to the side as he concentrated on the feeling. We were so close, separated only by a few layers of cloth but as far as our desire for one another was concerned? We might as well have been a million maddening miles apart.

"I don't think you're a damsel in distress, at least not completely. I just think you're woefully under-prepared when it comes to dealing with the Fae. You don't know the culture, the customs, therefore you don't know how to comport yourself," he said, but his voice was low and controlled. It took some serious concentration on his part to string that all together and it took a considerable amount more for me to process everything he said. In the end, I believed his assessment to be fair.

"Kiss me," I half asked, half demanded, and he tipped his head back offering his mouth up to mine.

I kissed him and he kissed me back, and even though I felt intact and unmolested, that thing – Gwynn – had touched me. He'd carried me away from my world and into this one and I wanted desperately to erase even that simple touch with Jack's much more tender and much more complicated one.

"Gods above and below, I want you in my bed. I've dreamed of it since the first moment I saw you, and I'd be a liar if I said otherwise," he growled against my lips.

"Good, yes, please, I want that, too," I whispered back and I'd given him the green light. His hands pulled my blouse and camisole from the waistband of my jeans at the back and his arms crushed me against his chest. I slid my fingers into his hair, holding it back from his face and kissed him fiercely as he worked his hands under the material and smoothed them flat against my skin.

I gave myself over to feeling instead of thinking for a while. It was much less stressful and the perfect way to escape all the 'could have been' that just wouldn't stop echoing in the back of my mind. I kissed him as if he were the only means to my survival and he held me on his lap as if nothing else in the world could touch me, as if he would protect me from all things great and small.

I took shelter in his arms. Kissed him, touched him, tried to give as much as I took and still felt like I couldn't come even with him.

He pressed his lips to the base of my throat and I tipped my head back and gasped, "Jack!"

"So beautiful," he murmured, and hauled me in tight against him.

Our bodies pressed close, still maddeningly separated by our clothes. Well, mostly, my clothes. He had no shirt on. His skin was warm under my touch, slightly slick with sweat from working at what looked like an honest-to-god forge.

I was amazed that all of that clanging hadn't woken me earlier, which was next-level terrifying. I mean, if you're dead to the world that close to a working blacksmith, what happened before he'd found me wherever he'd found me at? I shuddered and didn't want to think about it. I really didn't. Instead, I wanted to wrap myself up in Jack who was kind, Jack who wasn't terrifying, Jack who had been nothing but good to me since the first time we'd met.

Our kissing and touching became more heated before I knew it, my blouse and camisole were off over my head and Jack was laughing at the unfamiliar garment that was my bra, in his way again. I reached behind me and unhooked it and it was so worth watching his face as I did it. The heat and hunger in his eyes as he devoured every inch of my skin with his gaze set me on fire.

"You have the most beautiful skin," he breathed. "So smooth, so rich and bright." He brought his mouth to it kissing me between my breasts, lips drifting, dragging along my chest, tongue hot and wet against my body as he dragged a nipple into his mouth. I gasped, burying my fingers in his hair, clutching the back of his head, pressing his mouth into my breast as my hips began to rock unbidden.

"God, yes, that feels good!" I cried and his dark chuckle sent ripples of desire through the center of my being.

He picked me up completely and turned me to lay me on my back and I loved that he was strong enough to do it. It was different being manhandled when you wanted it, safe as opposed to terrifying. Still, butterflies took flight in my stomach when he did it. Like cresting a steep hill in your car, the tickling, light sensation as gravity took that split second to catch up as you came down the other side.

He didn't have any trouble kicking off his boots or unhitching his pants as he bathed me in light, wet kisses against my exposed body. I arched and went for my own belt and jeans but had a tougher time when it came to my boots. I had to unlace them, but Jack wouldn't let me up to do it. Instead, he stood at the side of the bed, nude and perfect, his cock thick and resting against his stomach, pulsing with his heartbeat, as he pulled up the cuff of my jeans and unlaced the boots himself.

I watched him, and he watched me and the simple act of undressing me while already nude himself, hair disheveled from where I'd bunched it in my hands, Jesus, it was hot. So incredibly hot, I felt myself grow wetter by the moment, my pussy throbbing and aching in time with his cock. I was so eager to have him inside me again I didn't know how to express it, but at the same time, I didn't have to.

He knew. We were totally on the same page.

Or so I thought until he went to his knees between mine. He wrapped his arms around my legs, one above each knee and jerked me bodily until my ass rested just on the edge of his bed's mattress. It was so fast, so sudden, I yelped and that sensation like momentarily falling took over for that split second again.

It was quickly drowned out by the sensation of his velvet tongue against my sex, his thick middle finger working its way inside me, stroking the walls of my body looking for that spot.

I arched luxuriously when he found it and moaned and he chuckled against my clit, his tongue working it expertly, causing me to jerk unexpectedly. He withdrew his finger and I felt momentarily bereft, but then he jerked me back against his mouth, barring my hips with one arm and pinning me from moving again. His finger returned and I gripped my breasts, arching again as he teased me higher, my body climbing in sensation to the top of Mount Everest.

I shuddered and shook beneath him and he pressed me harder to the bed, rolling his eyes up to meet mine over his arm and encouraging me with his intense stare. He wasn't going to stop until I came, and I was so close to that edge where pleasure wound tight with pain into a Gordian knot of sensation so tight I couldn't tell where one left off and the other began.

So sensitive, oversensitive, I relaxed and let myself go and the pleasure rushed through my system like the perfect drug, chasing all fear, all apprehension, chasing all bad things away so completely until it was just me, just Jack, and the pure shining bliss of the fall left behind.

16

Jack...

She came apart and back together so beautifully that it was almost a magick all its own. She lay panting, spent, her body trembling finely beneath mine as I climbed over the top of her, caging her protectively beneath my body so that I might taste her lips again. She kissed me languorously and slowly, drugged with the pleasure I'd given her, and yet she still wanted more.

Her legs wrapped lightly around my hips, her hot, slick flower rubbing tantalizingly against the granite of my cock, teasing me to the point of exquisite pain. The ache to be inside of her was a fierce and visceral thing. I wrapped my arms around her and walked her back further onto the bed so that I could grab purchase with which to love her, and laying her back gently into the bedding, adjusted myself with my hand so that I could slip inside her waiting heat.

I groaned, bowing over her, holding her close, sinking into her to the root and thrusting just that little bit harder, deeper, so that I could know her completely with no doubt. She cried out gently in passion, her arms going around me and pulling me closer, her legs falling open around me to allow me to do it again, and I obliged.

I couldn't get enough of her. I would gladly drown in her softness and light, her golden skin kissed from the inside out by the sun, her delicate curls softer than a summer wind and those freckles, like stars scattered against a deepening twilight.

I was beginning to absolutely adore her organic beauty. So natural and real against the surrealness of the Fae. Her innocence against the scheming and machinations of the Unseelie Court was refreshing. Her eyes held so many things beyond beauty. I could read her like a book, every expression, every nuance to every look, and I cherished that frank honesty for the treasure it was. She was so true to everything she said and everything she did. I wanted to show her everything, but at the same time, I knew what price the beauty of this place held and that price was unimaginable pain. I didn't want that for her. I wanted everything for her but that, and so I made up for it the only way I knew how. I gave myself to her for this moment in time completely, body and soul, never counting that I wouldn't be able to take at least one of those things back.

Her body wrapped around mine, smooth as silk, tight, warm, and so alive. She writhed just so in counterpoint to my slow, even thrusting as to drive me completely mad with pleasure. I could drown myself completely in her, and be perfectly content to never come up for air ever again.

She rocked her hips to meet mine and it was a perfect counterpoint to the rhythm I'd set. Our bodies moved in concert, creating a beautiful harmony, our whispered gasps and quiet moans a perfect melody. I shuddered, close to my own finish but I held myself back from that edge. If and when I came, I wanted to come with her.

She gripped me sure and sweet, and I kissed her as such, our bodies firmly rooted on the bed, but our souls soaring. I'd never quite felt anything like it before, our silent connection, the magick between us slipping like quicksilver through our veins. I half expected her skin to become luminous and emit a golden glow like a full-blood Sidhe woman's when she was wholly connected to nature and earth. She was such a thing of natural beauty, my American girl, my Quinn.

I lost myself in her so completely, so hopelessly, so irreversibly at that moment, I didn't know how there could ever be life without her ever again. I couldn't fathom living from one moment to the next without her, let alone the stretch of centuries, of eternity, that lay before me.

I suddenly knew such a bitter despair I thought I would never experience again, but only for a moment because she gasped and drew me down tight against her body even as it milked my cock with her fall. I closed my eyes and settled over her and let go of myself, of my worries, of my cares and concerns, and simply fell with her, plunging deeply into whatever it was I began to feel for her and realizing that whatever it was, it made me happy, content in a way I had been fooling myself into believing I was for many a year now.

"Oh, Jack! Mm," she moaned and held me close, wrapping her body as thoroughly around mine as our positions on the bed would allow. I held myself off of her just barely, to keep from crushing her lithe form. We lay gasping, panting, kissing one another between deep breaths of air as our heartbeats slowed and matched, throbbing in a steady conjoined cadence.

"I needed that with you," she murmured shyly and I smiled and kissed the tip of her adorable nose.

"Aye, I believe I needed that with you as well."

She tipped her head back and closed her eyes, letting out a gusty sigh.

"What are we doing, Jack?" she murmured and the slight distress in her voice was plain to me. It was a sentiment I was beginning to echo in the deepest recesses of my being.

"Taking things one moment at a time, love. It's all we can do."

She nodded and opened her eyes and I shifted back up onto my knees, withdrawing my softening cock from her body carefully. She shifted as well, moving over towards the wall and allowing me to stretch out beside her, tucking into my side and laying her cheek on my chest, near my shoulder. It had been many a long year since I had heard such a contented sigh from a woman.

She fit herself into my side so naturally and I held her close. She settled and murmured, "Just once I wish I could see you in the light." Her voice was wistful and I smiled. She was in Faery now, and in

Faery, all things were possible, limited only to your very own imagination.

"Rest now," I told her. "When I am sure the effects of the Sprite dust have left you, I would very much like to take you somewhere."

"Where?" she asked, curiously.

"It's a surprise," I said, chuckling.

"Okay," she murmured and it held a slightly shy edge to the tone. I turned and pressed my lips to her forehead.

"How did you know to look for me?" she asked a time later.

"That would be Mags," I told her. "Your Brownie."

"My brownie? What's a dessert bar have to do with anything?" she asked, perplexed.

I laughed, but tried not to do it too hard, I didn't want to upset her. Wiping a tear from my eye I said, "A Brownie is a lesser Fae. A house Fae that does small things, unfinished chores and the like. They're helpful folk."

"Oh, I didn't know. Was I supposed to do something back? I mean, to thank her?"

I chuckled. "Traditionally, you don't thank a Brownie. It is considered highly offensive. However, it isn't untoward to leave a saucer of milk and honey out without a word. I believe Mrs. O'Leary took care of that for you, so you needn't worry about that. I have it on good authority that Mags quite appreciated your discarded drawings. I don't believe it would be untoward to leave one or two for her in the future when you get back."

She went very quiet and both of us lost ourselves in thought. Truth be told, the only thing I didn't want worse than I didn't want her to go was for her to be cursed as I was.

She cuddled closer as if chilled, which was impossible with the forge and the heat of my chambers. She drew in a deep breath and let it out in a gusty sigh and didn't say anything to accompany it. She didn't have to. I knew precisely how she felt. I held her all the tighter for it.

"How come," she asked suddenly, "Gwynn Ap Nudd is a Welsh

name, but according to everything you've said, he's Irish. Shouldn't it be Gaelic if that were the case?"

"Ah, done some studying up on the subject, I see. You are correct, it is a Welsh name. The Tuatha Dé Danann have been known by many names and even worshiped as gods by a few of them. In Gwynn's case, he was worshiped most prominently by that name and so he chose to keep it."

"Worshiped as a god... wow," she said and I nodded.

"Not all, but enough."

"Is that how they became so powerful?" she asked, "And what exactly are their powers?"

"Partially, yes, and as for what powers each holds, that's very personal to each individual."

"Makes sense," she murmured.

"Their worship began with their power mostly," I informed her.

"So, say, for example, if one's power lay in, say, fertility, then it made sense that they were worshiped as a fertility god or goddess?"

"Precisely."

"Logically, it makes sense," she said.

I chuckled, "Logic only goes so far in Faerie. Magick defies all logic here, and the Rath and its power is as wild a magick as ever there were."

"Okay, why tell me that?"

"Because I'd like to show you some of that magick while you are here and I don't want you to lose sight of me or let me go when I do."

"Wait," she pushed herself up and looked down at me. "You're serious, aren't you? You're not just going to hurry me out of here?"

"I thought you might like to see the Summerlands, and perhaps take a peek at the Winterlands while you're here. There are other things, some too dangerous for you to behold, but there are wonders beyond compare, too."

"Jack, I would love to see whatever you would want to show me," she whispered, a little awestruck.

"I figure we could do it while we looked for your belongings," I said, though I had a feeling Gwynn had held onto them and it would be quite the chore to retrieve them.

"I only wish I had my sketchbook to draw some of it," she said.

"Ah, we'll find your things, Love."

She smiled a little and said, "We sort of have to. Can't go home without my passport."

I simply nodded and drew her tight against me. She laid her head back down and sighed. Truth be told, to find her things, I would have to call in quite a few favors. Damn Gwynn's eyes.

17

Quinn...

We were in no hurry, even with my excitement about seeing more of this magical place. We lay in the circle of each other's arms and spoke softly. I let my eyes roam his chambers. The bed was in a natural-stone alcove just off the main room. Though there was a door set in the opposite wall from us, on the far side of the room, it was as if we were in a cave. Iron lanterns hung from thick chains, dangling from the ceiling.

Sconces of the same iron, holding lanterns at regular intervals, were set into the stone walls. Every other available crag held candles, melting, the white wax cascading down the walls and pooling on the floors. Thick and heavy wooden workbenches were against the stone holding all manner of tools while the forge, a distinctly man-made thing, took up most of the center of the large chamber.

Another smaller alcove held a writing desk, the walls to either side of that alcove holding giant bookcases of live-edge, natural wood. They were big, heavy-looking things that held all manner of books stuffed and crammed this way and that. Books with thick old leather bindings lined the shelves, with paperbacks stacked haphazardly in front of them.

"Did you make them?" I asked, my eyes plucking out yet more metal-worked things, from a tiny wire sculpture of a raven to an old-fashioned, heavy metal cup.

"Aye, it keeps me busy. I find ways to sell some of it in the world above. It earns me the money with which to buy my books, if I can find a shop open late enough."

"I like that about you," I said.

"What, that I read?" he asked, amused.

"Yes! Not a lot of guys do in the States. Most of the ones that have ever shown an interest in me were all about the sports and TV more than the written word."

"I've been known to enjoy a pint at the occasional pub with a bit of footie on the telly."

I laughed. "Somehow, I just can't picture that no matter how hard I try."

"Well, I do tend to dress to modern convention when I do it."

"Now that would be a sight, but I still can't really picture it."

He smiled and it was so genuine but also almost shy. "Then I would love to take you with me some time, if you're agreeable."

"I think that sounds like the best date idea ever. Way better than running for my life and hiding in an old church." I smiled mischievously and said, "Though as far as pick-up tactics go, it was pretty effective."

He laughed and pulled my mouth to his and we kissed, which led to more fevered touching, which led to more of the mind-blowing sex we seemed to have with each other. We finished, trembling and gasping, smiling and laughing in a sweat-slicked, exhausted heap in the middle of his bed and I couldn't say I was sorry.

"Mm, I want to take you someplace," he murmured.

"I am okay with that, as long as you're sure we're done for the moment."

He laughed and asked, "I haven't made you sore?"

"Getting there," I confessed. "But not quite yet."

"Ah, well, I don't want to hurt you at all, if it can be helped."

"Yeah, me either. Hurting you, I mean." I lowered my mouth to his from where I straddled him and he kissed me back, his hands smoothing over my body, making me sigh.

"What did you want to show me?" I asked, ready for a break and to see all of the things he wanted to take me to see.

"Here," he reached off the side of the bed and came up with his shirt. "Put this on. We aren't going far and we aren't likely to encounter anyone so it will do for this first bit."

"Okay," I said, slipping the natural fiber material over my head. I swam in it, of course, but I liked that. It made me feel good for some reason, protected and cherished, almost. I don't know what it was about wearing an oversized piece of your lover's clothing. Like stealing your boyfriend's hoodie... although I could never picture Jack in one, no matter how hard I tried. It was just so weird.

He pulled on a pair of his pants and held out a hand to me. I took it, and he went to the door of his chamber, opening it up into a long, carved-stone hallway like something out of a castle. Doors like his, of rough wood banded in dark metal, lined it up one side and down the other, all out of beautifully carved, natural wood, their surfaces satiny and muted.

Vines grew from the cracks between the stone, climbing the walls between the door faces. Some were just ivy in various stages; the green of new spring, deep summer green, a riot of red and orange and some devoid of leaves altogether.

Other vines held roses, deep red, and some white, but both on the same vine, which I had never seen before. Others held flowers I had no name for. I stopped beside a big purple blossom on a delicate vine and said, "I've never seen anything like this before."

"Aye, extinct. Long before even my time," Jack said, and gave a gentle tug on my hand to get me moving again.

"It's all so beautiful."

He chuckled and said, "And I haven't even shown you anything. At least not yet."

I stared up at him and he took a corner. The next hall was nothing like the first, resembling the natural cave stone like the inside of Jack's room. I had to turn back to make sure we had really turned from carved to natural stone, the transition was just so abrupt.

I gasped when I turned back, to face no turn, but a smooth, blank stone wall glittering with bits of, I think quartz, an unfamiliar vine climbing a chain, and a lantern lit by something other than fire hanging from it.

"What is that?" I asked, squinting at the blue-white light.

"Slyph light, the same light that will-o-the-wisp use to lure traveler's from the road."

I shook my head in amazement and said, "What I really should be asking is: 'Where did the hallway go?'"

He chuckled deeply and I was growing to love that sound. He smoothed a hand up and down my back and said, "That would be the magick of the Rath itself at work."

"Okay," I ventured cautiously, "What exactly does that mean?"

He guided me forward, down the natural cave-hall that was alive with light and crystals growing from the very walls in thick patches, yet the floor was a soft carpet of thick, rich, green growing grass beneath our bare feet.

"The Rath is alive," he told me. "A living wild magick all its own. Constantly moving, constantly changing. You simply need to picture in your mind where you want to go and it will take you if it wants."

"And if it doesn't?"

"Well, then you're doomed to wander forever."

I shuddered and said, "That sounds terrifying."

"Aye, it can be. I was lost for a month, once."

"A month?"

"Aye."

"How did you survive?"

"Oh, there's food aplenty. I found myself in various courts. The Brownies gave me bread. That's how I met Mags."

"I wish I could meet her," I said. I felt guilty that she had apparently been taking care of me since I'd come to Mrs. O'Leary's and I didn't even know who she was or even that she was there.

"Aye, but not to thank her," he reminded me.

"Oh, no, not to thank her. That would be the height of rude, right?"

He chuckled, "Just frowned upon. One thing you must never do is move a Brownie to true anger."

"Why?"

He told me that they were, in all honesty, one of the more powerful beings of fairy, but also wholly-underrated. I thought about that some and decided that Brownies and I had something in common, then.

He led me through what he called the crystal caverns, down a gentle, spiraling slope to glowing blue pools that gently steamed below. The light was fantastic, subtle, muted and yet so very vibrant. Jack grinned as I took it in, looking up at the long spiral walkway leading down here, the high conical ceiling, the flowering vines littered with more of those lanterns and dimly glowing Slyph light things.

The rock glittered with crushed crystal and the expanse of ground between pools was covered in lush, deep green moss that was soft as velvet, and cushy under our feet. It was the height of luxury, so incredibly beautiful, and so beyond anything I could imagine.

"Come," he urged and drew me to the edge of one of the steaming pools. He dropped his trousers and lifted his shirt up and off over my head. I gasped as he stepped down the seemingly naturally-formed stones into the water, and as it was agitated, the blue glow intensified within it.

"Bioluminescence!" I exclaimed. I'd always wanted to see it up close, but it typically required travel to more tropical climates. Though I'd had plenty of money to make those travels, I hadn't had the bravery. The brave one of the two of us had always been Livvy and she had wanted to come here, so here is where I'd come.

I had to say, as of right now? Absolutely no regrets. I just wished that she could be here to see it as I sank to my chest in water that was as warm as a bath. I sighed and sat on Jack's lap and just let my eyes drink in the fantastical feast of eye-candy that was laid before us and sighed.

"I wish Livvy were here to see this," I murmured. "It was her that wanted to come to Ireland in the first place, and I feel like she's been so cheated of everything because of me."

"Are you certain she's not here with you?" he asked, and I looked down into his face. His arms were loose around me, his hands a comforting weight against my body, his expression cautious yet genuinely curious.

I hesitated and really thought about what he asked me.

In a way, it made sense. Livvy and I had loved each other deeply, as best friends, and as sisters. If either of us had been of the persuasion, we might have loved one another even more deeply than that. I knew deep in my heart that Livvy would want me to be happy, just as I knew I would want her to be happy if it were her here instead of me. It still did nothing to assuage my guilt over the role I played in her death, but yes, when Jack put it that way, I did derive some comfort from the thought that indeed, Livvy, with her belief in all things magical and unseen, would have absolutely had a hand in my being here like this, in this place, if she had anything to say about it.

"You heal bits of my heart I didn't even realize were so badly broken," I whispered and I kissed him.

His arms tightened around me and he held me close and firm. We sprang apart guiltily when someone cleared their throat nearby. I yipped and modestly pressed my body against Jack's, hiding as best I could from the nearby presence. I turned my face away from the tall, cutting figure of a man with long, straight, ankle-length black hair, so dark it held blue highlights, though that could have just been the blue cast of the light from the pools and glowing globes of fairy light that hung among the vines.

"Maebh requests your presence in the high court," the man said, and he stared down at us impassively, his dark eyes, a solid black from pupil to iris, fixed on me. I shrank down, hiding my front against Jack's.

In counterpoint, Jack seemed perfectly fine with this guy seeing the both of us naked. I took the time to study him more while Jack said, "It must be important if our Queen sent you, of all people, Doan."

The man, whose skin was as white as freshly-fallen snow, quirked a smile. "Who else could she send with a message for her messenger?" the man named Doan asked.

Jack grinned broadly and inclined his head in a bow. "My Queen's Consort, my King, we shall be along forthwith, as soon as we can find clothing suitable for such an occasion."

Doan's smile broadened and he raised a long-fingered hand, very white against the unrelieved black of his form-fitting garments. He snapped his fingers and a light, warm wind swept through the high chamber, rustling the leaves on the vines around their heavy fruit of lamplight.

"Do not keep Maebh waiting, Jack."

"Never, my King."

Doan smiled as if he appreciated the honorific and bowed his head before his form was swept by shadow and a huge raven took his place, winging its way high and out of sight over the lip of one of the grass-carpeted stone walkways jutting out from the cavern walls.

"Damn the man," an irritated female voice spat, and I jerked my head to the poolside.

Jack grinned and said, "Ah, Quinn Carter, meet Mags. Mags, may I present to you, your human charge."

The little creature almost reminded me of Yoda's grandmother. She was the same stature and held an almost identical cane to the fictional Star Wars character. However, where Yoda was green, Mags was brown and her face, which was very human-like, more resembled the face of a mummified one, the skin leathery and worn.

She had no nose and her eyes were wide and appeared to be lidless. Her cheekbones stood out in sharp relief and her mouth was drawn back from cragged and broken teeth. She was ugly to the point of being adorable, if that made sense, but I think that was more because of her tiny stature.

She reached up and patted her steely-gray hair in a carefully coifed, perfectly round bun atop her head and her mouth dropped open in what I think was supposed to be a smile. I smiled back and was afraid it was a bit weak, but it must have done, because she cackled and said,

"Oh, aye, I'm ugly by a human's standards, but by Brownie, I am and was quite the beauty. Quickly now, ye both wash up. I'll be finding ye both something suitable to wear."

I blinked in surprise as she winked out of existence and turned to Jack. He laughed slightly and said, "The Fae are very direct. They don't believe in lying to be polite and when one is trying to be attractive and obviously so, it is a grave insult to not acknowledge it. A compliment, even a small one, is expected. Remember that at court. It is best to take everything at face-value and at the same time, expect there are a thousand different meanings behind what was just said."

"That doesn't make any sense," I declared, and he smiled again but it held no humor.

"Welcome to Faery."

He said it rather dispassionately and I nodded my understanding. This was something I could understand as it had always been this thing in my life. Especially in America. The surface always looked so good, so beautiful and neat, but underneath the meaning behind things could be so ugly, so coarse. Nothing, especially for a woman, double or even triple for a woman of color, was what it ever seemed to be.

Jack's eye caught mine and he paused seeing the tired understanding in my face. He reached up, out of the water and cupped my cheek, sighing.

"Just remember, down here, nothing is ever what it seems but at the same time, the Fae believe in the literal and most direct meaning."

I swallowed hard and nodded, suddenly very afraid of what the Queen could possibly want from me.

"Why do you suppose she wants to see me?" I asked.

"I couldn't say, however, her brother Gwynn most certainly has a hand in it."

I nodded and he said, "Best get cleaned up. Mags will have my head if we aren't ready by the time she returns."

I nodded carefully and he handed me a sliver of soap from the edge of the pool, taking one up for himself.

18

J ack...

Damn Gwynn and his games. I feared what he was up to would have Quinn trapped into a life of service, and I didn't want that for her.

We separated and washed up, but still upon Mags' return she tsked and clucked, fretting over Quinn like a grandmother over her wayward granddaughter.

"Aye, ye best be washing that hair, girl!"

"Oh no, I couldn't possibly get it wet. I don't have any of the things I would need to get it into any kind of order. It'd be a frazzled mess and – oh! No!"

Mags had snapped her fingers and a deluge poured from nowhere over the top of Quinn's head. I climbed from the bath, laughing as she sputtered indignantly.

"Nonsense, ye wee lass, nothing that old Mags can't fix."

"I can't believe you did that!" Quinn cried.

"Get used to it, love. Mags is of that age that nothing stops her."

Mags cackled and told Quinn, "Aye, best listen to the laddie. Those curls are no match for the likes of me. Quickly now, wash up. It'll be a chore getting you into what I've found."

Quinn did as she was told with only a slight bit of grumbling while I dried myself and dressed. Mags had brought out my most fetching clothing for the occasion. I raised an eyebrow at her and she looked from me to Quinn and grinned a toothy smile. I rolled my eyes but couldn't help but smile in return.

I had been before the Queen many a time without the benefit of my best clothes and I found it quite amusing that Mags would think Quinn was more deserving of them than Her Majesty. Amusing, but not entirely surprising. There was no love lost between the upper nobility and the lower castes of Fae society.

"Off with ye, go wait up there," Mags demanded, once I was dressed and every thread and hair were in place to her satisfaction. Quinn was doing her best to dress behind a curtain of vines. Though we were far past a need for modesty between us, Mags was a different story and modern human convention where nudity was concerned was much more conservative than it'd been back in the days when the Fae were less Fae and more gods and goddesses.

"Be gentle with her, Mags," I cautioned and the Brownie narrowed her eyes at me.

"Off. With. Ye. Jack."

"Aye, aye, hold your temper," I muttered and did as I was told, but not before I caught Mags grinning. She was nowhere near angry, but she played her hand well and me for the fool. I chuckled and waited up the ramp around the first bend for her to produce my lady love.

I froze and bowed my head, heaving a great sigh. Admitting my feelings for Quinn to myself was probably one of the bitterest pills I'd had yet to swallow. I cared for her, entirely too much for either of our own good, but there was naught to be done for it.

My heart, for selective as it was, damaged as it was, was finally healed enough to love another woman and damn her luck, it had to be Quinn. Brave, intelligent, and trusting despite her own hurts, what was there that was not to love?

I didn't have to wait long for her and Mags to come up the way. Mags knew better than to keep Her Majesty, the Queen, waiting. Still, the old woman had outdone herself where Quinn was concerned.

She wore a light green dress in a style from long before even my time. The sleeves were long, coming to a point over the backs of her hands. She looked like a princess or a queen in her own right in the velvet and silk cloth, her curls dry and perfect, kissed gold by whatever magic the modern age held over them, held back by the magick Mags had woven a band of ivy into.

Quinn smiled at me as my eyes drifted along the long sweep of her throat, the hollow where the delicate bones of her collar met conspicuously bare.

"It's right here," she said gently, folding back the material of her sleeve to reveal the edge of the leather thong I'd used to craft the necklace to hold the nail I'd given her.

"Won't be any use against the might of the court and the Queen herself," Mags said. "But against an individual the likes of Gwynn? Perhaps it will give you an edge."

"Well," Quinn said and held her arms out, giving a little spin. "What do you think?"

"Beautiful beyond compare," I said with a smile and held out a hand to her. She took it and I placed it in the crook of my arm.

We proceeded up the ramp and spilled into the antechamber to the great hall. Quinn looked up and around and said in a hushed tone, "I don't think I will ever get used to that."

It pained me to think it, but I thought to myself that it was best that she didn't, though I admit a growing concern over why the Queen wished an audience.

"Jack," Quinn stopped mid-step and looked up at me as the court waited beyond the next archway, looking out at us. The Queen and her Consort sat upon their thrones looking on expectantly, and I swallowed and gave Quinn my attention.

"What do I even do?" she asked, eyes wide and a little frightened.

I smiled at her reassuringly and said, "Just be yourself. They know you don't know court etiquette. Simply follow my lead, speak only when spoken to, and you'll be fine. I promise you."

The Fae may not lie but at that moment, I certainly did, though I hoped I spoke the truth in that if Quinn made any misstep when it came to the court's social etiquette, that the blame would be placed squarely on me, despite the fact I wasn't the one to bring her into the Rath.

"Come now, Jackie-boy! Don't keep us all waiting," The Queen called in her sultry purr and Quinn jumped, startled.

"Of course, my Queen!" I called back. "Ms. Carter is simply a little awestruck."

"Come now, child," Queen Maebh called out to Quinn. "Let me have a look at you."

Quinn swallowed, and we moved forward again. She clung to my arm and I patted her hand where it rested on my wrist reassuringly. The court murmured behind their hands as we passed and Quinn's eyes became huge as she drank in the sights of the Tuatha Dé Danann in their curiosity.

"My, my, my," Maebh murmured, when we reached the foot of the dais. "She is quite lovely, for a human."

"Th-thank you," Quinn stammered nervously, then blurted, "Crap, was I not supposed to do that?"

The court laughed and I chuckled too, murmuring "You're fine, that's only Brownies."

"Teaching her our ways, Jackie-boy?" Maebh chuckled and leaned forward, her eyes roving over Quinn from head to toe.

"I am afraid Quinn is American, my Queen. While the humans of Ireland today still know a touch of the old ways, I am afraid they are all but lost and forgotten on the new continent."

Maebh frowned and leaned back in her seat. She held out a hand and one of the Queen's Guard stepped forward. Quinn perked up on my arm when the guard laid an all-too-familiar book onto the Queen's palm.

Maebh flipped through the pages and locked eyes with Quinn saying, "You're quite good, Ms. Carter."

Quinn swallowed nervously and said, "Thank you. I've been drawing since I was a girl."

"Mm, and just what were you planning on doing with the knowledge you gleaned here?" the Queen demanded and Quinn's grip tightened.

"Nothing," Quinn said. "That's my journal, those drawings are mine, for me alone. I don't share them."

"Hmm, a pity." Maebh sighed and shut the book with a snap.

"I'm sorry, I'm confused..." Quinn said her voice trailing off. She closed her mouth and blushed realizing she may have spoken out of turn.

Maebh sighed again and asked her, "Just what is it that you do, Ms. Carter?"

"I used to draw for children's books."

"Used to?"

My poor Quinn shifted uncomfortably and my heart went out to her. I knew she didn't like to talk about her friend with just anyone and I felt honored that she had with me.

"My friend, Livvy, she wrote the stories, I drew the pictures."

"I see. And where is your friend Livvy, now?"

"She died. That's why I'm here, in Ireland."

"Oh?"

Quinn sniffed, her eyes welling, and Maebh arched an eyebrow. She called out "Leave us!"

I felt the march of power, like the heat from my forge, prickling along my skin, my hair standing on end, but I wasn't affected by it. The rest of the court, however, had disappeared. It was just Quinn, myself, Doan, the Queen, and of course, the members of her Queen's Guard in their armor, standing to either side of, and behind the thrones.

Tactically, to a mortal, it looked foolish, but I knew better. I knew how fast the Fae guard were. I also knew that they need be nowhere near you to stop you, and that by standards of power, they were nowhere near the most-powerful thing in the room. The Queen and her Consort-King were warriors in their own right. Beautiful and deadly, they were a sort of formidable that not many in Faerie could boast to match.

Quinn turned, eyes wide and frightened at the casual display of the Queen's power. She held onto my arm more tightly and looked up at me. I looked down at her but kept my face impassive, placid. It was just good sense when you were with a people who would gladly exploit any sign of your weakness for their own gain.

"Leave us, Jack," Maebh ordered and I felt my stomach drop out in despair. This had Gwynn written all over it, but damn it all, I didn't know his game.

"As you wish," I told my Queen and reluctantly pried Quinn's nervous hands from their grip on my arm. She shot me a panicked look that begged me not to leave her, but I admit my cowardice. I did not want to wind up on Maebh's bad side. The price for that could be centuries of pain – and not for me, but for Quinn, as a means of hurting me deeply. The Fae, for as beautiful as they were on the outside, could harbor souls as black as pitch. Their cruelty knows no bounds.

Still, I couldn't resist the urge to reassure her. I bowed slightly and pressed my lips to her forehead before I complied with my Queen's wishes, which, depending on her mood, could merit punishment yet.

Still worth it.

19

Quinn...

I watched Jack's retreating back as he walked from the chamber, leaving me alone with the Queen and her –husband? I wasn't exactly sure what a 'Consort' was. It was an unfamiliar term for me and I would have to look it up later.

"I don't know what you want from me," I stammered, turning back to her.

She sighed yet again and looked so very tired, which struck a chord with me. I knew that kind of weariness.

"My people are barely the ghost of a memory. Our power fades," the Queen stated, and I felt the first trickle of unease make its way down my spine. Something was very wrong, though hidden from obvious sight. "I want you to help fix it," Maebh said simply.

"Me? Fix it? How am I supposed to do that?" I hated how my voice squeaked, but I had no idea how to accomplish what she was asking.

"We are not so very antiquated that we don't know what goes on in the land of men," the King said and I blinked.

"I didn't – I don't..." I was at a complete loss for what to say that wouldn't make me seem like a total asshole. The King smiled, but it was one that could mean anything.

I took my time to study the Queen while I waited for someone, either of them, to basically say something to save me from myself.

She was the kind of beautiful that was only a fable. Her long, black hair fell from beneath the silver circlet she wore as a crown. It cascaded over her shoulders and back like a shining living cloak, so black, that it held purple highlights under the lights, which I was startled to realize I had no idea where it came from. The light, I mean. It seemed to come from nowhere and everywhere and was bright enough to see everything by. In fact, I was a little sad to realize it was the best light I had seen Jack under so far.

As if my realization conjured it, the light intensified, slowly growing brighter, as if the sun rose in the throne room we were in, but nowhere near as warm as actual sunlight. More like a super-intensified moonlight filled the chamber. It allowed me to see the Queen and her King much better and I wasn't disappointed.

Her skin, like Doan's, was pale as milk and as smooth as cream. Her lips, as red as heart's blood, a deep crimson bordering on burgundy, were strikingly set below the most beautiful silver eyes I'd ever seen and I do mean silver, the color of winter storm clouds threatening snow.

"You're too beautiful to be real," I blurted and she smiled. Doan looked over at her and despite how dark his eyes were, they lit up with such a perfect light of love I felt my heart give a fractured ache. It was every woman's dream to have a man look at her the way Doan looked at the Queen right now.

She inclined her head gracefully and stood, her pewter gown, heavy in the bodice with velvet yet the sleeves and skirt a light chiffon material, floated behind her as she stepped down from her place on the dais with my sketchbook in her hands. She held it out to me, and I took it.

"We know who you are, Quinn Carter. You write books for children in the new world."

"I don't write them, though. I just draw the pictures," I said softly.

She cocked her head to the side and studied me and all I could do was stare at the leather binding of my book between my hands.

"You could do both," the Queen said judiciously. "It would be easy enough. We would give you our stories, our history. You would draw them and help us make them suitable for your audience."

"I don't understand how this would help you," I murmured.

It was Doan who spoke from his seat.

"My Queen is correct in that our people are dying. We slowly lose our magick the more we are forgotten. Several of the lesser Fae are beginning to fade. We had to seek out answers and so we did."

"The age of gods, and even your Christian God, is waning," the Queen said. "You humans have and always will be a fickle sort–" She raised an elegant hand, palm out to stop me, though I had no intention of speaking. I mean, she wasn't entirely wrong. "Please, I didn't mean any insult by that."

I shrugged and said gently, "Can't fault you for being right."

She smiled and I seriously wondered why I suddenly felt so comfortable and at ease speaking to her. Like, that had been way too casual, hadn't it?

"True, but I am asking you for your help. I can't and shouldn't be rude by human convention. I have learned that being too haughty has been a failing of mine." She cast a very serious look at Doan, who simply smiled serenely.

"I don't know," I said, staring at the book in my hands once more. Truthfully, her beauty, especially up this close where I still couldn't pick out any damn flaws, was super intimidating.

"Walk with me?" she asked.

I nodded, I could do that. It was a simple enough request, and I honestly didn't want to find out what happened if I said no. I mean, she was called the devil for what she did to help Jack. I fell into step beside her, Doan walking to her other side and a little behind her while the two armored knights fell into step behind us.

"I would show you what I speak of, perhaps it will sway you. Quite simply, I am at a loss, desperate to find an answer that would help our people. My spies among the modern world tell me that several of the new gods are gods of old re-imagined. Is this true?"

I thought really hard about what she was asking me and it

dawned on me, "What, you mean like Thor the god of thunder redone as a superhero in comic books and movies?"

She smiled and almost let off a glow. "Yes, that's precisely what I mean."

"Um, yeah, but he's about like the real god of thunder as Tinkerbell is really a fairy," I said, and the Queen frowned slightly.

"I don't know any Faery by that name," she said and I chewed my bottom lip.

"She's an animated character, part of the Disney franchise. Um, have you ever heard of Peter Pan?"

"Ah, by the Scottish author, J.M. Barrie. I've read that one to you, my love. About the boy who never wished to grow up." Doan smiled and the Queen arched a brow.

"Oh, that?"

"Yeah, that, except I didn't know who it was originally written by, just the Disney version. Um, do you have my pencils?"

We stopped our slow walk and the Queen snapped her fingers. My bag fell at my feet and my roll of pencils half out of it.

"Um, thank you." I picked it up, tucking the roll back into it standing upright, and slung the satchel across my chest. I dipped my hand back into the bag and withdrew a pencil, flopping my sketchbook open on my hands and roughed out a quick Tinkerbell on the page below the little fairy that'd landed on my book. I felt more than a little betrayed by her and it made me sigh inwardly.

I flipped the book around so the Queen could see, and said, "That's what people in America think when they hear 'fairy,'" I told her. Her shoulders dropped and she looked both sad and angry. I bit my bottom lip and wanted to help. I mean, I already had ideas on how to help, but then she nodded and gestured we should continue and we did, around a corner to face an open courtyard, except all that was in it was weathered, brown, and crumbling to dust.

"Oh, wow," I uttered and she sighed.

"It is a slow progression, yet every passing year it grows worse. I am at a loss for what to do, how to save my people."

"It's a cruel sort of death facing us," Doan said. "We have some Fae, lesser but no less our people, who wither and die just like this."

"We are immortal beings," the Queen said. "I am at a loss for how to stop this."

"I mean, I'm not sure how I can help. Children's books only go so far…"

"It is a seed, and from it, it is my hope, that a belief, no matter how small, can grow from it."

I pressed my lips together and really wanted to know what Jack thought, I mean, the circumstances were certainly different in my case versus his, but I figured if any of the old stories I'd heard were something to go by, any agreement with fairies could go badly for me in the end. Still, I could almost hear Livvy in my head and she wouldn't walk away from this. I mean, what kind of person would I be if I did?

What I said, even though I'd pretty much had already made my decision, was: "Can I take some time and think about it?"

The Queen and her consort exchanged a look and Doan gave a slight nod, the Queen didn't look at all happy about it, but drew herself up to her full height, which was really tall compared to most women, me included, and said, "Very well, I should like to have you announce your decision to the court. It has been many a year since we have had an occasion to have a garden party. Regardless of if your answer is yes, or no, I think this will suffice an excuse."

"I was just going to take a day or so," I stammered. I mean, I didn't think a party was in order, and –talk about putting me on the spot.

"Excellent, tomorrow night then?" she asked.

"Um, sure," I agreed.

"Very well, we await your decision," the Consort said and the look on his face screamed 'thanks for letting it not be an immediate 'no.' '

I nodded, and in a flash of light and a dizzying whirl of colors, I found myself outside the throne room, standing beside Jack.

"What happened?" he asked eagerly and I looked at him, confused.

"I was just about to ask you the same thing," I said. "One moment

I'm in a courtyard full of dead and dying plants, the next I'm standing next to you."

He frowned. "What courtyard? Up above? She took you outside the Rath?"

I felt my shoulders drop and realized that if I said no, that meant I was likely sentencing Jack as well as the rest of the fairies to a slow, sad death. I couldn't do that, but at the same time, there was no guarantee anything I did would actually help.

"How about," I said slowly, "You take me to get something to eat. This is going to be a long conversation."

He stood a bit taller and nodded, "The village pub?"

"Sounds great," I said, and let out an explosive breath.

"It should be late enough," he said and nodded.

"We should probably change."

"Oh, aye," he agreed.

⌒

IT TURNED OUT, that it wasn't late enough. While hours and hours had passed in the Rath, apparently only minutes had passed out in the real world, at least, judging by the sun. That, or it was a completely different day. I was scared about that as I powered on my phone.

I let out a breath I hadn't realized I'd been holding when the date said the same thing as when I'd left that morning.

"Go back," I murmured, and Jack drew back even further into the shadows of the alcove. I shut the door to my world firmly, and sighed.

"Back to my chambers, then. Let's hope the amount of iron I have in there will be enough to keep us from prying eyes and from being overheard."

I swallowed hard and nodded, letting him take my hand and draw me along the hallway back the way we'd come, but not. The next turn we took showed us to his door and I didn't think I would ever get used to that.

We slipped inside and he hung his lantern by the door, lifting its shroud with a turn of a little knob to illuminate the room. He turned back to me and looked weary, as if he carried the weight of the world in anxiety on his shoulders and I went to him, hugging him close.

"The Rath and everything in it is dying," I whispered. "The Queen thinks it's dying along with everyone's belief in your world."

I waited for him to scoff, to tell me it was nonsense, but instead, he sighed and pulled me closer, his arms going around me. He was quiet for a moment and when I looked up at him, I wasn't sure I liked what I saw. His eyes held pain, but not surprise, and he said to me, "I've known for a while, but as the Queen's messenger, I was sworn to secrecy."

I stared up at him, stricken. What a terrible secret to carry by yourself. He bowed his head and rested his forehead against mine.

"It's not just the Unseelie Rath, either. It's all across Faerie. The Goblins, the Sluagh, and the Seelie – all of them suffer equally under the blight of fading memory."

"I don't understand why their survival is tied to our belief and believing," I said and sniffed. I was fighting back tears, but it was so incredibly sad.

"It has something to do with the Iron Age," he said. "Something to do with the bargains that were struck to ensure the survival of the Fae during their darkest hour."

"I don't understand," I said.

"Neither, do I; it's not something that is often spoken of. It is a painful subject for those who lived through it."

We were quiet for a time, simply holding each other. I sighed and he asked me, "What did Maebh ask you to do?"

"She asked me to save you; she asked me to save you all," I said, and what he said next broke my heart.

"I don't know if that is the best idea, Quinn. Perhaps our time has come."

I pushed back from him and turned, covering my mouth with my hands so I wouldn't say something unfortunate. When I was sure I wouldn't, I dropped them and turned to face him.

"What are you saying?" I demanded. "That you, that all of these people deserve to die?"

"No, that didn't come out right..."

"You're damn right it didn't!" I snapped.

"Quinn, please! I need you to really think about this. Entering into any sort of pact with Faery, with the Unseelie especially, is almost always a very bad decision!"

"I mean, I don't even know if I can do it!" I said. "It all depends on things like my publisher and audience receptiveness. Who is my demographic? Will the stories even work for a young audience? Am I looking at converting to graphic novels for adults? If I am, do you know how much work goes into that?"

His shoulders dropped and he let his hands slip down my upper arms, sliding them in a gentle, soothing caress to lightly thread his fingers through mine.

"It sounds as if you've already made up your mind," he murmured.

I closed my eyes and asked him, "What kind of person would I be to just walk away? Who would I be if I didn't try? It's not about me, Jack. I was selfish once and it cost me my best friend. I'd like to think I learned that lesson."

"You are too beautiful for this place, Quinn. They may be beautiful on the outside, but I swear to you, they're monstrous."

I swallowed hard and said something unfortunate, then.

"Says the man who asked the Queen to help him burn thirty-two people alive in a church."

He smiled and it was the bitterest thing I had ever seen. He let my hands go and took a step back saying, "I, too, would like to think I have learned something from that time in my life, and I swear to you, by everything that I am and everything I still hold dear, helping them will cost you."

I covered my face with my hands and shook my head, letting out a shaky breath, "I'm sorry I said that. I feel like my decision just cost me big." I lowered my hands and looked at him, miserable. "I totally expect you to kick my ass to the curb right here and now for making that crack. That was a low blow."

He chuckled and said, "Aye, it was, but I see you're passionate about this. About saving something."

"Call it my need for penance," I murmured.

"Ah, now that is a concept I understand."

"Then support me in this, Jack. Please."

He looked at me, solemn at first, but then he smiled and cupped my cheek, grazing the skin with his thumb in a gentle caress.

"You have the soul of a warrior, passionate and willing to fight for what you believe in against all odds. This is the first time you have reminded me of why I fell in love with my wife... and you are making it incredibly easy to do the same with you."

I think I quit breathing. I stared up at him, searching his face and he bowed carefully to put his lips gently against mine. I let my eyes slip shut and opened my mouth to let him inside. His tongue darted against mine and we both just naturally moved into one another's space. The kiss was a gentle and soulful thing.

I had let him in, showed him a gap in my wall, and he slipped right through. I honestly liked having him there. Still, I was a bit rattled, as this felt really close to a first fight. I didn't know how to feel about how fast things were going. Not so much that we'd had the first fight, but how out-of-whack it left me. I mean, I was shook, and I mean shook so hard, so deep, that my hands trembled where they rested against his sides.

He gathered me close and the kiss intensified, melting some of the icy dread that'd filled me at the thought of this fight being the first, but certainly not the last. I didn't want it to be the last, but I didn't want there to be many more, either. I really liked Jack. I really loved that he made me feel not-quite-so-alone in the world, and selfish me, I didn't want to let whatever this was go, not yet. I knew that letting my feelings get too big, getting too attached, was probably the worst idea ever when it came to my heart. I mean, I would have to go home eventually, right? Right. I didn't have to think about that just now, though because clothing was beginning to fall like leaves to litter Jack's chamber floor and I was all for it, all for getting as close as possible to him.

"Jack," I gasped as his lips moved from mine to my jaw.He cupped the back of my head and pressed his lips into that sweet spot between my shoulder and neck. I felt my body bow into his as half my body went awash in a pleasant tingling sensation, and wound my arms around his neck and shoulders as my knees went weak.

He picked me up without a second thought and I yipped in surprise, my legs winding around his lean hips, clutching myself against him like a monkey to a tree as he carried me across the chamber floor to lay me back on his bed.

He slid down my body, all sensual lips and touch, almost worshiping me, inch by inch. I closed my eyes and let go, arching into his hands as they trailed over my skin, emitting a noise somewhere between a gasp and a cry when his tongue licked a velvet wet line from opening to clit.

He locked his mouth over that sensitive bud and a finger slid inside me. I swear, my eyes rolled back into my head and all I could do was grip the covers in my fists and try to hold still, even though my muscles had other ideas. I twitched with every stroke of his finger and every flick of his tongue against that sensitive bundle of nerves.

"Oh, god, Jack!" I cried out and he held me down. I loved that he did it because I knew that if it became too much, if I asked, he would stop. I loved that he did it because I trusted him.

I trusted him to take me high and higher and I trusted that when he sent me plunging over that precipice that he would be there at the bottom waiting to catch me. It was just that when I fell, I hadn't expected to fall in love, too... but I guess I did.

20

Jack...

I reveled in her softness, in every slope and curve of her beautiful body. She was so beautiful, so strong despite the cracks in her foundation. Still willing to reach out, so brave to let me in despite how often she had obviously been hurt in the past.

I wanted to know all of her secrets. I wanted to soothe those hurts and see her smile more than I wanted to ever see her cry. I wasn't surprised I wanted to be a part of her life to dry those tears when they came, but at the same time, I was so monumentally torn between wanting to keep her and wanting her to run, to go home, and to get as far away from here, from Gwynn, from Maebh, before any true harm could befall her.

While I was heartened that Maebh was asking Quinn for help, therefore would be less likely to hurt her because of her need for her, I couldn't say as much about Gwynn. He'd moved his piece across the board expertly and had bought himself more time to play with her and potentially get his petty revenge on me for thwarting him in the first place. It didn't sit well with me, but there was nothing I could do until he revealed his master plan.

As for now, my master plan was to try valiantly not to worry about anything except making Quinn feel amazing.

I laved my tongue over the most intimate part of her, watching her up the length of her gorgeous body, her deep and lovely gaze fixed on mine as she panted unevenly. Her perfect breasts heaved, her light golden brown skin nearly glowed with her pleasure as I worked a second finger inside her.

"Oh, god, Jack!" she half gasped– half cried, her head falling back, her hands gripping the quilt to either side of her hips, which rose and fell of their own volition. She worked herself against my hand and mouth and I let her, for now.

She was so incredible when she let herself go like this I couldn't help but watch, growing painfully hard. Never had I known a desire like the one she stoked in me. There was something so incredibly raw and innocent about her, so alluring in a way I couldn't speak to, but felt to my very core. She was someone special, a strange mix of jaded yet pure, a lovely contradiction that I wanted to watch bloom, layer by layer, much like a rose.

"Jack, Jack, Jack!" she cried, and I pinned her with an arm across those luscious hips of hers, working her into a frenzy, watching her cry out and arch, feeling her come around my fingers, her body pulsing and gripping them, pulling them deeper. I worked my tongue against her button and she writhed, laughing, crying out, over-whelmed, until she tried hard and harder yet to get away from me, her hands pushing at my arm, her hips twisting, her legs coming together to momentarily shut me out. I let her go reluctantly, as she curled onto her side, knees drawn up, and lay panting and shaking. I smiled and went to my knees on the bed, massaging her thigh, rubbing my hand up and down her smooth leg, enjoying the tactile sensation of her silky skin beneath my fingers and palm.

"Oh, god," she groaned. "Too much, you're just too much," she said, laughing between pants. I smiled and chuckled darkly and helped her turn onto her stomach, running my hands over her back, her shoulders, down her sides and over her hips, taking a long moment to really appreciate how perfect her heart-shaped ass was, how firm and lovely and how well it fit in my palms as I lifted and separated the cheeks enough to find her opening.

I straddled her thighs and locked her legs together with my knees, leaning over her and guiding myself to her opening. She lifted her ass, perfectly arching to accept me into her body, and she was so incredibly wet I slid in smoothly with no trouble, right up to the root.

I laid myself over her back, kissing her shoulders, protecting her with my body and drew my hips back, surging forward with a sure, smooth, stroke.

Gods, yes... she felt so good. In this his position, she was tight and welcoming, cradling my cock more intimately, somehow. She moaned and sighed out, her body relaxing below mine, her pussy tightening around me. I pushed myself up slightly and worked my way in and out of her, gazing down at the side of her face revealed to me as she laid one cheek against the bed.

Her dark lashes made a perfect crescent against her freckled cheek, her full lips curving into the most beautiful smile as she gave herself over to me. Relaxing fully, lying still and letting me have my way, whatever that may be, with her. Her surrender was so perfect it made me feel virile, like I hadn't in a very long time.

Everything about what it meant to be a man came to the fore. I wanted to protect her, provide a life for her and love her. I wanted her to bear my children, make her the center of my world. I wanted everything I had nearly had and lost all those many long years ago and those feelings were so complete, so completely overwhelming, all I could do was feel them, let them wash over and through me, and try so very hard not to become too terribly attached to any of them.

I only marginally succeeded at any of that, I think. Especially when her body tightened in that way around the head of my cock, that way that told me that she was close, so very close, to that shining fall once again.

She breathed my name and shuddered beneath me and it was so beautiful. I followed her over the edge and held her all the way down into the abyss of warmth and pure feeling. I floated with her along that stream of loose consciousness for several minutes while our bodies caught their breath, until my arms trembled finely with the effort to hold myself up, to keep from crushing her into the bed.

I pushed myself half up, laying light kisses along her shoulders, across her back from left to right, before pushing myself up completely, my cock slipping from inside her as we both shivered with our lingering over-sensitivity.

Moving off to one side, I laid on my back with a groan and turned my head to look at Quinn as she turned hers to look at me. We both laughed slightly and she dragged herself the half a meter over to kiss me. She rested in the cradle of my arms, propping herself against my chest to kiss me lightly and languorously, and I was certain this was what the Christian heaven felt like.

"Mm, that was nice," she murmured, voice husky with afterglow. She cuddled into my side and laid her head on my shoulder with a gusty sigh.

"T'was," I responded.

We were silent for a time and she reminded me, "I'm starving."

"Aye, I have some things here. Just give me a moment with you, like this." I didn't want it to end and I didn't think she did, either. She didn't protest, rather she simply cuddled closer. I held her, wishing it could be like this every day but knowing, deep down, that it was wishful thinking on my part.

Good things didn't happen to me. I didn't deserve them and I had come to grips long ago that was just the way things were going to be.

"Take me to your favorite place, here in the Rath?" she asked spontaneously and I smiled.

"Ah, now that would be my pleasure. A picnic, then?" I asked.

She looked up and beamed at me and said, "That sounds fantastic."

The glow from her, the light in her eyes. I swear it was a distant echo of what it had been like to be warmed by the sun. I smiled and nudged her lightly. I was tired, and reluctant to give up on sleep, but I wanted so very badly to take her to the Summerland, as I'd intended to do before we'd been so rudely interrupted.

We dressed once more and I admired her curves and sense of

fashion as she pulled on her jeans. She paired it with one of those little thin strapped cotton camisoles and a blouse that reminded me of something out of the nineteen-sixties, long-sleeved, but scoop-necked, edged in tatted lace at the neckline and cuffs. Three shell buttons adorned the front but were merely for aesthetic purposes.

A wide leather belt with a silver buckle threaded through her belt loops paired well with brown boots to finish it off, and the look suited her. She was a natural, earthy woman, which was part of her appeal. I could see why Mags had taken a liking to her.

"Do I need my coat?" she asked and I shook my head.

"Not where we're going," I declared, and finished wrapping and tying the last of my mortal provisions into a large square of sackcloth. I gripped the bundle at the knot and held out my other hand to her. She lifted her satchel over her head and with a smile, took my hand.

I led her out into the hall and locked my chamber door's iron lock with its iron key. She took up my hand as soon as it was available again and we set off.

I took the long way so that she could see more of Faery, the different hallways and antechambers, walking us through different lands for the different Faery tribes that lived within the Unseelie Rath.

It wasn't a long walk, but it was long enough for her to see some things. There were questions sliding behind her eyes when we reached the hall I'd been seeking.

The cornerstones were simple limestone, cut into blocks and resembling an almost modern-day take on a castle. The cuts, made by magick, were far too clean to be man-made. The walls between them were natural river rock bound together by the white earth. It was a short hall; at its end was a red painted door.

Windows were set into the walls to either side of the door, just before it. The light through the milk-colored glass, too white to be natural, was more for ambiance than anything. The red door was double, and bound in a black metal I had no name for. Only one side held a handle, the right side, but care and craftsmanship had gone into its construction. The red was as rich as a holly berry, the square tiles leading up to it smooth, but not polished.

Quinn paused at the end of the hall and dragged back on my hand slightly. Her eyes were wide and she studied every nuance of the scene before her. She looked at me with wide eyes, a hint of fear in their depths as she asked, "That light won't hurt you, will it? It's the brightest I've seen you set foot near."

I felt my smile grow with her concern and said, "That's why I've brought you here."

Quinn...

"What's behind the door, Jack?" I asked a bit breathlessly and his smile grew in a mischievous direction.

"Can't a man surprise his lady?" he asked and I bit my bottom lip and nodded carefully.

"I found this place by accident when I got lost in the Rath."

"The time you got lost for a whole month?"

"Yes." He nodded.

I stopped him from opening the door and placed my hand over his. He raised an eyebrow questioningly, but this was the best light I had seen him by and I wanted to take a moment. It was disappointing how much it washed him out, but he was even more handsome than I'd first thought.

He dipped his head and kissed me quickly before depressing the latch and swinging the door inward.

"Jack!" I cried, aghast as sunlight came pouring out of the portal. He laughed, and before I could smack him for scaring me, towed me through the door and into a perfectly sunlit meadow.

I gasped and stared out over the wavering golden grass, then looked up high at the blue sky stretching above us.

"I thought you said you couldn't go outside during the day!"

"Aye, I can't, but we're not outside. We're still in the Rath."

"What? How? I don't understand."

I knew my face was stricken, I was so scared for him, so scared I forgot to look at him right away. When I realized he wouldn't burn, that there was no screaming and no falling to his knees trying to protect himself from the sun's rays, I turned.

He was even more beautiful in the light. His cheekbones were high, his jaw masculine. The shadows chased away, I could better see that his skin, while pale from so many years without the sun, held certain flaws; there was a sharp scar under one eye, so old as to be nearly invisible in the dark. His long dark hair wasn't so dark in the light, either. Deep bronze highlights were naturally hidden in among the dark chestnut, indecipherable without the light. He smiled slowly, but before he did, lines I hadn't seen before, bracketing his mouth, spoke softly, subtly, of all the smiles that had gone before.

He'd been gorgeous in the dark, but he was absolutely, breathtakingly, handsome in the light. I swallowed hard and hadn't even realized I'd gravitated into his arms.

"What is this place?" I asked.

"I call it the Summerland," he said.

"You don't know for sure?"

"No, I haven't ever bothered to ask. I don't talk about this place with anyone down here in the Rath."

"Why not?" I asked.

"It's a blessing in my cursed existence. A gift. I tend not to look a gift horse in the mouth."

"How did you figure out it was here, or that it didn't burn?"

"You ask a lot of questions," he said grinning.

"Haven't you? I mean, even to yourself?"

"Aye, I do. I've read things in the old library –"

"They have a library down here, too?" I stopped him.

He laughed and nodded, "Aye, but it's not the kind of library you would be used to."

"We'll get to that later," I said looking up into the sky. "First, tell me all about this place."

"Walk with me," he said and took my hand, guiding me along through the grass.

I followed and he said, "It's a burial place," he said. "Mostly forgotten by the Fae. It's a battlefield of the first war of magick."

"Oh, so it's a memorial?"

"Precisely."

"A memorial that everyone has forgotten about?"

"Aye."

"That's incredibly... sad."

"Aye," he murmured.

For a long time, it was just the gentle swish of the tall, dry, yellow meadow grass against my jeans and his boots and trousers. He stopped me up short and pointed and I blinked. There was a glimmer of something around knee-height in the grass just ahead. I swept some of the yellow stalks aside, revealing a sword stuck in the ground.

It was a beautiful work of art, the silver blade etched in black, the crossbar a rich gold set with what looked like onyx and rubies. The grip appeared to be a textured bronze with two rectangular peridot stones set in it. The pommel, more of the rich gold in the shape of a crown, nearly brought tears to my eyes.

"It looks like it was just dropped today," I whispered in awe.

"Been here so many thousands of years, I can't even count them. The measurement of time is a tricky thing, here. It belonged to one of the very first kings of Faerie. A name so old it's been lost to text and time. I am sure there are a few among the Sidhe that remember him."

I let the grass spring back to cover the blade and straightened. I was concerned about whether I would be successful in doing what the Queen asked, but it was probably as good a start as any. It would be a heartbreak and such a shame to let so many years of history, an entire people, an entire race of beings, simply fade away into obscurity.

Jack unknotted his bundle and sat down, laying it out. I sat down carefully beside him and he broke off a chunk of bread from a loaf. He slid a knife from a hidden place and speared it, working it into two halves to lay some of the other things in the bundle into the middle.

I slipped my sketchbook out and put pencil to paper while he worked, doing some work of my own, drawing the sword among the grass, asking Jack questions, and scribbling notes in the margins. I was still unsure how I would put all of it together.

"Is this your favorite place because of the sun?" I asked, shading my eyes and looking up, glancing at the fiery ball in the sky, then quickly away.

"Aye."

I noticed it was warm here, but it was a strange warmth. Like it was all around, but it wasn't beating down on us. The pseudo-sun put off the light of the real thing but didn't put off any of the heat that should accompany that light. It was a curious thing and an odd sensation.

"You're sure you want to commit to this realm?" he asked gently, and the tone of sadness in his voice made me turn back to him.

"Why do you sound so down?" I asked.

He sighed and said, "Understand that even though Faerie is asking a great service of you, that nothing comes of doing anything for Faerie without some price."

"I think this situation is quite a bit different from yours, don't you think?" I asked, gentling my tone, trying not to reopen or aggravate old hurts, but it couldn't be helped. I mean, he was being a little ridiculous about this, wasn't he?

"Aye, it is. I asked the Queen for help, and in this instance, she is asking you, but I must wonder why. Who gave her the idea? What are their motives?"

"That's more than a little paranoid, Jack."

"No, Quinn. In the world you're in, down here, it's basic survival to expect the unexpected. Nothing is ever what it seems, down here."

His tone was ominous and full of warning, but I didn't know what to do about any of it. Instead, I chewed thoughtfully and swallowed my bite of sandwich, buying myself a little time to try and change the subject.

"So this garden party or whatever, what am I supposed to do? I don't really have anything to wear or know how to dress…"

"Ye don't have to worry about that," he said. "The Queen will send servants to handle it all for you. You're her guest, and as her guest, she can't have you looking anything less than your best."

"Okay," I said carefully. It felt like we were edging back into the dangerous territory of our fight and it was a place I didn't want to revisit. Jack's head came up at my tone and he frowned slightly, reaching out to push a stray curl off my forehead, tracing along my hairline until it was out of my eyes.

"I'm not trying to fight or argue with you, Quinn. I just don't want to see any harm befall you. I want to keep you safe, see you happy."

I felt my silent apprehension dissolve and sighed.

"It feels like you don't want me here," I murmured and he shook his head.

"Nothing could be further from the truth. I do want you here. I want to show you everything, I just fear the consequences of those actions."

"You act like everything has negative consequences down here."

"It feels like it, sometimes."

"That's a pretty depressing thought."

"Aye, it is."

I studied his face and sighed, turning to stare off into the distance.

"I mean it, Quinn. I just want you to be happy."

"I know, Jack… I'm just not sure what that's supposed to look like. You know?"

He smiled and that hint of sadness was there. He nodded and said, "I know. Truth be told, I wasn't sure what it would look like for me, either."

I cocked my head but didn't give my thoughts a voice. I was afraid if I did he would admit that it looked like me and I just didn't know what to do with that. I really didn't. I knew he was torn just as I was. He didn't want me here, but he did. I didn't want to go home, but I didn't want to stay if he didn't want me to. It was extremely frustrating being caught in this strange purgatory of mixed signals.

I tried very hard to set all of that aside and focus on the here and now. Just second by second, minute by minute, hour by hour.

What else was I going to do?

I STARED into the ornate mirror on the wall and almost didn't recognize myself. The dress was something out of a fairy tale, which *duh*. Its light, muted green brought out the gold buried in the depths of my brown irises, turning them to a molten caramel in my face. The material was an almost-velvety natural raw silk that floated when I walked. It brushed the tops of my feet and had a bit of a train to the back hem but the cloth was so light that when I walked, it whispered above the ground and against my skin.

Held up by thin, light straps, the dress's backline plunged so low as to almost be indecent. The front was high enough to cover everything adequately, the silk draping in a cowl. Still, the dress managed to cling in all the right ways and when I bent forward, it didn't gape and give everyone a view of what I didn't want it to. I was still having a hard time getting over not wearing a bra, though. The girls weren't floppy, thank god, but they were of a size that a bra was definitely warranted. I was so far out of my comfort zone it wasn't even funny.

Honestly, it felt more like I was wearing a thin, sexy nightgown versus an evening gown or what passed for one in Fairy. Mags stood on a tall stool beside the low bench I sat on, fussing with my hair. The curls were looser somehow, and smoother, sleeker than they were naturally. She had these tiny white flowers hidden like stars among them and through some sort of magic, dew drops sparkled here and there, reflecting the light but never absorbing into the hair itself.

She finished off my hair by creating a band of the blossoms, larger than what was hidden among the curls, to hold it back.

"There now, isn't that lovely?" she asked, grinning wide, her broken and stained teeth on full display. I couldn't help but smile too, I know it was awful to think it, but Mags was honestly so ugly it was adorable.

She clapped her gnarled hands and said, "Aye, get yourselves to work, you bloomin' faeries!"

Several of the doll-like fairies, like the one I'd sketched before she'd blown whatever-it-was into my face to drug me, flew out of the flowering vines draping the worn stone-block walls of the room. I flinched and Mags made a consoling sound.

"Oh, don't you be worryin' none about them, dearie. They pull anything like that Fearbán féir, I'll nail their wings down, I will."

"Who-da-whatsit?" I asked, and made a funny face to indicate how lost I was with some of the pronunciations still.

"Fearbán féir, Lass! The Sprite that helped that git of a brother to the Queen!" she said the last in a hushed tone, leaning towards me as she said it conspiratorially.

"Oh, so what's her name, then?" I asked, and pointed to the pretty little fairy hovering nervously nearby. Mags leaned back abruptly, taken aback. The little Sprite I spoke about zipped up and around into a perfect backflip and drew a little closer, cocking her head.

"Well!" Mags blustered, "She asked ye yer name, don't just fly there."

The little fairy chittered in a musical language I couldn't understand for the life of me and I looked to Mags for help.

"She said, 'Magairlín féitheach'," and at the face I made, she laughed. "It means Orchid, more or less."

The little Sprite cocked her head and looked me over, then said something. Mags translated, "She said to just call her Orchid."

"Thanks, Orchid. I'd feel really bad mangling your name. I feel terrible as it is that I'm basically the big dumb stereotypical American here." I sighed and thought to myself that if Livvy were here this would all be so different.

Yeah, Livvy would be the one with Jack.

I immediately felt guilty for the jealous thought and a wave of something like a cross between nostalgia and jealousy left a bitter tang on my tongue. I felt like I was tumbling from the sky. Overwhelmed, dizzied, like I was going end-over-end, the scenery whipping by, the emotions going through me and over me so quickly I couldn't grasp a single one. I swallowed hard and asked Mags in a shaking voice, "Is there a way to get a glass of water that won't trap me down here for seven years?"

Mags chuckled and said, "Oh, aye. A good thing Jack told ye about that." She snapped and a glass of water appeared on the stool by her tiny feet. I went to take it and frowned.

"He did, but he didn't tell me how I could tell if it was legit or not. You know, not a trick."

"The Fae aren't really known for outright lying, lass."

"Just by omission, and they're pretty fond of trickery," I said.

"Aye, but you're safe with me."

"I know that, thank you." I took a sip of the cool, sweet water and tried to stem the rising tide of panic threatening to choke me off. I was prone to anxiety attacks. Another reason I had loved and hated Livvy in equal measure. She was grounded, had her shit together, while I, I was a neurotic mess. It was a secret I was hoping Jack would never find out.

"Oh, now what's the matter with, ye?" Mags asked, even as Orchid chattered vehemently in whatever chiming sing-song language the Sprites had.

"Sorry," I said, dashing at the moisture trying to gather on my lash line.

"Aye, I know you can't do her makeup when she's in this state, shut up, ye git!" Mags waved her cane at the little fairy who immediately fell silent.

"I'm sorry, Orchid, and Mags, if you don't mind me saying, you really should try to be nicer to poor Orchid. I somehow doubt she asked to be here helping me." I turned to the Sprite and said, "I really don't mean to make your job harder. Just sometimes I get like this."

"Don't you worry your pretty head about us," Mags said, waving me off. "Just breathe, and pull yourself together, girl. You're expected in the Night Garden before long." Mags sighed, "Just know that I'll be here to talk if you need to, after."

"Thanks, Mags. It's like one minute I'm fine and then I'll think of my best friend, Livvy, and the whole world just goes topsy-turvy on me all over again. I miss her a lot, but sometimes I think such unfair things and-"

"Say no more, lass."

Orchid said something and Mags nodded tiredly. "Agreed, Sprite. Grief is an unpredictable thing and it doesn't always work how you or anyone else thinks it should. Grief doesn't care, it works on its own timeline."

I swallowed hard and nodded slowly. Coming from someone, undoubtedly as old as Mags, I had to believe what she said, right?

"Aye," she said with a sadder smile. "I know what you're thinking, lass. What does someone as old as me, an immortal, know about grief?"

"Oh, no, I wasn't thinking that. Honest."

She harumphed and sighed, "The truth is I know quite a bit. I was a child during the first Fae war. There have been seven, don't you know. I think it's sadder, more profound when one of us dies the true death. No offense, but you humans are such... impermanent creatures. To us, you're like a dog or a cat. You mustn't be surprised if some of the higher Fae treat you as such."

"Don't worry," I murmured. "I'm used to it."

"Are ye now?" she asked in a scoffing tone as if she didn't believe me.

"It's true. In America, that's the way a lot of my people are treated."

"What other people?" Mags asked with a frown.

"Um, black people?"

"Ye aren't black," Mags said with a scowl. "Now, Dubhlainn, he's black as soot from head to foot!" Mags cackled at her little rhyme and I smiled and laughed slightly along with her.

"Wait, how did you say his name? Dove-lin?"

"Aye, aye, it means 'black sword' in the old tongue. A fierce warrior. One of the fiercest. Lived through the fourth through the seventh Fae wars and fought in them all."

Orchid chirruped something and Mags scowled, asking, "Are ye sure?" Another silvery drawn out sound and Mags nodded once. "I stand corrected. The third through the seventh. Ye can't miss him, he's blacker than the night sky, from his skin to his hair to his eyes, that one."

"I'll remember that," I murmured, and closed my eyes for Orchid, who had gestured for me to do so. She'd already powdered my face and had stained my lips with a light shimmer, somehow. It felt strange having this tiny being basically finger-painting on my makeup, though with how small she was, it was more like she used her whole hand.

Mag chatted away telling me all about a myriad of the fairy men from a race that were called the Sidhe, which Jack had spelled for me but every time it was said it sounded like 'she.' I didn't know how I was going to get around the spelling sounding nothing like it looked. I wondered if it mattered or if it was the mere belief that counted the most. It was one of many things I worried about in making this whole thing work.

I wondered how Jack was faring. We'd left the Summerland and had gone back to his chamber, both of us tired and feeling it. I'd felt terrible when I'd realized he'd forgone sleep as much as he had on account of me. We'd made love again and had drifted off in each other's arms, only to be woken by a pounding on his door a short time later. He'd been called to duty, charged with delivering messages throughout this Rath and several others.

He'd bid me sleep some more, which I had, only to be woken by Mags. Jack had left a safe bite to eat and she'd rushed me through it before whisking me off to get ready for this gala. Jack still hadn't returned. I mean, I hadn't seen him again, but Mags swore up and down he would be there tonight.

"Aw, there we go, aren't you lovely?"

A light knock fell at the door and our heads turned in that direction. I think I forgot to breathe when I realized how much I wished it were Jack on the other side.

"Ah, that would be your escort," Mags said and gave me one more going over. I looked in the mirror and barely recognized myself. The woman staring back at me was something beautiful, out of – well, a fairy tale.

"You look lovely." Mags beamed and called out much louder, "Enter!"

I stood up and faced the door as it pushed in, the heavy carved oak groaning slightly on its hinges. It wasn't Jack, though. I didn't know the man who stepped through and I couldn't account for the frisson of anxiety that sent a tingling rush down my back, sweeping from the hair raising on the back of my neck, all the way down to the backs of my knees.

"Ah, don't you look a vision?" he asked, and I swallowed hard.

"Th-thank you," I stammered out.

He and I stood no more than twelve feet apart, his silvery eyes sweeping me from head to toe and back again. His eyes were familiar to me but I couldn't quite place them. I'd seen many unique colors of hair and eyes since coming down here, mostly on the little Sprites and Pixies.

His hair was long and white, falling easily to his knees and half pulled back revealing slightly curved and pointed ears. His features were sharp, and he was quite handsome, bordering on beautiful, but it didn't stir me like when I looked at Jack. If anything, standing across from this man, all I felt was nervous, anxious, and a vague sort of dread.

He held out a hand to me, the billowing sleeves of his white shirt, as white as his skin, draping from his shoulders and down his arm artfully. He wore a wide, black leather belt with a silver buckle and black, close-fitting pants tucked into knee-high black suede boots. The shirt collar opened in a V, showing a peek of his well-muscled chest.

"Ah, how rude of me," he said, his voice also familiar. "Allow me to introduce myself, I am the Huntsman, Gwynn Ap Nudd."

I turned to look at Mags, alarmed, but she'd disappeared, just gone in the blink of an eye, the way she had a habit of doing. I swallowed hard and tried not to feel like I'd been thrown under a bus somehow, but it was difficult. I realized with a bit of a start that the Sprites that had been helping me were also gone.

I turned back to face him and took a step back, as the twelve feet that had separated us had been reduced by half. I didn't like that. I didn't like him being closer at all, but he was between me and the only door in or out of the room.

"It's all right," he said. "I don't mean you any harm despite what Jack may have told you."

I brushed my palms which were suddenly damp along the silk over my legs and said, "You kind of kidnapped me."

"Ah, yes, that. I apologize, but it was the only way I knew to get you down here."

"I don't even understand why you would want me down here," I said. "Are you seriously that peeved that Jack stopped you from taking me on Halloween night?"

His eyes narrowed slightly and he dropped his hand back to his side. It'd been creepy that he'd held it out this long. I rubbed up and down one arm with my hand to try and stave off a chill that had nothing to do with the ambient temperature.

"Are you so certain that Jack's motives are entirely pure?" he asked softly, and it was my turn to narrow my eyes at him.

"Yes," I said simply.

He chuckled and shook his head. "I knew your drawings were special the moment I laid eyes on them," he said.

"What does that have to do with anything?" I asked.

"Maybe nothing, maybe everything. Now, please; my sister, the Queen, has asked that I escort you to the Night Garden. Jack awaits you there." He held out his hand to me once again and I contemplated it. He sighed, but it wasn't an impatient sound, but rather, a tired one. I looked from his hand to his face, which was impassive, and finally took a few tentative steps forward. He smiled thinly and his expression thawed a touch.

"Okay," I agreed. "I'll walk with you. Go ahead."

His smile grew slightly and he almost looked like he blushed, except there was no color to it. He chuckled lightly and said, "It's not the Fae way to simply walk with a lady, a proper escort is required. We are nothing, if not old-fashioned. I promise I don't bite."

My apprehension surged but I put my hand lightly in his, he stood a moment looking amused and raised an eyebrow.

"What?" I demanded, self-conscious all of a sudden.

"It's lovely to finally meet you, Quinn," he said and bowed deeply, gallantly, over my hand, brushing the knuckles with his lips. I stiffened, waiting for something untoward to happen, but it never came.

I wasn't buying it. There was something else at work here. I could feel it, sense it. It was like every time I had ever been thrown shade growing up by the mean girls club. I couldn't say anything without looking completely paranoid and crazy, and it was the worst feeling in the world knowing it was coming, but not knowing what. The just waiting for it to happen and that awful knowing that when it did, it would be horrible. The helpless, powerless feeling of knowing there would be a pain, but having absolutely no power to stop it, to avoid it.

I felt my shoulders loosen slightly when I realized I just had to go on with things and wait for it to happen before I could react. That reacting was the only thing I did have control over.

"Thank you," I said. "I wish I could say the same, but I'm pretty much scared to death of you." He smiled genuinely then, and straightened, turning to stand beside me and tuck my hand into the crook of his arm.

"How refreshingly honest and forthright of you," he said and we set off out the door and into the hall, the stone warm beneath my bare feet, which had ornate jewelry made from more of the same flowers that were in my hair. A chain of them wrapped around my ankle and along the top of my foot, the vine wrapping around my middle toe to give the appearance of sandals where there were none.

"I thought you might appreciate it," I said.

"Oh, aye. It was just unexpected. It isn't precisely a human trait."

Jack had warned me that the Fae didn't lie outright, but that they were extremely well-versed in deception without doing so. I tried to keep that in mind as I rolled my lips together and walked with him.

"I'm trying not to judge," I said gently, and it was true. My father had always taught me to never judge a person by what was said about them, to always give a person the benefit of the doubt until they proved to me they were as people said. However, in the very next breath, he told me to not ignore the warning signs either. So that is what I tried to do.

"I think you will like the Night Garden," he murmured after a slight lull in the conversation.

"What is it?" I asked. "I mean, why is it called that?"

I looked up at him and realized that all of what Jack called the pure-blooded Sidhe were really tall. I mean, I wasn't exactly a midget at five foot six, but where Jack was taller than me at six foot, maybe six-foot-one, even the women among the Sidhe were easily taller than even that.

Gwynn's lips curved into a genuine smile that didn't actually chill me to the bone for once and he said, "You'll see. I wouldn't want to ruin the surprise."

It was as he said this that we rounded a bend in the natural stone hallway. It wound to the left and spilled down a set of natural worn steps into an honest-to-god garden, only with a twist.

It was dark in the cavern, but the flowers glowed. So did little rock pools, tiny waterfalls spilling down the stone walls, the disruption of the falling water stirring up the blue bioluminescence in the pools to light the garden. Still, though I'd seen photos and video of biolumi-nescence on the internet, I'd never seen flowers harbor and emit a glow like these did. It wasn't just limited to one type of flower, either.

There were orchids growing in rock crevices, and amaryllis growing in clumps here and there. There were plumeria shrubs and water lilies floating idyllically in the pools. Flowering vines crawled up spiraling latticework, and drew my eyes up and up. Mica or some sort of quartz dotted the high, natural cavern's ceiling, reflecting the blue light, winking like stars overhead, and the whole thing just took my breath away.

There were men and women standing around, and they'd been speaking in hushed tones, but now, now they were just hushed and when I managed to bring my eyes back down to their level, I realized all eyes were on me.

The Queen saved me from their impassive expressions and cool scrutiny by stepping out of the crowd, her hand on Doan's arm. She smiled up at us and said lightly, "Quinn, so good of you to join us. Please, come here, let me have a look at you." She held out a hand and Gwynn took mine from his arm and holding it lightly, made a great show of 'helping' me down the three broad stone steps and onto the lush grass.

I went to the Queen and took her hand. She took a half-step back and looked me up and down. Her lips, painted a dark color that was indecipherable by the blue light, curved into a smile. I took the time to look her over, too.

She wore a very modern gown, halter with a plunging neckline, nearly to her navel. The gown was a light, airy material I had no name for, and left little to the imagination, but like the ceiling of the cavern, it was studded with crystals that refracted the light as she moved. The crystals were heavier toward the bottom of the long dress, dispersing at the top as if the stars exploded from the bottom and flew up into the sky rather than originating from up above.

So thick were the crystals at the bottom that when she moved, they rattled against each other and the sound was very like the whisper of scales against one another, like a snake, or perhaps a dragon, both equally lethal in their own ways.

"You look lovely," the Queen said, and I met her eyes, which were heavily lined with kohl making the iris seem completely colorless.

"Oh, thank you, but it certainly doesn't hold a candle to you, Your Majesty."

She laughed, a delighted sound, and taking my arm, settled at my side saying, "Walk with me." It wasn't a request; her voice was velvet-wrapped steel.

I fell into step beside her and the conversations around us resumed like they knew the Queen wanted the illusion of privacy. It was eerie and I bowed my head slightly to watch my step when really, I could feel their eyes on me.

"Do you have an answer for me, Quinn?" the Queen asked and her voice was slightly strained. I realized with a start that she sounded afraid.

I licked my lips and said, "I do. I would very much like to help you, Queen Maebh."

"But?" she asked, and I smiled and shook my head.

"No 'buts'," I said. "I can't guarantee how effective I'll be, but I would very much like to try."

She smiled and drew in a deep breath, standing a bit straighter, as if my decision bolstered her, and I realized that she had really been afraid I would say no.

"I am unused to asking for help in any regard, Quinn Carter," she murmured. "I am a warrior-queen, but this has simply been something I cannot fight." She stopped at the edge of a waist-high pool toward the edge of the cavernous Night Garden room. She trailed her fingertips through the water and the light flared. I studied her face by it and she looked both tired and sad.

"I am afraid I brought our people to this," she said in hushed tones. "I took us away from the sight of mortal men for too long. I was angry at their worship of this new, false Christian god." She looked back out over the small crowd of fairy nobility and a small smile of wistful pride flashed across her lips. She looked at them all like they were her children and she was a proud mother. It made me smile in turn. Someday, I wanted that look to be on my face.

"My pride, our pride, could very well be our downfall," she said. "I only hope it's not too late."

I pressed my lips together and finally, my curiosity won out. I said, "Queen Maebh, if I may be so bold as to ask..." She arched one dark brow at me and inclined her chin ever so slightly. "If you were all worshiped as gods in your own right, then..." I faltered, and her smile grew.

"Go on," she said.

"Then who do you find yourself praying to during times like these?"

"Well, perhaps this tale will start you on your way to helping us," she said, then asked, "Do you know what Tuatha Dé means?"

I shook my head, "No, I'm afraid I don't."

"Ah, well, Tuatha Dé means *people* or *tribe of*."

"Is 'Danann' a god or goddess, then?"

"Very good," she said, laughing.

"Which is it, though?"

"Danann is our mother and loosely translated means Mother of Earth, or Mother Earth."

"So the Tuatha Dé Danann are the people of the earth?" I frowned slightly.

"I like to think that we are born of nature, so after a fashion, I believe." She placed her hands flat on the rock and leaned over the pool, gazing into its depths.

"My beloved is far better at explaining our ancient origins than I. I would like for you to begin right away, if you can."

"I'm, um, here in Ireland only for the winter. I'm supposed to head back to America in the spring. I don't know if that is going to be enough time."

She smiled brightly, "Of course it is! Time moves differently in the Rath. I don't ask much of it, unlike many of the others, and I am the Queen. I can ask for as much time as you need. A year could pass here, while only a week passes in the mortal world if that would suffice."

"I- I don't know," I said, a little shaky.

"You aren't having misgivings now, are you?"

"No, I just. I guess it takes some getting used to, all the magic. I mean," I looked around again, "I've never seen anything like this on earth."

"I wish I could say I understood, but by now I am fair certain I take this world for granted." She looked at me fondly and I smiled.

"You'd probably think America was as ugly as sin."

"If the belief is strong enough, I might have the chance to see it," she said. I cocked my head and her smile widened. "You don't think we were always once limited to the land you call Ireland, do you?"

"No, I mean, I did think you were limited to the British Isles. You know, Ireland, Scotland, and England."

She laughed and it was a bright sound, "Oh, my dear girl. You have a lot to learn."

I grinned and said, "And I'm looking forward to it. Truly, I am."

The Queen's smile grew and she seemed to ease into a more natural state a little, leaving the stiff posture of her position off a bit. I was relieved, my misgivings left behind with Gwynn for the time being. I relaxed and really enjoyed talking with her, listening to what she had to tell me. I was fascinated, really. I could listen to her lyrical voice all night.

22

J ack...

I was, unfortunately, delayed to the gala by the need to dress appropriately for it after all my messages were delivered. When I arrived, Quinn was already standing beside the Queen, who was giving her speech. I adjusted my cravat slightly, unused to the garment, and stood at the back of the gathering, intent upon what was being said.

"...pleased to say she has agreed. It is my ardent hope that her wish to help us in these dire straits would afford her some respect and it is my ardent desire that you cooperate with your stories and recollections of our past to aid her in her endeavors. Ms. Carter has agreed to stay with us, in Faerie, for a year's worth of time in order to collect tales and imagery. While she is here, no more than a mortal winter shall pass. Then, she will return to America and attempt to foster belief in us once more."

A light smattering of applause rippled through the court and I studied Quinn's face. She looked nervous but determined, and I I'd be lying to myself if I didn't admit that, as beautiful as the Queen always looked, Quinn outshone her. I felt something in me soften as I realized that there was only one thing that could make me think any woman was more beautiful than the Queen of Faerie. It hit in the center of my chest like a physical blow, yet with none of the pain.

I was in love with Quinn Carter.

I drew in a deep breath, but before I could let it out, a most unwelcome presence disrupted my view. Gwynn stepped in front of me, an oily, malicious smile dripping from his lips.

"Huntsman," I said with a bow of my head only, so I did not let him leave my sight.

"So formal," he said with a feigned lightness.

"There are some among the Fae that require a certain amount of distance," I said. "Present company very much included."

Gwynn put on a mocking, scowling pout and said, "Oh, Jack. That very nearly hurt my feelings!" He placed a hand on his chest as if wounded and I scoffed.

"All one of them you have left, Gwynn? I hardly think so."

The next scowl was for real, when he said, "Well, in the grand scheme of things my feelings are hardly the ones that matter now are they?" I looked past him at Quinn and he stepped aside. I made to step forward but was halted immediately in my tracks by Eibhleann who raised a hand and placed her palm in the center of my chest, stepping into me.

I gritted my teeth and checked Quinn, who was speaking with the Queen and her Consort. I flicked my eyes back to Eibhleann's, which were simmering with something very akin to rage.

"And where do I fit into things now, Jack?" she demanded quietly.

"I honestly hadn't thought about it, Eibhleann. You are, and always have been, your own woman." It was perhaps a poor choice in phrasing, though I held no malice behind the words or in my tone. In fact, if anything, I'd said what I had with a gentleness that my former lover didn't quite deserve.

"Aw, do you feel I have been unfair to you, Jackie-boy?" she asked in a sultry purr. "Have I not given myself to you when you have asked?"

I felt my lips curve derisively and shook my head gently. "Eibhleann, I have ever been at your beck and call, not the other way 'round." Where anger had flared, a deep loathing remained as that anger ebbed. It shocked me to the core, but made sense to me, in a way. Quinn... Quinn had made me remember what a healthy relationship was like, had given me hope that I could, indeed, have something like one again.

"You're angry with me." Eibhleann's expression softened as she studied my face. She sighed, a deep and heavy thing and her shoulders dropped in seeming defeat. A moment of introspection flashed across her sharp features and she licked her lips. "No, I don't suppose I treated you very well, did I?" she asked and I couldn't tell if she were being genuine or not. I debated only briefly when a great sadness seemed to overcome her.

I frowned, "I never thought myself anything more than a passing fancy for you." I said softly. "All those times I suggested or hinted at something more, you plucked my hope for it from the air and dashed it upon the rocks." I took the hand on my chest between both my own and sighed.

"You care for her deeply, don't you, Jack? Deeper than you ever cared for me."

I shook my head, "I wouldn't say that Eibhleann. There was once I loved you, but I was certain and you said that there was no way, that you simply didn't want anything more."

"And so it was fairly easy for her to take you from me," she murmured, looking over her shoulder. I followed her gaze and saw Quinn, laughing at something one of the ladies of the court had to say.

"I believe we were lost to one another long before Quinn arrived. Likely before she was even born," I said, and Eibhleann turned to look at me.

She swallowed hard, tears trembling on her lashes and I let her hand go.

"So that's it, then," she said and it wasn't in the form of a question so I didn't reply. She looked at me and leaned in, her lips hovering above mine and asked: "One last kiss to say goodbye?"

Damn her. If I said no, she'd throw a fit, draw Quinn's attention. I didn't want that. I hadn't explained about Eibhleann. I gave a short nod, acquiesced and expected a quick, chaste press of lips but oh, no. Not Eibhleann.

She kissed me true, and I kissed her back, lest I raise a row, that, and we had been lovers for more than fifty years. I think I needed this goodbye and Quinn was occupied. Safely so – I could explain...

"Wow."

I jerked back from Eibhleann and looked past her. Quinn stood mere feet away on Gwynn's arm, Gwynn with his smug and oily smile. It had been a ploy, orchestrated by the both of them. I should have seen it coming. I cursed myself silently.

"Quinn, I can explain."

"Oh, I'm sure you could, Jack." She scoffed and shook her head, her anger a poor mask for her hurt. She shook her head and said, "I don't even want to hear it right now. In fact, just don't talk to me."

She wouldn't look at me. I kept my rage down while I felt my own heart crack in two, not for myself, but for her and what she must be feeling. I was used to this type of treatment down here. The games and manipulations. I wanted desperately to say to her, *did I not warn you? Did I not tell you they were this way?*

She turned abruptly and walked swiftly away, losing herself among the crowd, I made to go after her, but Eibhleann caught my arm in a vice-like grip. I turned to say something sharp but the cruelty in her eyes, in the curve of her lips told me everything. I shook her hand off my arm and she let me. If she hadn't wanted me to walk away, I wouldn't have been able to. She was easily a hundred times as strong as I, one of the many attributes among the pureblood Sidhe.

"I am sorry if I have hurt you," I murmured and her eyes flashed wide. I was angry, but what was more, is I was disappointed in her. Disappointed, but not surprised. Still, she knew and I knew, this was the last of it. This was the last slight the last hurt, the last bit of cruelty I would be putting up with from her.

She read my look and surprise flitted across her fair features. She was beautiful on the outside but far from it on the inside.

"You had me, Eibhleann," I told her. "Now you've lost me. You. Not because of Quinn, but because of yourself. I may have had a hand in the destruction of 'us', whatever there was of an 'us' to begin with, but that girl," I pointed after Quinn. "Had nothing at all to do with it." My chest felt like it was being squeezed by a fist and my breath heaved slightly with my fight to suppress the sudden, hot, and fierce rising anger inside me. As a parting shot, I said over my shoulder, "You could have done what you willed with me, against me, but you should have left her out of it."

She stood glaring at me, her hands balled into fists, several other Fae standing around our vicinity staring at her with amused looks. Some looked after me with much the same expression, though perhaps with an added shine of pride.

I had been blind to it, but no more. Now I realized precisely how much and why Eibhleann was disliked, even among other Fae.

I wandered the garden looking for Quinn, and found her in a secluded alcove with its own little reflecting pool and a thin trickle of musical water. A wisteria tree dripping with softly glowing blooms shrouded the alcove in privacy and I froze, stepping behind a crag of stone to listen when Gwynn stepped into view, holding out a square of cloth to Quinn. She took it and dabbed at her eyes.

"Thank you," she said quietly.

"Of course," he murmured and his tone was consoling. I ground my teeth together, clenching my jaw, but held still.

"I'm sorry," she said after a moment and Gwynn knelt on the carpet of grass before her so that he could look into her face. She shook her head and tipped it back, staring up at the glowing canopy above her.

"For what?" he asked gently. "You've nothing to be sorry for."

"I may have judged you unfairly..." she said, trailing off. She pursed her lips and looked back at him. "That's definitely something for which an apology is owed." Gwynn chuckled and bowed his head, nodding in agreement.

"Aye, I suppose you're right," he said. "Still, I can't blame you for being deceived."

I frowned. He didn't lie. She was being deceived but by the same token, that deception wasn't entirely of my making, though by not telling her of Eibhleann, I had to admit my duplicity in the deception. A prime example of the Fae's ability to craft the truth in such a way as to deceive without actually outright lying. It was infuriating, maddening, and it might be costing me dearly. I went to move into the alcove but my arm was caught by an intervening hand. I snapped to, turning swiftly in the direction of the interloper, and discovered Doan, the Queen's Consort, a serious look upon his face and a finger pressed to his lips in a command for silence.

I cocked my head and gave him a questioning look, and he rolled his eyes and pointed gently in the direction of Quinn and Gwynn. His expression was dour and begged silence, and my respect for Doan tempered my anger into a steely resolve to commit to patience.

Still, I didn't like it. I didn't like any of it, and I wanted to protect Quinn from any more damage to her psyche and any more hurt to her soul. I didn't want to see any more of her tears.

23

Quinn...

"Aye, I suppose you're right," he said. "Still, I can't blame you for being deceived."

I huffed a bitter, broken laugh. "I should have guessed he was like any other guy. If it's too good to be true, well, then it usually is."

He gave me a bit of a rueful smile and a slight nod before standing fluidly. I swallowed hard and closed my eyes, trying to collect myself so that no more tears fell. I turned to look into the water beside me. The little alcove had seemed perfect. Draped with softly fragrant and glowing blossoms from the tree at the back and to one side, it held a little reflecting pool with two seats to either side formed naturally out of the gray rock face.

Gwynn gave me some space and sank into the seat across the pool that was very table-like. I supposed it was some sort of magic that kept it from overflowing. I didn't see a drain or a way for the light trickle of water to escape the basin, yet it didn't overflow.

I closed my eyes again and took a very deep, cleansing breath, letting it out slowly. Before I opened my eyes and fixed him with my gaze I asked the tough questions.

"Who is she? I mean, who are they to each other?"

"Her name is Eibhleann. She is," Gwynn cleared his throat, "Of minor Fae nobility." I winced on the inside but didn't let it show. *Stupid, stupid, stupid, Quinn. What the hell makes you think that Jack has any real interest in you when he's hooked up with fairy royalty?*

Gwynn went on, "They've been lovers off and on for the last fifty years or so."

I felt ill.

"Do you think I should apologize to her? I mean, I really didn't know..." Gwynn chuckled lightly in that way that said a person thought you were adorable. It was slightly condescending and I blushed with embarrassment. I mean, yeah, now that I'd said it out loud, it sounded pretty stupid.

"No, I don't think that would be wise. I would give it time to settle, but it was a very sweet and kind thought."

I nodded miserably and stared at my hands clutched in my lap. He drew a breath to speak but stopped, seemingly thinking better of it, and closed his mouth, contemplating me.

"Ask," I murmured quietly and his mouth set into a grim line.

"You'll still help us, won't you?" he asked.

"I already committed. I already said I would. Just because Jack is a jerk and not the person I maybe thought he was doesn't mean I'm going to condemn an entire race of people to burn out and fade away." I shook my head and asked, "What kind of petty monster would that make me?"

He smiled and it was a sad one, his expression going far away for a moment before he sighed and said, "Some of the Fae wars were fought for reasons far pettier."

I swallowed hard, my mouth dry, and tried not to think too hard about those stories. I mean, I would listen to them, I would have to, but wars didn't make for good children's books. I didn't know what I would do when it came to those parts of the fairies' history.

I guess I would just have to cross that bridge when I came to it. Just like I would have to, embarrassingly, cross the bridge here very soon that would be the humiliating request for my own chambers. I didn't know if they had assumed I would be staying with Jack, and broaching the topic was going to be painful in its humiliation. I mean, they all had to know, didn't they? This world was a small one. Much smaller than the human world, and that world was a small one, too.

I watched the water ripple in the pool in front of me and tried not to get the damn song stuck in my head.

"It will be all right," Gwynn said, and I swallowed hard.

"Yeah, no, I know I was just thinking about my things and, um, where to stay." I shifted uncomfortably and looked up at him. He smiled and inclined his head.

"Already taken care of."

"Really?" I blinked.

"Aye, Mags should be getting your chambers ready as we speak."

"Thanks..." I murmured at a bit of a loss.

"Ah, there you are!" We both turned toward the voice. Doan stood in the natural stone archway leading into the little alcove.

"I'm sorry," I said immediately. "I just needed a moment. I'm not used to being the center of attention. Livvy always used to do it, so I didn't have to."

"Perfectly understood," Doan said. "Jack had to be sent with an urgent message to one of the other Raths. Our Queen has told me that you wish to begin at the beginning, with the old history. Is that correct?"

I nodded slowly. "Yes, that would be great."

"I believe there has been enough excitement for one evening. I'm sure this all has to be overwhelming to Ms. Carter to some degree," Gwynn said, and I appreciated that he was giving me an out.

"Aye, I see your point, Huntsman."

"Thank you, Consort. I thought, if Quinn was ready, I might escort her back to her chambers. See that she gets settled."

"Aye, I believe that would be best."

I stood slowly while Gwynn rose from his seat swiftly, and fluidly, like a cat.

"Thank you," I murmured.

"Of course." Doan inclined his dark head and added, "I shall see you tomorrow if you are ready to begin?"

I nodded, "I'd like to get to work. I'm actually pretty excited to be working on a project." Doan smiled and stepped aside so that Gwynn and I could pass.

"Excellent, I shall see you after you've had a chance to rest."

"Thank you."

I ghosted past him and Gwynn shadowed me. He held out his arm to me and I took it, though I was uncomfortable still. I mean, he had admitted that he'd manipulated things in order to 'expose' Jack, but I still didn't trust him or his motives completely. I somehow doubted I would trust anyone fully while I was down here, but I couldn't pass up the sights and wonders to be seen! I couldn't pass up the opportunity to be the one to draw the fantastic, and to, hopefully, be a real-life hero.

Besides. I wanted to do this, I wanted it to succeed, and I wanted desperately to do it all in Livvy's name. I just didn't know how I was going to do it all. I mean, the magic time-disparity was definitely going to help, but – I had a sudden thought.

"What about Mrs. O'Leary?" I asked. Well, more like blurted. I stopped in my tracks and Gwynn humored me, looking at me with amusement and I rushed out, "If I don't go back to the cottage anytime soon, there'll be questions. She might report me missing and that could get... complicated."

"Calm yourself now," Gwynn said and patted my hand where it rested on his arm. "It's been taken care of." I blinked long and slow and tried to process what he'd just said.

"I'm sorry," I said, the hair standing up on the back of my neck. "But just how has it been 'taken care of'?"

"We've sent a changeling in your guise to pose as you while you're here. It won't be difficult at all for her to fool the few villagers you had regular contact with. She has a strong glamour about her."

"I see."

Actually, I was fairly unsettled. I felt like Gwynn was being a little too helpful at this point. Like he'd perhaps, successfully kidnapped me anyway, only in such a way that I'd fallen right in line. Like one of the mice right after the Pied Piper. Which, if I remember the tale, he then took the village's children or something because of their refusal to either pay him or follow through on their end of the bargain.

"Don't be upset, Quinn," he murmured and stopped in front of what I presumed was going to be my chamber door. "We are simply eager to stop or reverse the damage being done, and at the same time, we want you to be comfortable."

What he was saying sounded good, but I couldn't shake the nagging feeling that something else was at work. Jack had tried to warn me, but, of course, Jack had also been lying to me this entire time.

Still, I had learned the hard way to trust my gut and my gut was telling me this was all wrong, that something about Gwynn was all wrong.

"I'm sorry, I guess I am just having trouble trusting anyone or anything right now. I'm pretty well shook."

Gwynn smiled but it wasn't a happy thing. He gave a nod and said, "Well, here we are." He reached past me and depressed the latch on the ornate door handle that appeared to be some sort of oxidized pewter. The door swung inward and I smiled at him and gave a nod in return.

"Thank you," I said. My father raised his daughter to be polite, after all.

"As Doan said, he will be by to collect you at some point. If it's alright with you..." he picked up one of my hands and brought it up between us, "I should quite like to see you again." His eyes locked with mine, an intense look, as he brushed his lips lightly across my knuckles.

I swallowed hard, my throat so tight with anxiety I didn't trust myself to speak. Instead, I simply nodded. I didn't want to tell him no. I had a distinct feeling, the impression, after the look he'd just given me that 'no' wouldn't be well received.

"Until then," he said and let my hand go.

"Good night," I managed to say, and he smiled, dipped a rather formal bow, and turned, striding up the hallway.

I slipped into the chamber and shut the door tightly behind me with a sigh. He hadn't threatened me overtly. He hadn't said anything out of turn, hadn't held my hand too tight, or done anything to make anyone witnessing our exchange think anything was out of place... but that look he'd given me over our hands had been absolutely chilling.

He'd lived up to his title with that one look, 'Huntsman', because I most certainly had felt like prey pinned in place by that one look, like a butterfly to a board.

I shot the bolt on the inside of the door and turned to see where I would be staying and, like everything in this strange land, the room, or rooms, were beautiful. Of course, if there was one thing that stuck with me when it came to Jack, it was his tale of how he'd once lost himself in Faery for over a month. I didn't want that to happen to me, and with the exchange I'd just had with Gwynn, I suddenly felt like rather than staying as a guest of the Unseelie Fae, I was, in reality, their prisoner, locked into a gilded cage.

24

J ack...

I did as Doan asked only after he swore to me that he would see to it Quinn remained safe. I rolled through the halls of the Rath like thunder through the sky, my rage boiling around me though, by all outward appearances, I was calm in the thick of things. I was the eye of the storm, as it were.

I went to my chambers, unlocking the door and slamming it behind me, but still the anger marched along my skin, eating me alive. I needed to move, I needed to work; I needed an outlet for some of my rage. I ripped the finery off a piece at a time and threw it onto the bed until I stood shirtless in just my breeches and boots.

I stalked over to the forge, lifting my lantern from its peg and snapping open the shroud. I dumped the accursed coal into the cold hearth and wrapped fingers around the handle of the bellows chain. I pumped and stared into the depths of the forge, working it hot and hotter still, for what I would need.

"You've gone and done it now, Jackie-boy," Mags' voice crept out of the darkened corner of my room. "What were y' thinkin', y' git?"

"Not now, woman!" I barked and she drew herself up straight to her full height, which would be funny were it not for the potential of sparking her temper, as she nae came to my knee.

"Don't you be talkin' to me like tha', boy!"

I turned with not a care at the moment. If she were spoiling for a fight, I would give her one. Whatever she saw on my face had her cocking her head, the depths of her eyes glowing with a faint light, a trick of reflection from the forge as she fixed to set into me.

"Why didn't you stop him, then?" I demanded, to head her off, and she scowled.

"Aye, were I angry enough I may have done him harm, but he's the Huntsman. It's not as easy as all o' that," she said and shuddered, settling down like a hen over her nest.

I gave a short nod and demanded, "Then what would you have had me do?" She scowled and looked contrite, heaving a reluctant sigh.

"Why haven't ye gone to her then? Tried to explain yerself?" she demanded. "There's more than one way to fight for yer woman."

"Aye, there is! What is it you think I do?" I roared at her. Contrition gone from her weathered face, her scowl returned in full force.

"What ye always do when ye get angry, hurt, or sad! Ye bury yerself in yer work, Jack! You sulk for days and sometimes weeks, and then you do a lot of the same. Nothin'. You've let them hold you down, a boot on yer neck, for nigh on two hundred years."

"Oh, aye, and ye've done the same for a lot longer than that!" I shot back.

The truth hit a little too close to home for her liking. I believe it was the first time I'd ever seen Mags gobsmacked. She recovered, her face splitting into a wide toothy grin after a moment, and she cackled clapping her gnarled hands.

"Oh, but it's different this time, eh, Jackie-boy?"

"Don't call me that accursed name!" I seethed and turned back to the forge, thrusting a bar into the flame.

"What are ye doing, and how can I help?" she asked at once.

"What Doan asked," I grated. "And ye can check on Quinn, make sure she's alright."

"Already done that, and she's as fine as a woman whose heart's been betrayed can be at the moment."

"I didn't betray anything," I ground out, and worked the bellows.

"Aye, I know that. Feckin' Eibhleann."

"You know what's happening, Mags?"

"Aye, I know."

"They've put her at the center and I don't like it."

"It's their boredom and their never-ending greed for power that leads them down this road, time and time again."

"Aye, I know."

"This is bigger than Gwynn and his thirst for power. Bigger than all the lot of us, Jack."

"Aye, I know that."

"So what are ye going to do?"

I stared at the heating rod in the coals and sighed, "For now? As I've been asked by Queen and Consort, Mags."

"Why?" she asked.

"Because it's what Quinn has chosen."

She harrumphed and made that settling motion like a worried mother hen again. I didn't like it either. I liked even less that Quinn could very well be collateral damage in Gwynn's machinations despite her pure heart and good intentions.

"He's not as smart as he thinks he is, Jack," she said and I looked her way. It was an icy comfort.

"No, he's not, but that doesn't put Quinn in any less danger. He has no care for her insofar as an instrument to slight me back for my perceived slights against him. His ego knows no bounds."

"As much as I hate to say it, I believe in the Queen and Consort's plan. The full-blood Sidhe may be pompous, egotistical gits, but as far as those two go, Her Majesty and lover aren't so bad as compared to the rest."

"I believe that's one of the main reasons why she's Queen, Mags," I said dryly, and she nodded once.

"Aye, that, and she can be right scary."

"Aye, she can be that. Be grateful we are at least on her good side in this."

The silence that stretched between us was separated by the occasional pops and crackling of the forge's heating coals. Finally, I asked, near-hypnotized to a calmer state by the conversation and forge fire, "Why are you still here?"

"Aye, aye, I'll be looking in on your lady love for you again, then." I nodded and she asked more gently, "Shall I deliver a message, Messenger?"

"Nae, if she is going to hear anything from me, it will be from me."

"Do you think that wise?"

I shook my head, "I don't know."

When I didn't say anything further she harrumphed and said, "Do your work, then."

I nodded and continued making the necessary calculations in my head. I'd never forged a cold iron sword before. Forging a weapon of any kind had been forbidden by the Queen, until now. I'd forged my knife for myself, true, but it had been necessary to my personal safety. I'd justified it by telling myself what the ruling class didn't know didn't hurt them in that particular instance.

This was going to be a new and interesting challenge for me, forging something the length of a sword and there would be some magick required. Magick I certainly didn't possess. I sighed and felt my shoulders drop, my love for Quinn and unending worry over her fueling me once my anger was spent.

25

Quinn...

My things were here already. I opened the wardrobe in the corner and all of my clothes were hung and the rest were neatly folded in the two drawers the free-standing, live edge cabinet held. My mouth went a little dry and for a moment it felt like the walls were closing in on me.

What did I get myself into? What had I exactly agreed to?

I pulled out some of my more familiar things, my favorite jeans and one of my favorite tops and quickly changed into them. The quarters they'd arranged for me were much like Jack's and even the Night Garden. An almost-natural stone cavern with modern (at least by comparison) amenities included.

I explored my surroundings further, feeling a little better, comforted, by being in my own clothes. I hung up the dress and moved through the little suite of rooms and realized it was like I had my own little studio apartment, but larger than the cottage I'd been renting.

As you came through the door, it was an open floor plan of sorts. To the left and in front of the door was a little kitchen area, much like the cottage's, although where there was a little iron potbellied stove back in the human world, this one was made entirely from stone. A neat little pile of split firewood was stacked beside it. Likewise, the little kitchen counter and sink were stone with an addition of a slab of natural, live-edge wood to extend the work surface.

Flowering vines dripped from the ceiling between the kitchen and main room, swept aside and gathered, held back by a cabbage rose, larger than I had ever seen, in a delicate rich yellow that bled to a russet orange at the petals edges. I touched it, and yes, it was real.

The main living area of the space wasn't set up as such. Instead, there was a nook with a drafting table in it. One of those fairy light-globes hung above it by chain, casting a nearly- perfect white light to draw by. More vines hung around it, allowing me to close it off from the rest of the room if I so desired. A tall stool was tucked under the table for me to sit.

My sketchbook sat on it already, my roll of pencils with it, but what was really nice was the square cups set at regular intervals at the top of the table with every sort of pencil and color I could want in them. It was as if someone had gone to a high-end art store, looked at the pencils and Copic pens in their displays, and said, 'I'll take the lot,' and brought them here.

That, at least, made me smile.

The bed was large, a four-poster canopy bed; the canopy was made from morning glories of just about every color, the comforter, a rich green velvet. Pillows were everywhere and were different purples, blues, whites, and magentas, of course, to match the blossoms.

Past the bed, against the back wall, was the final doorway, leading into a very modern bathroom, complete with a working flushing toilet. The shower was set deep into the back wall, in yet another natural alcove, but when I turned the tap, the water poured like a waterfall from a slot near the ceiling. There was a modern drain in the stone floor for the water to go and these details, too, helped me feel a little bit more normal.

I went back to the little kitchen and wondered if any of the food or drink were safe to drink when I realized it had to be. It was all from the little cottage I rented. I put the kettle on to boil and made myself some tea. With a sigh, I took the steaming mug with me over to the drafting table. There was another, smaller table, just perfect to set my mug on, placed near my right hand. I set my mug down and pulled out the stool, popping myself up onto it. I let my fingertips roam the tools of my trade and sighed.

Truth was, I wanted to draw, and so I chose a pencil, lifted a sheet of drawing paper down from the shelves of it above the little station and clipped it into place. I lost myself in sweeping lines and shading, drawing the Night Garden as I'd seen it when I'd first walked in. It was freshest in my mind, and seeing as I didn't have anything else to draw for the time being, it would do, just to get me drawing.

I tried very hard not to think about Jack and the fairy woman whose name sounded like 'evil-lynn'. It wasn't her fault Jack had behaved as he did. Still, I wanted to believe that there was something else at work here. That it wasn't true. The stricken look on his face as he'd looked at me made me want to believe that this was all some cruel or sick joke on Gwynn's part. Sadly, if that were the case, wouldn't Jack come find me? Wouldn't he have been here already? Trying to explain, trying to fix it?

If he were serious about you, yes. He's not, that's why he's not here.

I sniffed, my eyes welling, and rotated my head on my stiff neck and shoulders. I set my pencil aside and gave in to my insecurities. I mean, she was beautiful. Ivory skin that was so smooth, with just the barest hint of lavender undertones to it. Long lilac hair, and not a strand of it out of place. Her makeup was done to perfection to accentuate that even her eyes were a startling shade of amethyst. And she was so poised, so slender and regal and, well, perfect.

I didn't hold a candle to that woman and I knew it, and it hurt because it meant everything, and I do mean everything, with Jack had been a lie. Probably just a lie to get me down here. To get me to do what they wanted, needed, to ensure their survival. Of course, now that I was committed, now that I was clearer minded, I wondered what they'd done in the first place to warrant such a fate. A slow death, fading away like that...

"Oh, don't cry, lass. None of the lot of them are worth your tears," said a sympathetic voice to my right. I nearly leaped straight out of my skin, letting out a startled little shriek, my hands immediately going to my chest to try and hold my pounding heart in place.

"Mags! You scared the life out of me!"

The little old Brownie woman grinned and I think it took everything in her not to cackle in glee, even though she apologized, "I'm sorry, girl. I just wanted to look in on ye."

I frowned slightly and asked, "Where did you go, earlier?"

"Oh," she waved her hands at me and 'tsked'. "Never you mind that. I heard what happened in the Night Garden." Her look crumbled into lines of worry and I sighed.

"Yeah, I'm sure everyone has," I said, my face flaming. "But don't worry about it. Not my first time and it doesn't change anything. I'm still going to do what I can for all of you."

Mags looked sad then and shook her head, propping both her gnarled hands on her little knob-headed cane in front of her. Again, she reminded me of a certain little pop-culture green guy and I smiled, even though I knew it was weighted with sadness.

"We don't deserve the likes of you, love," she said with a sigh, and when I opened my mouth to protest, she raised a hand to stop me. "Truly, we don't. You're all things sweetness and light, you are."

I shook my head. "That couldn't be farther from the truth, Mags," I said softly and she sighed again.

"Is it true about that woman and Jack?" Her mouth flattened into a grim line and I nodded, suddenly tired.

"I thought so," I said. A silence ensued, heavy, weighted, not uncomfortable but not comfortable, either.

"Aye, it's true they were lovers, but it wasn't like that," she said spontaneously, and I raised my eyes from the floor.

"What was it like, then? How come he hasn't come to see me? To talk to me?"

She sighed a third time, and it looked as if she were warring with herself over what to say, and I suddenly felt bad.

"I shouldn't ask these things," I said. "I'm putting you on the spot, in the middle of all of this, and that's not fair."

"You're hurt, it's understandable," she said with sympathy, and she kind of shuddered and it reminded me of a chicken, fluffing its feathers and settling in. I picked up the empty mug that'd held my tea to get it out of her way and she smiled at me and relaxed a little more.

"Jack cared for Eibhleann far more than she ever had a care for him," Mags said, and she raised her chin, almost defiantly. "Until you came along and took the attention off of her, that is."

I scoffed. "How can someone as beautiful as her possibly be jealous of someone like me?" I asked.

"Eibhleann may be beautiful, but she's not well-liked. She's a petty, cruel creature. A right git if you ask me." Mags looked uncomfortable and I frowned.

"You... you aren't supposed to be telling me any of this, are you?"

She looked off to the side and wouldn't make eye contact with me. I felt my shoulders drop and she sighed, "It's Jack that should be telling you this, but he's otherwise indisposed."

"Doing what?" I asked curiously, and Mags shook her head.

"Don't you be worrying about that," she said. "I've said far too much already."

I didn't want Mags to get in any trouble, but I had one burning question that was nagging at me and I couldn't let it rest. I asked her, "Mags, am I a prisoner here and I just don't know it?"

"No!" she said emphatically. "We desperately need your talent, Quinn. This is the first plan that may work to save us. It's a pity Gwynn was the one to suggest it, but there's more at work here than we can say. No, lass. You're no prisoner, but there's some court intrigue afoot. It's nothing you need to concern yourself with." She gestured that I should give her my hand and I did. She held it with both of hers and sighed.

"I hate to see you hurt, lass. Jack feels terrible, but one situation at a time. Doan will be here, come morning to show you more of Faery and to tell you the old tales. I know it hurts, but remember, the Sidhe are a cruel lot and to show any sort of hurt brings them no end of joy. Be angry, but don't give that Eibhleann what she wants."

"I don't understand," I said. "Thousands of years old and some of them, it's like they're a bunch of high school mean girls. How is that even possible?" I asked. My suspicions, that feeling that Gwynn was up to something, just intensified with Mags' revelations.

She sighed and looked distressed saying, "I've already said far too much, lass, but I like you."

I smiled and said, "I like you, too, Mags. You're honest. Feels like for a people who abhor lying, they're all awfully damn good at it."

"Ah, well, they do love their intrigues and their games."

"I'm at the center of one of them, aren't I?" I asked softly, and Mags' silence told me everything.

"I best be getting these old bones of mine to bed," she said and let my drawing hand go. She'd massaged the hand and it felt loads better. Sometimes it was prone to cramping when I worked for as long as I had tonight.

"I'm pretty tired myself by this point," I confessed.

"Get you some sleep."

"I will," I promised and in a blink, she was gone. I looked down into the mug I gripped by the handle with my off-hand, staring into its empty depths, and sighed. Mag's revelations, without honestly giving anything away, were both welcome and incredibly frustrating.

I washed my cup, squinting in the dim light and realized that the fairy lights around the rooms had slowly dimmed into deep twilight. I hadn't remembered them doing that, the change had been so gradual. I had been wondering how I was supposed to turn them out when I went to bed, but now they were so dim, I could barely see enough to change into my pajamas by them. I crawled into bed and laid down and, as soon as my head touched the pillow, was plunged into near-perfect darkness. The only light was a single, deep-blue, dim one emanating from the bathroom archway.

I swallowed hard and a bit of a worry bordering on a mild panic gripped me. That was when the stamens lit softly on every blossom in the room, providing just enough light as to feel like moonlight coming through the window – if there'd been a window.

"Thank you," I murmured and there was a slight rustle among the hanging vines of the room.

I closed my eyes and tried to relax, and in the blink of an eye, I think I was asleep.

THE LIGHT WAS what woke me. All of the lights in their globes among the vines and atop their sconces on the walls were blazing. I squeezed my eyes shut after the initial assault and when I opened them, they were at a much more tolerable level.

"What am I supposed to know? Why do I need to be awake?" I groaned and pushed myself into a sitting position just as a knock fell at the door.

"Oh," I said a bit sheepishly and I got up. "Thanks," I murmured, though I wasn't entirely sure who I was thanking. It was a little creepy, thinking someone was keeping tabs on me enough to mess with the lights. Just before I reached the door, it unlatched itself and opened revealing the Queen's consort, Doan.

"I see the Rath is excited for us to begin," he said with a smile.

I blinked in confusion, "What do you mean? I thought someone was controlling the lights and the doors."

"Not someone, something. The Rath is a wild magick and, as far as we can tell, sentient all on its own." He smoothed a long-fingered pale hand along the satiny wood of the door's jamb.

"You're serious," I said, heart quickening. I had never considered that the Rath itself was sentient. I wasn't quite sure how to feel about that, that a building, (which wasn't quite right by way of a descriptor, but I didn't know what else to call it,) might have thoughts or opinions on a person or things.

"Quite," he said with a smile, hands clasped behind his back.

"Um, if you could give me just a minute, I'll find some clothes and we can get going. I, uh, just need to grab a few things."

"Of course," he said and bowed his head which I found strangely polite considering I was the visitor and he was the royalty, I guess. I mean no one really referred to him as the king. It was always Consort to the Queen, The Queen's Consort, or even just Consort. I wasn't used to a female being the higher power while the man was referred to as, basically, just the husband. I was surprised to find how mind-boggling it was to me. *Let's hear it for the patriarchy, I guess.*

I gathered the things I wanted to change into and went into the bathroom to change. I blinked, startled when I looked into the mirror above the sink. The flowers were gone from my hair and my face, which I had pretty much expected to be embarrassingly makeup-streaked, was clean and freshly-scrubbed. I couldn't remember doing any of it, but I wasn't complaining, by the same token. The last thing I wanted to contemplate was looking ratchet as hell in front of the Queen's significant other.

Doan waited patiently out there while I put on my clothes and pulled my hair up into twin, poof-ball pigtails. It was a cute look with this boho-chic outfit of jeans with holes patched behind them in ivory lace and an ivory peasant blouse. The jeans were rolled up at the ankle and I paired them with some high-heeled but comfortable brown suede boots.

When I went back out, I found the Consort standing at my drafting table, hands still behind his back as he looked over the piece I had worked on the night before.

"It's nearly all lined out. I was trying to decide if I wanted to go with colored pencils or if I wanted to color it with Copic pen."

"I am eager to see it complete," he remarked, and he looked back at me with a smile.

He wore unrelieved black, like the Dread Pirate Roberts from mine and Livvy's favorite fantasy film growing up. It was an old film, out before I was born. There was another fantasy film that she and I had loved growing up. Someone told me it was the first time ever that computer generation was used in a movie and I had tried to argue with them that computers capable of that hadn't been around in the eighties, but I had lost. I'd had to go back and watch it as an adult and sure enough, the owl at the beginning and end credits wasn't a real owl at all.

"Tell me," Doan said conversationally, interrupting my train of thought. "What have you already seen of the Rath?"

I swallowed and said, "Um, well, the Night Garden, obviously. Um, Jack's quarters…" I felt myself blush at that and Doan's smile grew, but he wisely didn't comment, sparing me from making my humiliation complete. I was grateful for that.

"I've also seen a few other places, but I don't really have the names for them. There was this spiral leading down to glowing hot springs and then there was a section that I guess housed pixies. My favorite was a place that Jack called the Summerland, but he told me that was just what he called it. Not that it was its actual name."

Doan had frozen and was looking at me much like a cat looks at a bird. I stopped what I was doing, gathering my supplies, and he said rather quickly, as if barely suppressing his excitement, "This 'Summerland', can you describe it? Was there anything unique about it?"

I was suddenly afraid to say anything. The way he was looking at me, it felt as if I were about to accidentally dime Jack out about something I shouldn't and I sort of stopped in my mental tracks. *He made you the 'other woman,' what are you worried about him for?* I struggled with the sharp emotional pain that radiated out at the concept and thought about my conversation with Mags the night before. I didn't dare bring it up to Doan. I wouldn't break Mags' confidence for anything. I was stuck between a rock and a hard place and had to think fast! I was taking too long to answer.

"Jack said that he once got lost in the Rath for over a month. To not wander too far or without an escort. He said he found the place when he was lost and that he'd also found out later that it was some kind of burial ground or battlefield, although I'm not sure how he found out about that."

Doan took a step forward and pure excitement lit him up from the inside out. I relaxed some and he asked eagerly, "Please, describe the place itself for me?"

"Um, it was a stone hall leading to a red door, and through the door, you kind of went outside, but Jack told me we weren't outside at all. The door opened onto a summer meadow, the sun shining brightly. The grass was tall and dry. Golden for almost as far as the eye could see. There was a sword..." I grabbed my sketchbook journal off the drafting table and opened it to the page I'd drawn it on and passed it to Doan. His dark eyes devoured the image and his face broke into a broad grin.

"Quinn, I am going to need you to do me a favor," he said, and I frowned.

"Okay?"

"Are you done gathering your things?"

"Um, almost." I held my hand out for my sketch journal and he handed it back. I tucked it into my satchel and slung it over my chest. I added my pencils and a few other things and turned back. "That should do it."

Doan held out his hand and said, "Come, I shall see if I can teach you how the Rath works."

"How it works?"

"Aye, if you please. Close your eyes and clear your mind."

I looked at him skeptically at first, and with a sigh tried to do as I was told. I was miserable at the whole 'clearing my mind' part. Always thinking, it never wanted to stay quiet for long.

"Now, picture that door, that hallway leading to your Summerland," he said gently.

I popped open one eye and said, "It's not my Summerland, its Jack's." He gave me an impatient look and I closed my eye again and said, "Okay, okay!"

"Concentrate and tell me when you can see it," he murmured.

"I can see it."

"Come then," he took my hand and led me to my chamber door. I opened my eyes and he sort of hissed at me, "Concentrate!"

"Alright! I'm sorry!" I closed my eyes and let him lead me out and down the hallway.

We paused after a few feet and he asked, "Have you got it?"

"I think so," I answered.

"Excellent, open your eyes."

I did, blinking to adjust them to the hall light, and he gestured ahead of him. I steeled myself and went around the corner and exclaimed, "That's it; that's the door! Oh my God, it worked!"

"Indeed, now I would very much appreciate if you would take me to see this sword in the grass."

I nodded and went to the door and placed my hand on the handle. I opened it, and sunlight, warm and bright poured out. Smiling, I stepped through with Doan close on my heels. The door swung gently shut behind us and I raised my face to the light and reveled in the warm summer breeze.

"The sword, if you please Ms. Carter?" He wasn't harsh, irritated, or mean-sounding when he asked. Rather, he sounded like a man who was desperate, who was close to his very own personal unicorn or Holy Grail, and I didn't know what warranted all the fuss.

"Okay, while we walk, can you tell me the story behind it?" I asked, striking off in the direction Jack and I had taken, toward the line of trees.

"As in most wars, there is death. During the Fifth Fae War, we had a King. He had been our king from the beginning, Quinn, and was a much-beloved man. He had several children and one of them wished for the throne. He thought the king had grown old and the court was, unfortunately, split down the middle on the subject."

I stopped Doan and swept the grass aside, and there, the sword glittered, point stuck in the earth as if freshly dropped.

Doan looked like he was going to cry when he knelt before the blade and he reached out, trailing fingertips over the hilt. A sad half-smile graced his lips and he said, "Hello, King Nuada... my old friend. Fare thee well across the veil?"

I watched the Consort bow his head and he looked up at me with tears in his eyes that he stubbornly refused to shed.

I cocked my head and lowered myself to the ground and said, "No bullshit, did you know him? Like, know him personally?"

"Aye, aye, I did. He was my closest friend, and me one of his advisors."

I nodded and said, "I'm sorry for your loss."

He shook his head, "It's been many a long year, millennia in fact. I thought this place lost to us but you have done me a great service in bringing me here."

"Maybe nothing is really lost, here in the Rath." I looked up at the sky, a little unsure what made me say that but at the same time damn sure it was correct. I mean, it made sense.

Doan looked me over and sat beside the sword in the grass. "Sit," he asked and I sank down near them and flipped open my satchel. I said, "Thinking about it, maybe it's just forgotten for a while and the magic or whatever is still here, it's just the Rath concentrates on the important stuff. You know? The stuff that you guys need the most. It's like a building when the power goes out and the generators kick on. The generators don't run everything. Typically, just the emergency lighting and essentials until the power comes back on."

He looked at me a little strangely and so I had to launch into a full description of electricity and generators and how the human world got on in these modern times. He watched me with an utter fascination which was fine. I was roughing out a sketch of him, a poignant one of him sitting beside the sword, arms propped on his drawn-up knees, head bowed.

"Truly," he murmured. "Any bit of human history could potentially be at your fingertips, with the touch of a button?"

I laughed a little, "Yeah, but with the way the internet works, it's not all on there. The individual stories get lost and facts eventually get shuffled. Misinformation gets woven in at some points and before you know it the whole world starts spouting myth as fact over some of the silliest things. Like, if you ever get your hands on a laptop and go looking? Avoid sites like Wikipedia as the be-all and end-all on any given subject."

He frowned and nodded, thinking about it, and said, "So the individual tales are the important ones?"

"To me, I think, and honestly, to most other people, I would think, too. Like Nuada there, what happened?"

Doan sighed, "He tried to keep his people together, the Sidhe united as one tribe."

"And?"

"One of his own sons struck him down. Here. Took the crown for himself, but not all followed him. He became the King of the Seelie Court. His sister, a Warrior-Queen in her own right, led those who dissented to form a new court labeled the Unseelie Court."

"Queen Maebh?" I asked quietly.

Doan smiled, "Aye."

"So you were her father's advisor?"

"Aye."

"And," I blushed, "You became his daughter's lover?"

"Many years after his death, but aye. 'Tis how it happened."

I folded my sketchbook shut over the pencil and sighed, "There's quite the story there."

He laughed and nodded. "Aye, I suppose there is."

"You guys really don't age past a certain point, do you?" I asked. "You and the Queen don't look a day over five or six years apart in age."

He laughed again and said, "Compared to our Queen I am thousands of years older. I was there for her first steps. Quite a bit younger for certain, but appearing no older, no younger, than I do now."

I jotted some notes down in my sketch journal on the page behind the drawing I'd just made, nodding.

"Okay, um, do me a favor and take it from the top," I said. "Tell me a story, no, tell me the story of how all of you first came to be."

26

Jack...

My chamber door swung open despite my having latched it. I straightened from my work and felt my shoulders drop as Quinn was revealed, her fist poised to knock. She blinked at the door in surprise, but then her gaze locked to mine and the surprise was quickly snuffed by shrouded hurt. I'd seen the pain just before she could veil the emotion and it tore at my own heart.

"Hi," she said simply, but she didn't come in. Instead, she sucked on her bottom lip, which sent a shot of desire through my blood. Her words zinged me but good when she said, "Apparently the Rath likes me and is keen on opening doors for me. Definitely makes it a better boyfriend than the guy who's using me as a side chick without telling me."

I turned away from her, checked the heat of the forge and, satisfied I could leave the iron to sit, turned to her.

"It wasn't like that. It was never like that," I told her, and pulled a rag from my back pocket, wiping the dirt and soot from my hands as best I could.

She came in and shut the door behind her with a palm flat to the wood. She turned back but wouldn't look at me, fixing her gaze on the floor instead. She asked; "Don't you think you should have told me there was someone else, Jack?"

Her misery was apparent and my heart twisted painfully that I was the cause. I bowed my head and said, "I'm sorry, love. I didn't think Eibhleann was serious about me, I didn't realize there was a relationship there... it was always just a bit of fun. Nothing like with you. Truth be told, I thought Eibhleann and I were long past due to dissolve our arrangement. I should have done so, before starting anything with you. I'm sorry for that."

I looked back up to Eibhleann's glare and frowned.

"You don't get to decide such things, Jack!"

"Aye, I do," I shot back. "You may be Sidhe and full-blood at that, but I choose who, what, and when I fuck."

Eibhleann marched across my chambers and let fly, slapping me soundly across my face. I went with the blow, seeing stars, and shook my head to clear it just in time for the second blow to catch me on the other side. Before she could land another, I caught her wrist. She grinned savagely and tried to step into me, for a kiss.

Strong she might be, but I used her imbalance to my advantage and threw her to the floor, stepping back and pulling the iron from the flames to put between me and her, to be sure. I hadn't thought she could set foot in here, let alone use her glamour as far as she had, with all the iron in the room. It must have cost her considerably.

I didn't feel a bit guilty about anything that I had said. None of it was anything I wouldn't have said to Eibhleann's face or just to Quinn. I shook my head and sighed. In some ways, I'd spoilt Eibhleann by letting her have her way, by not speaking up on my own behalf. It had seemed easier to let things pass without comment and now I was reaping the consequences of my passivity. No more. It was time for Eibhleann to hear some harsh truths.

"You're a vain, manipulative woman, Eibhleann. I could have loved you once but you tore those feelings away bit by bit and cast them to the wind with your petty cruelties. You had me and it was by your own doing that you lost me. You can't fault Quinn for being herself and you can't fault me for falling for her, for the kindness she gave me that you denied me all the times you did."

She pushed herself up into a sitting position and gave a haughty laugh. Shaking her head, she climbed to her feet and shook the dust and soot from her dress.

"You don't deserve any of my kindness, Jack. Not now, not after what you've done. Do you honestly think that she'll have you back? She saw us kiss in front of everyone, and trust me when I say Gwynn will have her writhing underneath him, one way or another, before the week is through."

I didn't like this time disparity placed just upon my chambers within the Rath, but I understood Doan's request for a weapon that could be used effectively against other Sidhe. My only consolation was that the time spent here and now with Eibhleann, as distasteful as it was, was only a fraction of a second in the rest of the Rath outside my door. Or at least, I hoped it was.

"Get out, Eibhleann. Your tantrum is noted, but it changes absolutely nothing."

"Oh, I think it does, Jack. You aren't in nearly enough agony for my tastes. I believe I shall have to get creative where the little human is concerned. After all, just what is it she has that I don't?" she demanded.

"A soul, for one," I shot back and rage contorted her expression so that finally her outside matched her insides.

"I'm going to make you pay for humiliating me, Jack O'Laughlin! You remember, the price will be paid, and whatever it may be it is on your head."

"Do anything to harm her, Eibhleann, and I will end you."

She spit at my feet and turned, making her way to my chamber door and ripping it open, shrieking as the iron door handle burned her palm. She whirled, holding the door open with her foot, her good hand wrapped around the wrist of her injured one and gave me a look of contempt before she went out into the hall, the door slamming shut behind her.

I was a lot less worried that she would do anything anytime soon.

She'd depleted her magick to the point she couldn't open the door without physical means. That said something. It told me that maintaining her glamour inside my chambers had cost her. I was heartened that she couldn't keep it up for very long. I wouldn't have been surprised if she had attempted to bed me in Quinn's guise. It would be something she would do. It also made me wonder if it hadn't been Eibhleann sending Quinn nightmares, as it was very close to what Quinn had described.

I wondered who had approached whom, and had to surmise that it was Eibhleann who had gone to Gwynn. The petty banality of recent events was all something Eibhleann would do. Gwynn was much loftier in his goals. His end game would see him more powerful, with what he wanted. Eibhleann and Quinn were simply a means to an end for that bastard.

I'd place good coin that he was using Eibhleann for his own ends, and whatever those ends may be, he was just getting a small measure of petty revenge on the way for my having initially thwarted him where Quinn was concerned. He was on his way to a far more serious endgame and that endgame was likely the throne.

It was no secret that Gwynn was power-hungry, nor that he disagreed with his sister when it had come to humankind. When humans had turned their back on the Fae in favor of their new God, the Queen had decided Faerie would turn their back on the human world, save for their loyalest followers, those who still believed.

It had been Gwynn's contention that the Fae should make a show of force, should enslave the humans of Ireland and make them their thrall, to crush this new Christian God beneath their heel. The Queen knew that the might of the Fae could probably hold Ireland, but defend it against the rest of the world? No, she had been smarter than that. She realized the zealous nature of this new Christ's followers. Additionally, she held no desire for world domination. She understood that the time of the Sidhe had passed and now it was the time for an era of man. She had seen the rise and fall of many empires; unlike Gwynn, however, she had learned from them.

Once, long ago, before man was even thought of, the Sidhe had been the oppressed. That oppression had been the subject of at least two of the seven Fae wars. They had risen, they had conquered and carved out a place for themselves, which is really all that they had initially wanted. It was as her father had taught his daughter. Now, she held no desire to become a conqueror in turn. Rather, she wanted what any good ruler wanted for her people: to protect her people, to watch them thrive, to watch the Earth heal and to return to the Fae's original purpose as stewards of the earth, as Danann's protectorate.

I went back to work on the iron sword requested by Doan and tried not to think about what was, or what could happen to Quinn in my absence. I missed her terribly, I worried about her awfully, and as time crawled by for me, even though intellectually I knew the passage of time was dissimilar for her, I was afraid that every moment that ticked by without my being there to explain myself was a moment too long for Quinn to ever forgive me or wish to listen to me.

I did the only thing I could do. By order of Queen and Consort, I worked tirelessly to finish the weapon they'd asked for.

27

———

Quinn...

Doan was a wealth of knowledge about Fae history and I was learning so much from him. I'd found myself outside of Jack's door more than a time or two over the last two days, but I just couldn't bring myself to knock.

I moved freely through the Rath, now that I knew how to ask where to go and I tried my best to never take it for granted and to always be polite. Like now, I needed a break from my drafting table, my shoulders and back knotted painfully, my arm and hand cramping at inopportune moments. I wanted a long hot soak but my chambers only had the shower, so I had gathered a set of towels, had donned a robe, and had visualized the room of pools Jack had taken me down into.

I'd made my way there, carefully, and had found it. I'd silently thanked the Rath and had found a nice, hot pool and had slipped in, hair piled high and clipped at the back of my head to let the heat work its magic. I had discovered an icy-cold pool on my quest to find one the perfect temperature. There were cushions and pillows around the edges and I'd been here all alone, so when I was through bathing, I'd dried myself and knotted the large towel at my chest.

Piling cushions at the icy water's edge and lying on my stomach, I lowered my drawing hand and arm to the elbow and hissed, sighing out, closing my eyes and wishing I at least had some music or something to listen to.

Instead, I closed my eyes and let ideas and imagery play out in my imagination. I was working on a few things at the moment, keeping in mind what had worked well for me and for Livvy in the past, but also branching out in a more adult direction with a graphic novel idea. I was working closely with Doan and the Queen and was surprised that they listened to what I was saying when it came to humans and their natures, in making the tales relatable to bolster their believability, which truthfully wasn't hard.

A light touch traced my spine from the back of my neck to the top of my towel. I jerked and a palm rested against my back while a lyrical masculine voice that wasn't Jack said, "Sorry, couldn't stop myself. You looked so peaceful and your skin is so beautiful." I pushed up and turned, clutching my towel to me and frowned at Gwynn.

"Yeah, not used to people just randomly touching me. It's not exactly something humans do to each other. In fact, it's actually pretty frowned upon."

"My apologies, a clash of cultures, a misunderstanding. Among the Fae, it would be considered a grave injustice to ignore such beauty and not admire it up close and personally."

I tried not to shudder, the whole touching-without -ermission had thoroughly creeped me out. Gwynn smiled but it didn't look apologetic in the slightest. In fact, he rather looked like the cat that swallowed the canary.

"You're hurting?" he asked.

"Happens sometimes," I said. "I get bound up in what I'm doing and spend too long doing the same thing and my back and arm like to give out on me. It's nothing I can't handle."

He chuckled and said, "I have no doubt, but what kind of hosts would we be if we didn't see to your comfort?"

"Where I come from, that's going way above and beyond what a typical host does for any guest unless the guest is paying to be there. Like at a five-star hotel with a spa package or something."

"Are you not?"

"Not what?"

"Paying us with your help."

I jerked back as if I had smelled something bad, and I had. I shook my head and said with a scowl, "That's not why I am doing any of this."

"Is it not?" he asked, cocking his head. "If you are successful, you do stand to make a lot of money, don't you?"

Wow. The nerve of this guy, but maybe not. His expression was one of genuine puzzlement. My frown deepened. I couldn't tell if he was trying to sell me on a line of bullshit or if he genuinely didn't get it. I decided to err on the side of caution and went with the latter.

"I'm doing it because it's the right thing to do, Gwynn." He smiled at the use of his name and I pressed on. "I mean, granted, we don't know if it will work or have any effect, or if my publisher will buy into it, or any of those things. Still, I can't hear your guy's story and not do anything. I at least have to try."

"You have a beautiful nature and soul, then. Far grander than mine."

"Um, thank you," I said.

"I should like to take you somewhere," he declared and I blinked.

"What, now?"

"If you please."

"Where?" I asked.

"Mustn't spoil the surprise," he said coyly.

"I'll um, need to go by my room. I only have a robe here."

"That is perfectly acceptable attire for where we're going," he said cheerfully.

He stood and held a hand down to me to help me up. I gave him my off-hand, my dominant arm still tight and throbbing and now suffering pins and needles from the temperature change.

He held out my robe for me and I shrugged into it. He was nice enough to turn around, a small smirk on his face while I slipped the towel out from under it, overlapped the two edges and knotted the belt at my hip securely.

I picked up the towel and draped it over my shoulders in an effort to somewhat increase my modesty.

"Okay," I murmured and he turned around, holding out a hand to me. Not his arm, not like before when we were being so stiffly formal. I rolled my lips, hesitated briefly, and took it in my own. He chuckled and set off at an easy, sedate stroll.

"What has been your favorite part of Faery so far?" he asked conversationally.

I told him the truth, that there was far too much beauty and far too many amazing sights for me to pick just one right now. He laughed and said that living here, it was easy to take these things for granted.

The conversation was a nice one, and eventually, we turned down a hall that was the exact duplicate of the one leading to the Summerland, only instead of red, this door was painted a rich blue, the color of a Steller's Jay.

"This is my favorite place," he declared and he opened the door. Cold swirled out and a puff of random snow landed at my feet, melting immediately. I jumped back from the cold and he laughed.

"Have a look," he said. "We won't go in."

I did and one of the most serene winterscapes stretched out before me. This must be the Winterland Jack had mentioned. I said, "It's beautiful."

"If you should need to find me, you can find me here," he said. "I wanted to show you."

"Um, thanks," I murmured.

"Of course." He closed the door and I shivered.

"Not exactly dressed for the cold," I said with a nervous laugh and he smiled at me.

"No, it was simply on the way to where I wanted to take you."

"Okay..."

He took my hand again with a smile and gave it a little shake, an indication I should loosen up. I tried, but my nerves were getting the better of me. We set off back down the hall and made idle small talk until Gwynn stopped in his tracks. He was frowning and I turned to face one of my worst nightmares.

It was the woman with the lilac hair and eyes, the lavender undertones to her beautiful skin. The one Jack had been kissing. She cradled one hand against her chest with the other, a thick white bandage around the palm. I blinked and said the dumbest thing. I said, "Um, hi."

Her eyes narrowed and welled with tears and she blew past us, the hall we were in narrow enough that Gwynn and I either let go hands or she would crash into them. I let go and stepped back against the wall and she went right through us as if we weren't even there. I looked after her and suddenly had no desire to be out and about. All of a sudden, I just wanted to be back in my room. Deep, deep down, I just wanted to go home. It seemed like the most efficient way to get far away from here, crawl under the proverbial rock, and die.

I knew it wasn't my fault, but it sure felt like it. I sighed and Gwynn looked solemn. He nodded in what seemed like understanding and said, "Perhaps another time, then."

I nodded and said faintly, "Thanks." I guess I didn't need to say anything more. I mean, it must have really been written all over my face.

"Allow me to walk you to your door."

I did, and when we reached just outside my quarters Gwynn sighed and put a hand on my shoulder.

"If you should need anything, or want to see anything, come find me. You at least know where I am, now."

I nodded and said, "Thanks, I will."

"Try not to be sad. Truly."

I mustered a smile I didn't feel and nodded. My door swung open and I said, "Thank you for being willing to take me around."

"Of course." He leaned in awkwardly, and I stiffened. He paused, seemed to think better of it, and placed a gentle kiss on my cheek, straightening quickly. I forced a smile I didn't feel then and he gave a short bow and a smile of his own, and went up the hall.

I went into my quarters and shut the door and immediately fought the urge to go into the bathroom and scrub the simple, sweet gesture off my face and I had no idea why I was having such a violent reaction to what was supposed to be this nice thing.

Because your gut is telling you there's something off about that guy. That, and something is screaming that none of them are telling you the whole story.

I mean, I believed they were telling me the whole story when it came to their history and when it came to their predicament but I also got the distinct and nagging feeling that something else was going on, too, and damn it, there was only one person I thought I could ask.

I got dressed and made sure to have the nail Jack had given me close to my skin. He hadn't seen fit to come see me in over three days and there was giving a woman space, but damn. I wanted badly to believe that what Mags had told me was true. That he was busy with tasks set forward by the Queen, and honestly, that may very well be.

Everybody saw. It wasn't just humiliating for me, but for his partner when it should have just been embarrassing for him. But you know, these kinds of things typically ended with way more collateral damage than the person at its core counted on, which is why you shouldn't do it. He'd had enough time to come to me. I wanted some damn answers, so it was time for me to suck it up and actually knock this time.

It was entirely too soon that I was standing outside his door, fist poised to knock and really rethinking my choices. I didn't have time to back out, though, because the door unlatched and swung open.

Jack stood from where he was bent over the grinding wheel and leveled his gaze at me. I stepped through the doorway uninvited and took the door by the handle to push it closed. When I turned around, his posture had eased some and I took a deep breath and let it out slowly.

"You owe me an explanation," I said coolly, and he set what he was working on aside, the wheel slowing now that he no longer actively worked it into a spin by the pedal system.

"Aye," he said. "That's fair."

He gestured over to his desk chair and I went and pulled it out, dropping into the seat. He dragged a low stool over and sat across from me.

"Is it true that you and she were in a relationship?" I asked.

He was quiet for a moment and sighed, gripping the back of his neck to ease a tension there. He nodded reluctantly and said, "I suppose she thought so, though it wasn't necessarily our arrangement."

"I don't understand what that means."

He explained and I listened, and it honestly made sense. I couldn't tell you why I believed him, but I did. Maybe that was just me being like every other dumb side-chick on the planet. I don't know, but I did know that listening to his version of events, my stomach wasn't in knots like it was around Gwynn. I wanted to chalk up my nervousness around Gwynn to all of the notions Jack had put in my head but I couldn't.

As a woman, I knew. It was like that guy trying to be slick and pick you up at the bar. The vibe around Gwynn was just all wrong. I bowed my head and uncrossed my arms over my chest and tried to relax, but the damage, I think had been done. Jack looked wounded by my closed-offness, and for some reason, that, in turn, wounded me. Tears of frustration wet my eyes and I couldn't help myself... I spilled everything.

I'd been holding it all in, keeping it to myself with no one to talk to about it for days and despite all appearances, despite what I'd seen with my own damn eyes, I still trusted Jack.

"It feels like something is going on. Something that no one wants to tell me but I'm smack in the middle of, Jack, and I'm scared. What's going to happen to me?" I sniffed and rubbed my nose with the back of my hand and he reached for me, slipping off his seat and crushing me to him.

"Nothing, love. Nothing is going to happen to you, I promise. I'd die before I let anything happen to you."

And holy hell, I believed him.

"I missed you," I confessed and he sighed, kissing the same cheek Gwynn had, only instead of skeeved-out, I felt safe. Warm and protected and maybe, yeah, even loved.

"I missed you, too, Quinn and believe it or not, I've been separated from you far longer than you have from me."

"What are you talking about?" I asked, miserably. He rocked back so he could look at me. Cupping the side of my neck, his thumb playing back and forth along my jaw.

"Gwynn is planning an insurrection," he said and I blinked.

"What?"

"He brought you here, planted the seed for you to help the Fae in the Queen's mind. He and Eibhleann have aligned themselves for petty revenge, using you against me but Eibhleann is short-sighted. Gwynn isn't interested in mere petty revenge. He has placed you as his pawn, his Trojan horse, but has no intention of letting you actually help or follow through."

"Why? I don't understand..."

"He plans on driving you off. I don't know how, yet. I imagine, however he plans to do it, it would be quite unpleasant for you. He believes in a more straightforward approach. He wishes to foster man's belief by invading and oppressing them. He wishes ardently to be worshiped once more. He thrives on fear. It is his nature."

"That would go really, really bad for you guys, though," I said, chilled. I mean, did Gwynn have a clue about modern warfare? Somehow I doubted it. Jack sighed and looked about a million years tired.

"Are you even supposed to be telling me any of this?" I asked.

He shook his head, "No. It was the Queen and Consort's decision to let things play out. Right now, there's no hard evidence that Gwynn plans to overthrow the Queen."

"So, let me get this straight, Gwynn brought me and my job to the Queen's attention. The Queen went along with it and asked for my help, and all the while Gwynn is planning on basically bullying me out of my commitment – to what end?"

"To prove that the Queen's faith in humans and humanity is

faulty. To sow doubt among the rest of the court in her ability to lead us and to suggest himself as a suitable replacement monarch."

"Yeah, we can't let that happen," I said. "So what do we do?"

He stared at me, dark eyes wide for a series of heartbeats I thought would never end, before he lunged forward and pressed his mouth to mine.

I admit it, I was weak. I should have stayed angry, I should have pushed him off, slapped the shit out of him for not being honest with Eibhleann, for not telling me about their... the arrangement, because I dare not call it a relationship. I mean, if Jack were a woman and Eibhleann a man, it would be a textbook case of domestic abuse. Just because their gender roles were reversed didn't make any of it okay.

His mouth on mine did for me, though. It was like I'd been a nearly-completed puzzle and that night, in the Night Garden, someone had come along and flipped my pieces in the air. All I knew is that when he kissed me, like this, the pieces felt like they finally landed, and mostly in place. I couldn't help myself. I kissed him back and even though I knew we had some things to work on, to work out between us, they took a back seat for the moment in face of a bigger need for our attention... which, the longer he kissed me, took a back seat to a more basic demand to connect.

He ripped his mouth from mine and reached down, working up my long skirt with his fingers. I parted my knees and he went up on his, tugging me to the edge of my seat, working himself out of his pants.

"Jack!" I gasped as he moved my panties aside and slipped himself into me. He brought me down from my chair and I rode him. He was as far up inside me as he could go and I shuddered from the pleasure of it. He smoothed a hand along my cheek and I held onto him, arms around his neck and ground my hips in a circular motion. He cried out and brought my mouth down to his.

Our tongues clashed, our breathing deepened and was ripped from our lungs in gasping pants as a warm glow began low and centered in my body. I closed my eyes and sucked in a sharp breath, tossing back my head and moaning out. His hand found my ass, encouraging my rise and fall over him, the other hand and arm bracing me, securing me against any feeling of falling except for the one that counted.

"You amaze me," he growled and I smiled.

"Ah, yeah?" I said breathlessly, sliding down his length. He bottomed out against my cervix with that sweet, sharp pain that sent waves of tingles sweeping through my entire body. I wasn't sure what precipitated this wild moment of passionate abandon, but I liked it. No, I loved it.

"Aye," he grunted, and bodily he picked me up. I wrapped my legs around him and he carried me to the bed. Somehow, some way, he managed to stay inside me, laying me back and thrusting all the way forward. His strokes were hard and deep, neither fast nor slow.

I wrapped myself around him and relaxed for the first time in days. I Lifted my hips to meet his thrusts, frustrated by how much clothing was still between us but not wanting to stop to do something about it. I was wetter than I could ever remember being before in my life. Tightening around his shaft, tensing my pelvic floor muscles as the pleasure rose to a fever pitch and the orgasm took us both in a crescendo of gratification.

He pushed his upper body up off of mine, both of us panting, struggling to draw breath as satisfaction curled low in my belly and swirled out through my veins. He gazed down into my eyes and whispered, "You would still help them, help us, despite it all?"

"Of course I would, Jack," I replied, low and gentle. "I don't have any control over what a few bad people choose to do. All I have control over is what kind of person I am and who I choose to be. It's not yours, or Mags', or even Maebh's or Doan's decision to be this way. It's Gwynn's and Eibhleann's, and maybe a few others. Why punish the many over the actions of a few? That would say more about my own poor character than it would about theirs." I smiled a bit wanly, my heart cracking in two as I thought about my father who had instilled these values in me, and of Livvy who had carried those lessons on. I certainly hadn't gotten it from my mother, but then again, when my father had died, I think her grief had maybe twisted something inside of her. Still, it was no excuse for her overbearing nature, for some of the things she said.

All I could do in situations like these was do my best to be better.

Jack shook his head and heaved a deep sigh before saying, "You make me wish I were a better man."

I smiled and said, "Then be better. Only you have the power to change that sort of thing."

He grinned and barked a short laugh, asking, "As simple as that, is it?"

I nodded. "Yeah, the choice is pretty simple, but I'm not going to lie, committing to something like that can take some work."

"I know what I choose," he said gently.

"Oh, yeah? What's that?" I asked, smiling faintly. Still, I wasn't prepared for what came out of his mouth.

"I choose you," he said. "I choose you because I love you. It'd like to tore my soul asunder, the hurt in your eyes." He choked up. "I never want to be the cause of such hurt again."

I sniffed and stared at him through eyes blurred by tears and said, "I didn't want to believe it. What I was seeing. It was awfully convenient that Gwynn chose precisely the moment he did to so helpfully take me to you right then."

"You've good instincts," he said moving from between my legs and stretching out beside me, propping his head on his hand and pulling me near with a strong arm around my waist.

"Well, it's not exactly my first rodeo. It's classic high school mean girl tactics they're employing."

Jack chuckled and said, "Doesn't sound very sophisticated."

"You'd actually be pretty terrified at how sophisticated some of the tactics teenaged girls employ against each other are. It's disgusting. A lot of them made my life a living hell all through junior high and high school. If it weren't for Livvy, I'm not even sure I would still be here."

His face became impassive as he mulled over what I'd said.

"I don't want you in any danger."

"I don't want to be left in the dark anymore. I get that you guys are well-meaning and are trying to shield me from the ugly side of life, but Babe, I'm a half-black, half-white, raised-in-the-city American woman. I've seen a lot of ugly."

He leaned forward and kissed me soundly, murmuring "And a fierce one at that."

28

———————

J ack…

  "Is this not how we arrived here in the first place, Jackie-boy? A defiance of my will as Queen?"

  Maebh was displeased, and I immediately took a knee saying, "It was not my will to defy you, my Queen. I was weak in the face of my emotion. I plead mercy."

  Doan chuckled and put his hand on Maebh's. They exchanged a significant look and she sighed.

  "My ire isn't with you, Jack. It is with my brother," she stated, and leaned back into her throne. She sighed and pinched the bridge of her nose with her free hand.

  I had hated her for the longest time for going through with the bargain we'd struck and cursing me to this life. However, years later I'd had to admit she was correct, in that she'd but given me precisely what I'd asked for, and what was done was done. I thought I had been at peace with it, but it took Quinn completing me to be so. Without that decision, that fateful day, I would have never been around to meet her. Now, I would do anything to keep her, to protect her, to watch her thrive.

"What would you have us do, my Queen? You have only to wish it."

She made a contemptuous sound that almost sounded like a laugh and asked in return, "What would you have me do, Messenger?" Her voice was bitter and I straightened cautiously. It was rare for her to show any emotion and what she displayed now was a form of despair. I understood that well enough. Betrayal was a hard and bitter pill to swallow.

"Perhaps, you do nothing, my Queen," I suggested humbly.

"Nothing?" She barked a bitter laugh that felt like razors against the inside of my skull. I fought not to wince.

"I humbly suggest you hear him out, my love," Doan said gently, the voice of reason in the little bit of chaos. It was just he, the Queen, and I in the throne room, yet that could not and would not ensure we weren't heard. I withdrew a parchment envelope from the inside of my coat. A letter to the Queen and Consort from my Quinn.

Maebh raised an eyebrow in curiosity and the envelope flew from my fingers to her hand. Doan gave her back her other one and she cracked the wax seal keeping the envelope closed.

She read the contents, a plan that I confess was mostly Quinn's rather than mine. We'd lain together after our too-short dalliance and had spoken at length about things and I must say, her American love of television crime dramas and procedurals had come in handy. She had suggested a sting, and though I didn't like it one bit that she wished to play the bait, I didn't see another way.

"Remarkable," Maebh said, and she sounded impressed. "She has spirit, your human."

"Aye, she does," I said and couldn't keep the polish of pride out of my voice.

She handed the letter to Doan, whose dark eyes rapidly skimmed the page. He nodded slowly.

"It would certainly be a simpler solution than what I had suggested. The evidence to prove to the court beyond any shadow of doubt Gwynn's power-hungry intentions would be invaluable. She is quite a bit more cunning than I have given her credit for. I, too, am suitably impressed."

Another significant look was exchanged between Maebh and Doan. Maebh's lips curved into a nasty little smile, one I had only seen when she bestowed the cruelest of punishments. I waited for her to come to a decision and she finally looked in my direction.

"Yes, I think so. Tell your lady-love that I agree to her terms. The bargain will be struck once Gwynn's true intentions are exposed."

I nodded, keeping my face impassive. It would seem Quinn may have outsmarted even me. In the letter she'd had me read, there was no mention of any terms, nor of any bargain. My pulse spiked painfully on the side of my neck and my collar suddenly seemed too tight.

I swept a deep bow and said, "As you wish, my Queen."

She gave a sharp nod and said, "Also tell her that Doan will follow up with her on the morrow. Now, as for that other thing..."

I nodded and swept the iron sword off my back and laid it flat on my palms. I presented it to Doan and said, "I would wear gloves, were I you, Consort. I've wrapped the hilt in silver wire, but it may not provide the protection you require."

Doan inclined his head and whipped out a handkerchief. He wrapped it around the hilt and withdrew the blade from its scabbard, giving a nod of approval.

"This is fine work, Jack."

"Thank you, Consort."

"You've done well," Maebh said and sighed. "What would you ask for this service?"

"I only ask that we keep Quinn safe."

She cocked her head and swept me with a somber gaze and smiled a little sadly.

"I cannot promise that no harm will come to her with such a dangerous operation ahead; the best I can promise is that we all shall try to the very best of our abilities." I dipped another deep bow and Doan took the scabbard from me.

"My Queen," I said reverently.

"You are dismissed, Jack. Deliver my message and my gratitude to Ms. Carter accordingly."

I straightened and, with a slightly less-formal nod, left the throne room and made furtive haste to Quinn's door.

I knocked twice and she opened it, pulling me quickly inside, asking, "Did they go for it?"

"Aye, Doan will be gettin' with you in the near future."

"Ball is in their court," she said breathlessly. "Guess all we can do now is wait."

She smiled and I felt an answering one of my own grace my lips. I pulled her to me slowly and she giggled. The mend in our relationship was still fragile and new and I wished to prove to her how very ardent I was when it came to doing right by her from now on.

"I am still so very sorry for not telling you –"

"Shhh," she interrupted, placing her fingertips lightly against my lips. "It's all right now."

I smiled against her fingers and closed my eyes, basking in the warmth of her love and forgiveness. She replaced the light touch of her fingers with a kiss that felt almost reverent and I knew I didn't deserve her. I also knew that I would forever strive to be a man who did.

We spent forever kissing, touching, undressing, and connecting. I ghosted fingers and lips over every inch of her skin, worshiping her as my own personal goddess of mercy and all things good and right in my life. She was as sweet as sin and I loved her like I never thought I would love another ever again.

She was soft as silk beneath my hands, around my cock, and I immersed myself in her completely. I moved over and inside her, drawing our lovemaking out for as long as possible, refusing to rush no matter how much the ache in my balls demanded it of me. I made certain my lady was satisfied first. It was the least I could do.

I slept the best sleep I'd had in a century of time with Quinn lying against my chest, her soft, lithe body tucked against me, her leg over both of mine. I slept deeply, dreamlessly, and it was a good thing for what lay ahead.

29

Quinn...

I drew in a deep breath, held it for several seconds and let it out slowly over several seconds more as I stared at the blue door. The plan was in place but I was never a very good liar and it was pretty much all me from this point forward. Doan had been surprised at my ideas on how to get this done. He'd frowned and had said to me, "The Fae don't lie directly," to which I'd responded, "Good thing I'm not Fae."

He'd laughed, and taken my plan to the Queen, who had basically said it was going to take a buttload of power to pull it off, but that it could be done. Enough power that it was a real gamble, but honestly, we didn't see another way. It's not like he was going to confess it in front of everyone, but he was just egotistical enough to spill it in front of just me. After all, who in their right mind would believe the human? From Gwynn's own mouth, though? Still, it was all predicated on his cooperating and that all relied on me actually being able to lie convincingly.

No pressure.

Jack didn't like it. He said there were far too many 'ifs' when it came to this plan and I couldn't disagree, but it was still honestly the quickest route between both points. I twisted my head around on my neck to loosen the tight muscles and shook out my hands, let out another breath, and reached for the door's handle.

I'd dressed just for the occasion in my warmest clothes, even putting on a pair of leggings beneath my jeans. The blast of cold that greeted me was still considerable. I had never been a fan of it but still stepped over the threshold and onto the path. My boots gave that satisfying crunch through the top snow crust and I let my breath out in a plume, closing the door tightly behind me.

Into the lion's den... I thought and let my eyes wander the pristine scenery.

The Winterland was more trees than field, in counterpoint to the Summerland. The path I was on wound around a lake to a blue-roofed gazebo of sorts out over the water. Something seemed vaguely wrong about the landscape as I wound my way through it to the structure, and I finally realized it was the plant life. None of the plants had lost any of their leaves, but none of the plants I was seeing should have any during winter. The birch trees should have been naked sticks and branches thrust toward the sky but instead those branches were lush with leaves that were not only white as the snow that rested on them but also glimmered beneath the frosty sparkle.

I blinked and went up near a blade of marsh grass which should have been golden, brittle, and dry but instead also appeared to be silvery beneath the crust of frost and snow. It was beautiful, and I wished I had a working camera to take images back with me to draw later and to get the colors right.

I rose and continued to make my way to the structure, and when I reached it, found several benches surrounding a frozen fountain underneath. I walked to the railing overlooking the lake, which was surprisingly unfrozen, the waters a deep abiding blue. Snow-covered stones peeked out like constellations in a midnight sky.

Nothing stirred here. No snow fell, no creatures were moving among the snow-covered ground or through the frosted and frozen trees. I rested my hands on the stone-topped railing and let the quiet that only a snow-covered landscape could provide sink in. I closed my eyes and breathed out and wondered how I was supposed to find Gwynn in here. The flap of bird wings had me open my eyes just in time to see a bird, very much like a crow, only not solid black but rather black and white, come in for a landing beside me. I blinked as it landed on the railing near my hand and it cocked its head, contemplating me with one beady silvery eye.

The bird really did look just like a crow but I knew that couldn't be right. Its body was mostly white, its head and face black. The wings were white at the shoulders but the long flight feathers were black. The same for the tail feathers; white at the base, closer to the body, but black at the tips.

It was a very unusual bird, but beautiful. Of course, the flash of light that it emitted wasn't normal at all, and when I lowered my hand, Gwynn stood less than a foot away, smiling, the black markings the bird had borne shrinking away as an ink stain absorbed in reverse, the black of his face receding into his hairline before disappearing completely, leaving only his usual pure-white skin behind.

He wore black and white and I swallowed hard, realizing that he really did look good, but also that he matched the scenery a little too well. The whole effect came off a little too contrived.

"What?" he asked smiling, and I smiled too, deciding I could at least speak the partial truth.

"You match the scenery," I said and he laughed.

"I'd never thought of it that way," he said and then cocked his head in a way that made me think that the echo of having been the bird hadn't left him completely.

"You came, was there something you needed?" I bowed my head in a way that I hoped would come off as shyly and shook it.

"No, not need, just um," I shifted and cursed myself inwardly that I hadn't thought of the most basic thing I should have when coming here. A reason why. I sighed out, mostly to buy myself a moment to think, and finally said, "I don't know. A change of scenery? Maybe some company..."

"You're having doubts?" he asked and it was almost a little too eager.

"About getting the Fae's story told?" I frowned and shook my head. "Not at all! I think it's honestly a great idea and that people are going to love it back home. I think the Queen is really on to something."

He laughed like what I was spouting was the most naïve thing he'd ever heard and I fought down a surge that was a mix of triumph and irritation, with maybe a healthy shot of anger in there for good measure.

I put on a frown, which wasn't hard, and said, "What? This whole thing was your idea, you don't believe I can do it?"

His hand flashed out of nowhere and caught me around the back of my neck. I cried out in panic and put my hands up as he hauled me the last few inches into his chest. I pushed back away from him but he was too strong!

"I have no intention of allowing this charade to carry on for much longer. It's loathsome and to be honest, quite bothersome. Did you actually think you could make any kind of a difference? Our power fades minute by minute, hour by hour and my sister allows it! You were nothing more than an experiment, proving to me that Maebh has gone soft."

"So, what?" I demanded, voice tight with mixed fear and rage. "You set all this up and won't even give it a chance to succeed?"

He cocked his head to the side and considered me. "It has no chance for success because this is what you're going to do," he said, and nearly put his nose even with mine. "You're going to fail, and if you don't fail, I will destroy everything you have left that you hold dear."

"Newsflash, there is nothing left!" I snarled and brought up my knee; he was expecting it somehow, though, and turned, my knee glancing off his thigh. He spun me around and shoved me up against the railing and tears sprang to my eyes as he pushed himself into my ass.

"Are you so certain?" he whispered in my ear. "What about your Jack? I could kill him, you know."

I kept up the game, the fact that the Queen and the rest of the court hadn't appeared told me that I didn't have enough. I swallowed hard and asked him, "So what is this, then? You're seriously willing to pit what's left of your people against the might of the world armies? Do you know what that would do to you? To the earth? Do you even know what a nuclear bomb is? What will happen if they decide to drop one on your head?"

Gwynn laughed and reached around me, going for my belt, I struggled in his grip at the back of my collar as he kicked my feet apart.

"We are the Tuatha Dé Danann, girl! The rightful custodians of the earth. My sister is weak, it was her mistakes that lead us to this. Skulking in the shadows beyond the fringes. Leaving us to be forgotten, leaving the earth to your race's utter folly!"

"And you aim to fix it all by force, destroying what we are sworn to protect in the first place? I think not, brother. This is treason, but what's worse is you sought to achieve my throne through outright lies."

He let me go and I nearly fell to my knees in relief, my hands going to the button on my jeans to refasten it. Hands fell on my shoulders and I cried out, but Jack's voice stopped me from going into a full-blown panic.

I didn't even care about what was going on behind us, I just tucked myself into Jack's front and let him shelter me from Gwynn's presence as I fumbled to tighten my belt again. That had been close. Terrifyingly close.

Voices rose, a shouting match I didn't care to really listen to rising up. Finally, I was able to get it together, to focus back in on what was going on. I was shocked and surprised when I looked, and the Queen stood in armor, the iron sword Jack had created in her gauntleted hand.

"If you want it that badly, come and get it, brother!" she said coldly. For the first time ever, Gwynn looked more than a little nervous.

"You would have me fight you, Sister? You would strike me down? Your own flesh and blood?"

"I would suggest you stop talking, and either draw your sword or take a knee, Gwynn," Doan said coolly, his voice as frosty as our surroundings.

Gwynn looked from Doan, to the rest of the court gathered behind him in a semi-circle beyond the fountain, to his sister who looked both fierce and murderous. He focused on the sword in her hand and his eyes widened. Finally, he sank slowly to one knee.

"Seize him," Maebh ordered and several of her guards marched forward to surround Gwynn at his back. They relieved him of his weapons and lashed his hands behind his back with a thick leather thong.

"To the Hall of Reflection with him."

"For how long?" Gwynn demanded.

"For as long as I like!" The Queen's voice rang out, rolling across the lake with the power of thunder. Her guards gagged Gwynn and hauled him to his feet. She turned to me and her posture eased, her expression softening.

"You still wish to remain here?" she asked and I looked at Jack and nodded. His eyes widened.

"I do, I can still do all that you ask, go to New York, make the pitch and get the ball rolling, but I don't really have anything to go back to. Everything I want is right here."

Maebh inclined her head and said, "It is the least we can do for the service you have done us today."

"I just hope this other crazy plan works," I said with a smile.

The Queen smiled but looked tired. The glamour she had had to employ to shroud herself and everyone else had been a considerable use of her powers. I honestly was glad that Gwynn had backed down. With how gray around the edges she looked, I didn't think she would have been capable of standing up to him, even with an iron sword at her disposal. She swayed on her feet and passed it to one of her guards.

She'd had to work even harder with it in her hand, but I understood why she'd wanted it. If she had fought Gwynn, she would have needed to kill him. She may yet need to, in order to keep her people safe.

"It will work," Doan said with certainty, and his belief in me meant the world to me. I looked to Jack, who stared at me with a wide-eyed sort of wonder on his face.

"You would truly give up your life out there to stay down here with me?" he asked softly.

"If this works, wait and see what I ask for next," I said softly and kissed him. He wrapped his arms around me and held me tight and I'd never been anywhere else that felt so much like home.

EPILOGUE

Jack…

It had been too long, this time away from Quinn. She had, with the subtle help of some charisma charms and a potion or two, managed to land a deal for both a series of children's books and a series of adult graphic novels. She had released the first book in each under very different pen names and already Faery had begun to recover.

I had been very busy walking messages between the different Raths as powers long forgotten began to stir and old portions of the various parts of Faery began to reveal themselves once more. It had begun rather quickly, with the dying portions showing new signs of life as Quinn's tales took hold and the buried messages of caring for mother earth took root.

It was a start, a good one, and Queen Maebh had been all too happy to grant Quinn her second wish. I smiled as I stepped over the threshold into the Summerland and set off down the trail to the edge of the wood.

It was a long walk through the sun-dappled trees, but eventually, I spilled out the other side, my lantern loose in my grip, a slight burden, but one I would be glad to set down none the less.

The light grew as I reached the other side and stepped out into the clearing that held our home. Quinn opened our cottage door and smiled as brightly as the false sun in the glamoured sky.

Her second wish, like her first, both selfless and self-serving at once. She had asked, for my sake, permission to build our home in the light. She smoothed her hands over her swollen belly–the first child in Faery in over five hundred years– and met me on the light stone path, halfway to the door.

"Welcome home, husband," she murmured, raising on her toes to give me a kiss. I smiled against her lips and kissed her back.

Everything I'd ever held hallow in life was at my fingertips because of Quinn's light.

ALSO BY TIMBER PHILIPS

Hallowed Be Thy Light

Hunter's Choice

Love in Purgatory

ABOUT THE AUTHOR

Timber Philips hails from a land filled with beauty and steeped in magic; the Pacific Northwest. She swears you can see fairies and goblins, magic and promise around every tree and in every drop of water and she shares that magic whenever she can. She loves welcoming everyone to her worlds of romance rooted in fable and fantasy.

Stalker Information:
www.timberphilips.com

Facebook Group
https://www.facebook.com/groups/timberswolves

facebook.com/authortimberphilips

bookbub.com/authors/timber-philips

instagram.com/authortimberphilips

twitter.com/timberphilips